Build Your
WINGS
on the Way
Down

JUDITH STAPONKUS

For Charlie, Max, and Mickey and all dogs everywhere.

Sometimes you just have to take the leap and build your wings on the way down.

— KOBI YAMADA

CHAPTER 1

The room was cool, almost chilly. Its walls were painted an icy blue-grey, and opposite the slate-colored leather sofa hung three abstract pictures, living room art suggesting smooth blue water melting into a cloudless summer sky. Maureen sat sunken into the sofa and glanced at the clock on the end table. Eleven minutes had passed in silence. Across the muted grey rug, the woman perched in the white occasional chair positioned beneath the pictures removed her glasses and leaned forward.

"I believe it's your turn to speak." Her voice was calm and cool, like the room. "Tell me one thing about any person from this scene you're trying to rebuild."

"I've told you everything I can remember." Maureen gazed down at her newly manicured nails, longing to gnaw them until they were ragged, but not wanting to give Dr. Taylor the satisfaction of witnessing her neurotic compulsion.

"You said it was a summer day, and there was a girl in a ruffled dress swinging on a swing." Dr. Taylor put on her glasses and rested back against the chair. "Are you the girl?"

"You always ask me that question. I don't know who the girl is."

"Who else do you see?"

"A woman. She's struggling against the wind as she's hanging a sheet on the clothesline."

"That's the first time you've mentioned the woman."

"She's not important. A bit player." Maureen dismissed the woman so she could forget her.

"We'll set that aside for now. Tell me about the man you saw coming into the picture."

"I don't know. He's just a big, ugly man, holding a box."

"Hmmm."

"Do you realize I detest it when you do that?"

"I'll try to refrain from responding in such a manner. I want you to know I heard what you said."

"Of course, you heard what I said. You're a few feet away from me." Maureen wasn't sure why she was filling up with anger.

"Good point." Dr. Taylor hesitated. "Look closer at the man. Do you recall any details about him or the box he's carrying?"

"Inside the box is a present for the girl. It's doll."

"Another thing you have never mentioned before."

"I can only talk about what I remember when I remember it, unless you want me to make up stuff."

"Have you been making up stuff to tell me?"

"At $150 an hour, once, sometimes twice a week, for two years? Not likely." Maureen was lying, of course. It was much easier to make up fictional details of her life, than to face reality. Still, she stayed with Dr. Taylor, unwilling to admit she hoped the truth, whatever it might be, would rise to the surface.

"Not likely? I'm glad." Dr. Taylor laughed, a soft, controlled laugh and glanced at her wrist watch. "How would you like to end today's session?"

"I'll tell you how the story ends. The man hugs the girl, there's a loud bang, and he falls forward like cut timber, shot in the back of the head. Spattered in blood, the girl begins to scream. How's that for an ending?"

Maureen was in a panic. Today was her presentation to the Board of Directors and their biggest potential client, Wexler Global, an account she had devoted the last year of her life to obtaining. She thought she was more than well-prepared, addressing any predicament that could arise. With some convincing, David had even agreed to take her old Chevy for the day while she drove his new Lexus.

"This would be unnecessary if you had taken my advice and bought a new car."

"I like my car. Lately, it's been sort of temperamental, and I can't afford to take any chances today."

"Which substantiates my reasoning. Now I'm the one taking a chance."

"It's this one time, David, not a permanent swap."

"All right, but, for Pete's sake, don't let some valet drive the car, and be sure you're not parked close to anyone else." David continued packing his duffle bag with power bars, bananas, and water.

"Ted and I are doing a long run this morning, so I'm meeting him at 7:45. Good luck today." He threw a kiss in Maureen's direction, tossed the bag over his shoulder and was gone.

Maureen watched him leave and tried to ignore the empty feeling growing in the pit of her stomach. She reassured herself he was preoccupied with meeting his running buddy and not pulling away from her or being distant and uncaring. Besides, this was not the time to analyze their marriage, and she vowed to give their relationship the attention it deserved as soon as work settled down. She hurried to get ready for today's meeting and, because she was ahead of schedule, decided to leave early for the office, just in case. Assembling everything she needed, Maureen swore at David when she realized he had taken her key ring with the keys to both of their cars. She bolted upstairs to search for David's keys, which he rarely carried, since he always used his phone app to start his own car.

After an excruciating ten minutes of searching, Maureen decided she had to call David, but her call went straight to his voicemail, and she remembered he often left his phone in the car while he ran. She didn't leave a message because he was running and couldn't help her anyway, and he already disapproved of her needing to use his car in the first place. She hung up and instead called her younger sister, Jasmine, who arrived fifteen agonizing minutes later.

"Is that what you're wearing?" Jasmine, barely in the door, pointed a critical finger at Maureen. "You have to change, and let me fix your hair."

"We don't have time for any of that."

"Give me ten minutes, and I guarantee it will be worth it."

It was. Maureen had to admit her outfit felt much more put-together and professional, and her unruly, brown frizz was arranged in a sleek and fashionable knot at the back of her head.

"Like I said, the I-10 is a parking lot." Jasmine was digging in her designer bag for car keys. "We'll never get downtown on time, so I'll drive you to the train station."

They arrived at the quaint, red brick station as the 9:25 Blue Line was closing its doors. Maureen leapt from her sister's car, knowing there was little chance of boarding, but she had to try. It pulled away as she stepped onto the loading platform. The next train was scheduled to arrive in twenty-two minutes, minutes Maureen didn't have.

Jasmine caught up with her sister on the platform, with Maureen's brief-case, laptop, and coffee in hand. "You forgot these. Probably a good thing you missed the 9:25."

Maureen took the items, willing herself to calm down. There was still time to get to the meeting as long as nothing else went haywire.

"Thanks for everything, Jazz. I wouldn't have made it at all if you hadn't given me a ride to the station."

"You could have called an Uber."

"True, but you were quicker and went that extra mile figuring out what I should wear, not to mention taming my hair so it looks almost normal."

"Hey, look at me, taking care of my big sister, instead of you taking care of me!"

"Miracles never cease."

They both laughed, knowing how Maureen had taken care of Jasmine for most of her life. Following the arrest of their mother, Peggy, when Maureen was fifteen and Jasmine was five, the two began living with their Aunt Toni, but it wasn't much of a life. Toni made it clear the last thing she needed was two more brats to add to the four she already had. Maureen and Jasmine had been forced upon her, and all their aunt wanted from the arrangement was the money she earned by renting out Peggy's farmland and the free hous-ing the farmhouse provided. When Maureen turned eighteen, she became Jasmine's legal guardian and took her far away from the chaotic uncaring household and the aunt who told them, "Good riddance to bad rubbish." Through all the tough years that followed, Maureen was her sister's rock.

"The next train will get me to the office with time to spare," Maureen told Jazz, giving her a quick hug. "Now get out of here. I know you have a busy day ahead."

Waiting for the 9:47 train, Maureen opened her laptop and double checked the graphics and final talking points. She was ready. Now, all she had to do was make it to the office.

The train arrived on time and was less crowded than Maureen antici-pated. It was fifty-one minutes to Layton Station downtown, and she used the precious time to review every aspect of the past eleven months in which she had worked nonstop to acquire the Wexler Global account. If all proceeded as planned, the deal would be finalized today, and Maureen would be promoted to the position of Midwest Regional Manager.

Nearing the Layton stop, Maureen sent a text to Andrea, her secre-tary, saying she would be arriving soon. When Maureen stood to gather her belongings, the train sped up without warning and jerked to a stop, throwing the few remaining passengers stumbling into the aisles. Maureen managed to remain upright, but the last ounces of her coffee exited the cup and took a leap onto the front of her crisp, once immaculate, white blouse, the coffee dribbling down from where it landed on her chest in an ever-widening stain until it disappeared into her waistband.

Cursing under her breath, Maureen worked her way to the exit, where another commuter squeezed past her, pulling a tattered suitcase, which dragged alongside Maureen's leg, tearing a hole the size of Cincinnati in her new thirty-dollar pantyhose.

"Nice job! You wrecked my stockings with your stupid suitcase."

"If you weren't blocking the exit with your wide-load behind, I wouldn't have had to squeeze past." The guy yelled an obscenity and was off the train before Maureen could respond. She had intended to yell back at him, but he had disappeared into the crowd of passengers.

Maureen needed to let it go. She wanted to give the idiot a piece of her mind for his rude behavior and derogatory comment, but not today. Every ounce of energy she had would be essential at her meeting, but first, she had to get there.

CHAPTER 2

The Anson-Chambers Office Building was a free-standing example of modern architecture stretching across nine levels. Designed for commercial use, its overall atmosphere was one of calm space, natural light, and connection to nature. Whenever Maureen approached it, she took a moment to admire its free-flowing lines and shimmering glass. Except for today. Already behind schedule, she did her best to hurry without running, head down and mouth set like a thin layer of mortar. Security waved her through to the lobby and the nearby open stairway meandering in a spiral of marble steps and platforms along a wall of windows pulling one upward through light and sky. Every day, Maureen used the stairs, not because she was a fitness fanatic or anything like that, but because she hated small enclosures like elevators. Today, she had no other choice, and she crossed the lobby to the elevators, where she pushed all of the upward arrow buttons. When two elevators arrived at her level at the same time, she stepped onto the empty one on the right, pressed the button, gripped the metal handrail stretched around the perimeter, and prayed for the ninth floor. The elevator had other ideas, stopping at each floor for every slow person on earth who strolled on. Maureen didn't think she could be any closer to elevator rage than she was at that moment.

When the doors opened on her floor, Maureen pushed past the three other passengers on board and rushed out, nearly colliding with Andrea.

"I was about to text Don and have him stall the start of the meeting." Andrea, a stickler for punctuality, reached for Maureen's laptop and briefcase, while giving her the once over. "What happened to you?"

"Car keys disappeared, freeway at a standstill, coffee leap due to sudden train stop, panty hose mishap, speed walking in jungle weather, and elevator hell."

Glancing at her reflection as the two women hurried down the mirrored corridor to the office, Maureen was dismayed that her dark, naturally curly hair had sprung from the sleek knot Jasmine arranged at the nape of her neck, and now it stood out from her head like emancipated cotton candy, framing her sweaty, flushed face. She looked more like a circus clown than a business executive about to land a multi-million dollar account.

Entering her office, Maureen felt a sense of serenity wash over her. The place was her oasis. Thanks to Andrea's organizational skills and the added benefit of not having to battle David's cluttered lifestyle here at work, Maureen's office remained clean, tidy, and spartan.

"Here's what we're going to do." Maureen began removing her suit jacket. "Take off your blouse."

The two traded blouses, despite the fact Maureen was a size fourteen and slender Andrea was a couple sizes smaller. Somehow, Maureen managed to fasten the front buttons, her generous chest straining against the fabric as she put on her suit coat.

"If I don't take any deep breaths or laugh, I think the jacket will hold in most of me."

Andrea had started to put on Maureen's coffee-stained blouse, but changed her mind. "I think I'll put this one in the sink to soak."

Instead of the blouse, she slipped on a sweater she kept for emergencies on the back of her desk chair. "What about the hole in your panty hose?"

"Oh, darn, I forgot. Guess I'll have to show some skin." Maureen stepped out of her stockings, looking grim. "Not a good look for someone approaching forty."

"I'm wearing pants, so I can't help you there. You have no other options." Andrea always chose practical, classic pantsuits, never requiring leg exposure.

They tackled Maureen's hair next, brushing and wrangling it into a ponytail, spraying it until it surrendered. It wasn't the elegant style Jasmine had given her, but at least it didn't look like Maureen's head was on fire. Andrea was blotting Maureen's nose with face powder, when Don knocked on the office door and entered without an invitation.

"It's eleven o'clock, Moe. I thought we had agreed to be in the conference room at 10:30. I must have gotten it wrong."

Always deferential, yet somehow insulting and accusatory where she was concerned, Don had a manner which had grown to rub Maureen the wrong way. Together, they worked on this project for almost a year. All during that time, she never felt like they were a team, or that he, the new kid on the block, respected her, despite the fact she was the senior account executive for their state with fifteen years' experience. Maureen suspected Don used her contacts as though they were his own and inserted himself into relationships Maureen had taken years to foster. It was maddening, because he won people over with little effort, taking advantage of his golden boy good looks and magnetic personality.

"I'm finishing up some last minute tweaks of the project." Maureen was hoping to throw Don off his game a little, knowing how he hated being excluded from anything, insisting on knowing every detail of what Maureen was doing. "Meet you in the conference room in five."

Board members were still milling around the doughnuts and coffee when Maureen arrived. She walked straight toward Howard Wexler, the CEO of Wexler Global, who reached out to shake Maureen's hand.

"This is the day we've been working toward, Maureen." Wexler pumped her hand with enthusiasm. "Let's see what you've got for us."

Don seated himself beside Howard and began engaging him in deep conversation, but Maureen ignored Don as she walked straight for the head of the table. The presentation she designed and produced was her baby, and it was time to show it off.

Bending to arrange her computer and hard copies, Maureen heard a pinging sound and glanced up to see the top button from the front of her blouse ricochet off the metal coffee carafe in the center of the table, and roll away to settle in front of Robert Chambers, her boss, who stood at the other end of the table.

"Maureen, you have my attention. Let the games begin!" Chuckles around the table increased Maureen's embarrassment, and she felt herself redden from her cheeks down to her chest which was now overflowing from her open blouse.

"Thank you, Robert. Welcome Board Members and a special welcome to Mr. Howard Wexler, CEO of Wexler Global Energy Corporation." Don, on cue, started the applause, while Maureen smiled and tugged the edges of her suit jacket together in front of her.

Maureen's presentation lasted twenty-five minutes, with only one slight technological glitch, which Don corrected, thus saving the day. When she was finished, Don led the applause once again, and Maureen sat down, pleased with her work, the blouse disaster forgotten.

Wexler was impressed and spoke with appreciation about the work Maureen and Don had done to meet the demands of his company. "I want Anson-Chambers to handle all of our business from now into the foreseeable future," he said, indicating the deal was secured.

It was a huge victory, and Maureen and Don were congratulated by the Board members as they exited. When Robert invited them both into his private office, Maureen couldn't help but smile.

"This Wexler deal was an enormous win for the company, and for you two, in particular." Robert motioned for them to sit. "I realize this was a team effort, and, Maureen, your leadership and experience were a key component to what your team accomplished."

"Thank you, Robert."

"Don, your enthusiasm and technological innovation proved invaluable in getting this accomplished. I especially appreciated being kept in the loop regarding how things were progressing, and I looked forward to your emails, calls, texts, and, yes, every visit you made to my office."

Maureen stared at Robert in disbelief. From the beginning, she and Don had agreed she would be in contact with all parties involved, and with Robert, in particular. The fact Don had ingratiated himself to Robert while double crossing Maureen made her feel undermined and deceived.

"Maureen, you are well-suited to the position of state senior account executive, and I would like you to continue as such, with additional salary compensation to reflect our appreciation."

Swallowing hard, Maureen felt her heart pounding in her ample chest. "Thank you, Robert. While my primary goal has always been about the success of this company within our state, I was lead to believe landing this account would earn for me the job as Midwest Regional Manager, a position for which I have proven myself more than capable."

"You're not wrong, Maureen. This time, for a variety of reasons, the Board has decided to go in a different direction." Robert dismissed her without a second glance and turned to her young co-worker.

"Don, you have demonstrated you are a loyal Anson-Chambers team member, whose tireless work has impressed the Board. You are the face and presence we need in the position of our Midwest Regional Manager. Congratulations to you both."

Robert reached to shake Don's hand. By the time he was slapping the young man on the back, Maureen had marched out the door. Despite being blind with rage, she managed to walk back into her office where she flung her laptop and files onto her desk. Andrea came in and closed the door.

"That snake. That two-faced, job-stealing, ass-kissing snake." Maureen kicked at her desk chair with the silent wheels and leather seat, the one she earned after ten long years on the job.

"What happened? Didn't the presentation go well?"

"It went very well, I thought. What I didn't think was Don had been hijacking the project all along, sucking up to Robert and taking all the credit, I'm sure."

Before Andrea could respond, Don peeked his head into Maureen's office.

"Moe, you've got to understand, I didn't know anything about this. I am as surprised as you are."

"Are you serious? We agreed I was the liaison person and would keep Robert, and everyone else, informed. Now, you're surprised, despite the fact you were working behind my back all this time."

"You were so busy, the information wasn't getting relayed. I was only trying to help you out and keep everyone up-to-speed on our progress."

"The reason I was busy is because this entire project was all me, and you know it. There was no "our progress". The last year of my life, every waking hour, was dedicated to Wexler and his needs. I planned his kid's birthday party, picked up his dry cleaning, even helped him with his wife's Christmas present."

"In my defense, Robert knew everything you were doing, because I told him. I was blowing your horn for you."

"I'll bet you were, which is why you're the loyal team member who is a tireless worker. Give me a break."

"Look, it's business. Neither of us has control over the actions of Robert or the Board. We'll have to learn to live with their decisions to prove we are all team players."

"Get out of my office, Don!"

"Let's agree to disagree on this one. Please say we're still friends."

"We were never friends, Don, and you've proven it. Now, get out."

"I'll stop back later when you've cooled down a bit."

Maureen lunged toward him, but Andrea, who'd been captured in the middle of the exchange, caught her boss by the arms and held her back.

"He's not worth it." She didn't release Maureen until Don backed out the door and disappeared down the hall.

Andrea reached in Maureen's bottom drawer for the emergency bottle of Tito's vodka stashed there and poured a shot into their coffee mugs.

"What's going to happen now?"

"Nothing. A big, fat nothing. Same title, same job, same everything."

In one gulp, Maureen swallowed the booze in her cup, and then grabbed Andrea's cup and drank hers, too. The vodka seared her throat and chest, and she savored the burn.

"I have to get out of here." Maureen began tossing random items into her briefcase: pictures of David and Jasmine, a tape dispenser, stapler, post-it notes, tissue box, the Wexler files and flash drives, the bottle of vodka.

"How do you want me to handle your absence? I could say you had another client meeting or you were asked to make an on-sight appraisal." Andrea had her pen and notepad ready.

"If anyone asks, although I doubt they will, say my head exploded, and I needed a sick day." Maureen started out the door, but walked back to embrace her long-time secretary.

"Thanks, Andrea, for your loyalty and friendship. It has meant a great deal to me."

Before Andrea could talk her into staying, Maureen headed for the stairs. Outside, she hailed a taxi, which was something she never did, and directed the driver to her home address. Maureen needed to be where she was safe and secure. She needed to be home.

CHAPTER 3

The taxi ride was going to be a long one, and after fifteen minutes, Maureen snapped open her briefcase to retrieve the bottle of vodka and discovered it had leaked, dampening most of what was inside, including the Wexler files she had taken with her.

"What a waste of perfectly good vodka." Raising the bottle to her mouth, Maureen took several long drinks and then slowed her pace to occasional sipping. She studied the damp Wexler files, their alcohol-scented sogginess generating none of the panic Maureen would have experienced had this happened a few short hours ago.

The taxi rolled to a stop in front of Maureen and David's two-story brick home. Worth every penny, Maureen told herself, handing the driver a $100 bill. The garage was closed, so Maureen plodded up the front walkway, feeling a little tipsy. She was relieved when she managed to unlock the front door after only three tries.

Inside, the house was quiet. David taught several classes at the university and would be gone until late afternoon, so Maureen had hours to sulk and feel sorry for herself before regrouping. She reasoned her practical, computer science husband would be empathetic to her situation, but would find her feelings of betrayal and entitlement to be self-indulgent and non-productive. If she wanted a pity party, she would have to party all by herself.

Tossing her purse onto the counter, she set the vodka bottle and the damp briefcase into the kitchen sink, located an open bottle of pinot noir, and poured herself a generous glass full, the perfect complement to the hot bath she craved. Glass in hand, Maureen climbed the soft, carpeted stairs to the master suite, promising herself this was her last alcohol for the day. She kept a careful eye on the wine sloshing around in her glass as she pushed the partially open bedroom door. David had a thing about her drinking upstairs, so spilling was not allowed.

In the doorway, Maureen halted, staring in disbelief at her bed. The woman's back was slender and smooth, one arm resting across the man, her creamy blond hair a tangle of curls tumbling over his bare chest. Her long legs were awash in the bedclothes, and beside the woman's body, the man had stretched a tanned and muscular leg, the leg of a runner.

Maureen stepped to the end of the bed. "David?"

The woman lifted her head.

"Jasmine?"

"What the hell?" David sprung to his feet, pulling on his boxers, stumbling in the process. "Geez, Maureen, you scared me half to death."

Jasmine was pulling the sheet around her. "Maureen, I'm so sorry."

"You're sorry you slept with my husband or sorry you were caught?"

"David and I never meant for this to happen."

"I think you mean you never intended for me to catch you in the act." Maureen's voice sounded calm, not because she felt relaxed, but because she felt dead inside. She pitched the wine glass to the floor and left the room.

David caught up with her before she could open the door to the garage. He was barefoot, dressed in faded jeans and a university faculty tee-shirt, his long, dark hair pulled back in a messy pony tail. Maureen envisioned Jasmine's fingers entwined in his thick curls, their lips pressed together. Before David could say a word, Maureen pushed past him and ran for the guest bathroom, locking herself inside. She knelt beside the toilet and vomited until her insides ached.

"Maureen, listen to me," David pleaded through the closed door.

She flushed the toilet and wiped her face and mouth on the expensive towel David had insisted she buy when they had remodeled. "Go away."

"I'm not leaving until you at least hear what I have to say."

"How long, David? A month, six months, a year? Longer?"

"You've been so consumed by your job this past year, it was like I was alone in our marriage."

"Unbelievable. It's my fault you are unfaithful, you arrogant, Machiavellian cretin."

"Come out, Maureen, so we are face to face. Talking to the door feels cold and insincere."

"Golly, David, we wouldn't want to offend your warm, sincere disposition."

"I'm trying to be rational, Moe. We need to talk about what's happened."

"What's happened is you're sleeping with my sister. What else is there to say?" Maureen thought she might implode if she stayed in their house any longer. "Go away, and I'll come out."

"All right. I'm going into the living room. Please come in there so we can have a calm, adult discussion."

Maureen could hear the domineering, superior tone in David's voice. It made her furious. She listened as his footsteps moved away from the bathroom. With a click, Maureen unlocked the door and stuck her head out, glancing in both directions as though she was pulling out into oncoming traffic. There was no one in sight, and she hurried away from the direction of the living room into the kitchen, where David and Jasmine waited to ambush her.

"I don't want to talk to either of you." Maureen snatched her purse from the counter and began digging for her car keys. "Where are my car keys?"

"Moe, you have to know this was nothing David and I planned. I can't bear the thought of hurting you."

"Too late. Guess you'll have to suffer under the terrible burden of my hurt feelings because you were screwing my husband."

"Don't take it out on Jazz. This is my fault."

"Nothing's ever Jasmine's fault. She's as innocent as the driven snow."

"This is all on me. I guess I was feeling abandoned with you so emotionally unavailable and . . ."

"Spare me your psycho-babble. It's your same old tune, how I'm devoid of emotion and unable to connect. Where the hell are my car keys?"

"I never said such a thing, but we both know your past has cast a shadow over every relationship you've ever had." David dug into his jeans' pocket and handed Maureen her keys.

"David, you are being unfair." Jasmine spoke in her little-girl pouty voice. "Maureen had no control over what happened in our family. You can't blame her." Jasmine attempted to place an arm around Maureen's shoulders, but she bolted away.

"I know she shouldn't be blamed," David said, "but it doesn't change the fact she internalizes everything and is emotionally closed off. It's why she has problems with overeating and drinking too much."

"So now I'm not only unloving, but also a fat lush."

"Don't put words into my mouth in an attempt to misconstrue my message."

"Oh, I'm getting your message loud and clear." Maureen attempted to leave, but David gripped her arm.

"Let go or I swear you're going to lose an eye." For emphasis, she jammed her car keys toward his face.

"Making physical threats, Maureen, is not a sign of someone in command of all their mental faculties."

Maureen laughed. "I have not even begun to lose command of my faculties. Believe me, you have no idea what things look like when I'm out of control."

"Losing control runs in your family, I suppose."

"David, I'm begging you, please stop." Jasmine hung on David's arm, her long blond hair resting on his shoulder. "Maureen is nothing like our mother, and you know it."

Maureen watched the familiarity between the two and felt her insides lurch. She considered throwing up in the sink, but when she leaned into it, there was the vodka. She picked up the bottle and stuck it upright in her purse. Then, she opened the briefcase, grabbed the damp photos of Jasmine and David, and tossed them into the trash. She slammed her soggy case shut, and used her purse to ram past the happy couple. In the garage, Maureen threw herself into the car and jammed the keys in the ignition, as she willed the Chevy to start. She flattened her foot on the gas pedal, and the car burst out of the garage, missing the opening door by a fraction. The old car roared down the driveway into the road, and Maureen caught sight of David in her rearview mirror, watching her drive away as he stood in the center of the street, still barefoot and handsome, and still a son of a bitch.

CHAPTER 4

It was a miracle Maureen didn't cause an accident on the expressway, considering she had no recollection of driving on it. The car and Maureen traveled on autopilot as she swore, sobbed, wiped her dripping face and nose on her sleeve, and pounded the steering wheel. Maureen turned onto the tollway where, at the first toll, she made the mistake of entering the bus lane. When the gate dropped in front of her vehicle and lights began flashing, it was enough to snap Maureen into a more alert state of mind. With no other options, and, as luck would have it, no bus behind her, she put the car in reverse and backed out. A cacophony of honking horns surrounded her, accompanied by yelling and obscene gestures, but it didn't matter. At that moment, there was not one thing that did matter to her.

Lacking any plan and with no destination in mind, Maureen continued driving northward, eventually leaving Illinois and entering her home state of Wisconsin. When her gas tank icon blinked an alarming shade of orange, she turned off at the first exit indicating it was the location of a gas station. The place was well-lit and busy, something Maureen looked for when traveling, and it was modern and clean, with enormous restrooms. Fifteen minutes later, with an empty bladder, a full tank of gas, bags of snacks from the Ito family (Fritos, Doritos, Cheetos), and an enormous cup of coffee, Maureen pulled back onto the interstate, still feeling like she'd been run over by the 9:25 Blue Line. At least she had managed to stop sobbing.

In the southbound lanes, a torrent of cars and semi-trucks were using their wipers and scattering road spray, as Maureen and the countless other vehicles heading north traveled beneath ominous clouds cut by streaks of lightning. Although she was accustomed to driving in hectic traffic, doing so during heavy rain or a thunderstorm made Maureen feel closed in and panic-stricken.

The rain was pounding her vehicle, and she decided to leave the interstate. At the end of the exit ramp she hesitated, straining to read the road sign for a clue about which way to turn. Digging into her purse, Maureen located her phone, which showed one bar and a low battery. She fumbled for her cord to recharge the phone and remembered she had lent it to Jasmine yesterday. The phone charger wasn't enough, Jasmine? You had to help yourself to my husband, too?

With no other choice, Maureen was forced to trust her instincts. She turned right, hoping it was north. David had nagged her to buy a newer car with a navigation system, but Maureen liked her comfortable Chevy, with the exception of its lack of a working compass thing on the dash.

The car was smothered in darkness, perhaps because the rain was falling in opaque sheets, or the more likely scenario, because she was in the middle of nowhere. Whatever the case, Maureen alternated between cursing and crying, alone on the road, stuffing herself with cheese encrusted junk food. Focusing on the white line hyphenating the center of the pavement, Maureen drove at a slow pace. Whatever her destination, she wanted her body to arrive in one piece, even if her entire life was shattered.

Up ahead, something was in the middle of the road. Through the blinding downpour, Maureen thought it was an old lawn chair or a cooler that had flopped off the back of a north bound camper, but, no, the object was moving forward at a pace slower than Maureen's. She leaned on her horn as she pulled up behind the thing, which paid no attention to her. Maureen decided she would have no problem passing the plodding animal, who resembled a pig and seemed oblivious to the two-ton vehicle bearing down on it, but as the old Chevy moved left to pass, so did the pig.

"Are you kidding me?" Maureen shouted at the blurry blob now obstructing the lane.

As Maureen's car was forced to hang back, the moving road block re-established its course down the center of the highway. Option two was a right side pass, so Maureen increased her speed, turn signal on and car horn blaring. With an unexpected speed and agility, the animal took over the right lane. Maureen's tires skidded as the car veered onto the narrow shoulder. The alarming movement of near flood-stage water roiling in the ditch and her proximity to the mushy gravel caused her to slow the vehicle to a crawl and ease it back onto the road, pulling in behind the creature who had stopped moving altogether.

The road block parked itself in the center of the pavement and turned to look in Maureen's direction. It was a dog. Honking the horn had no effect. Yelling through the windshield was useless. There was nothing left to do but confront the thing up close and personal. Maureen stormed out of the car and sloshed to where the dog had taken up residence.

"You need to move," she yelled as she approached it. "Stopping in the middle of a road is not a good idea."

Its eyes were droopy, its ears uneven and clipped off with jagged edges, like someone wielding a dull scissors had chopped with abandon. Uneven teeth protruded from a wide mouth stretched across a broad face creased with wrinkles. Despite the rain, Maureen could see it was white in color, except for the patches of raw pink skin covering its boney back and sides. Several long, loose nipples hung under its belly, a tale of at least one litter of puppies. The dog's legs were short and bowed, and its body was squat, ending in a stubby tail hacked off close and ugly.

Maureen realized she could not leave the pathetic creature. She had to do something.

"Come on, road dog," she said, gesturing for it to follow her.

To her surprise, the animal dragged itself to its feet and trudged toward Maureen, following her to the car. Maureen opened the back door and patted the car seat.

"Hop up," she said, realizing that was not going to happen. The distance from the ground onto the back seat was too great, and the exhausted-looking dog was too short.

There was nothing else to do except hoist the dog into the car, which Maureen did with some trepidation. It was, after all, an animal she did not know, and lifting it up by its belly was a personal gesture. With care, Maureen reached her arms around the dog's middle and lifted. When the dog's front paws connected with the car seat, it pulled forward as Maureen shoved its rear end with both her hands until the animal was inside.

"Don't look so insulted. It had to be done." Maureen couldn't help but smile.

With that, the dog lowered itself onto its belly. Releasing a deep sigh, she dropped her head and closed her eyes.

CHAPTER 5

The rain pummeled Maureen's car as she started to drive, but despite the drumming sound outside, she could hear the dog's loud snoring from the seat behind her. The sound was strangely soothing, and Maureen began to relax a little.

After awhile, in the distance, there were lights, too many for a residence or farm, and, when she drove closer, Maureen could see it was a burger joint, attached to a gas station and car repair business. Her mouth watered at the thought of eating something not in the junk food category, and she turned into the parking lot and stopped.

The weather front appeared to be moving off, because the rain had dwindled to a light shower, and the air was warm and breezy when Maureen stepped out of the car. The smell of fried foods drew her toward the restaurant, when she remembered the dog and turned back to see it pressing its already scrunched face against the window.

"I'm guessing you are hungry, based on your skin and bones appearance," Maureen said as she reached in carefully to roll the back window down a bit. "If you promise to be good, I'll bring you a burger." Never having had a dog, she wasn't sure what foods they preferred, but she felt confident any dog would eat a burger, given the chance.

"Stay here," she ordered, knowing it was an empty gesture done to prove her false control of the situation, when it was obvious the dog would do what it wanted when it wanted to do it.

As she entered the crowded restaurant, heads turned to stare at Maureen. She was certain it was because she was an overweight, thirty-nine year old woman with crazy hair, wearing a too-small blouse and a skirt with no stockings, but, as she approached the lunch counter, she wondered if it could have been the cheese dust on her face and sprinkled down her front. Maureen found an empty stool and sat, brushing away the orange evidence of her recent eating frenzy. Despite the family-size bag of Doritos and the 12-ounce bag of Cheetos she had eaten in the car, she felt weak with hunger.

Gazing around the room, Maureen wondered why it was so busy, considering the storm, the fact it was 8:00, and the far-flung location of the restaurant. She hoped it was the quality of the food drawing the crowd, and with high expectations, she placed an order.

"The food is excellent here," the handsome man rising from the stool next to her offered, as he finished the last of his coffee.

"Good to know," Maureen said, taking a sideways glance at him. He was tall, slender, and maybe in his thirties, with stubble shadowing his face and curly blond hair in need of a good hair cut.

"Storm's letting up." He gestured toward the steamy windows, picked up his bill, and left the restaurant.

She watched him approach a Jeep parked near the door. Instead of getting in, he grabbed a backpack from inside the vehicle, locked the doors, and walked toward the building with the sign 'Premium Auto Repair'. Maureen's gaze shifted to inside the room, where she noticed a couple seated near the door. The man wore a running tee-shirt, and his dark hair was edged in gray and pulled into a ponytail at the nape of his neck. The woman was young and blond, with pink-lined lips smiling as he reached across the booth to tuck a stray curl behind her studded ear. Maureen felt physically shaken, imagining the two as David and Jasmine. How many times had they shared stolen moments, laughed together, touched one another?

Within fifteen minutes, her order arrived. Maureen bit into the burger, done to perfection, and she sampled the crispy, hot fries, but she had lost her appetite and pushed the food away. She thought about going to the restroom to throw up again. Instead, she scraped the onions and condiments from the burger, tore it and the fries into dog-sized chunks, and requested a bag from the waitress. No reason why the food should go to waste, Maureen thought.

When she attempted to pay her bill, Maureen discovered she could not use her credit card. "Cash Only at the Counter" read the poster at the register, and, as the frowning woman with the outreached palm pointed out, so did the large sign hanging above the length of the counter.

"If you're short on cash, there's an ATM out front, next to the soda machines."

Maureen found enough cash in her wallet to pay for the food, but her funds were shrinking fast, so she grabbed her doggie bag, located the ATM and dug for her card. After inserting the card and before she could enter her PIN, the screen flashed "Invalid Card" in large, black letters. Several more attempts ended in the same result. Maureen considered pounding and kicking the contraption, like when she had to kick the vending machine at work to get a Snickers bar to drop, but chose the more civilized option and walked inside to complain. The same woman was still at the register.

"Your ATM isn't working." Maureen attempted to sound friendly but firm, not sure she sounded either way.

"Been working all day so far, until you tried."

"At some point, it stopped functioning. Says my card is invalid."

"I guess your card's invalid."

"Isn't there something you can do?"

"Yup, I can help this next customer paying his bill. Evening, Harold."

It was apparent Maureen had been dismissed. She walked to the restroom, entered a stall, not bothering to lock it, and tried, without success, to throw up. Doggie bag in hand, she left the restroom and the restaurant.

At the car, Maureen opened the back door and tossed the pieces of food towards the dog who sat squatting on the seat. When the animal growled and showed her crooked teeth, Maureen retreated, moving faster than she had in a long time, slamming the back door. The dog lunged, pressing its snarling face against the glass, and Maureen stood outside in the rain, feeling shaky and reluctant to get back into the vehicle. When it appeared as though the dog was concentrating on the food and not on attacking her, Maureen opened the driver's side car door and slipped inside. The sounds of chomping teeth drifted into the front seat, and in spite of her trembling hands, Maureen felt relieved the dog had eaten.

The blond stranger was correct about the weather. As Maureen pulled out of the parking lot, the western horizon showed the last glimpses of the setting sun tucked beneath the remnants of the storm, its final rain falling with less enthusiasm, even as lightning flashes etched fine lines across the clouds. Maureen was thankful the visibility had improved, and hearing a groan, she glanced over the car seat as the dog lay down with a deep sigh and closed its eyes. Telling herself to take a lesson from her passenger, Maureen loosened her grip on the steering wheel.

Mesmerized by the soft rain and the flip-flopping of the wipers, Maureen drove on in a kind of daze, when the appearance of a man standing by the side of the road grabbed her attention. She drove past him, but wondered if she should go back and offer him a ride. In the life Maureen had fled, she would never dream of picking up a strange man on an unfamiliar highway at night. Now, that life was gone, and she had nothing to lose. She pressed her foot onto the brake, positioned the car in reverse, and backed up until she was alongside the tall figure walking in the rain. He wore a hooded poncho, and Maureen was relieved when she realized it was the blond-haired man from the diner.

"Do you want a ride?" Maureen called through the passenger window she had cranked open.

"I'm okay. Thanks anyway." He started walking again. It began raining harder.

"We're going in the same direction. Might as well share a ride."

He glanced skyward as lightning flashed overhead, shrugged and opened the car door. Removing his backpack, he threw off his poncho, gave it a shake, rolled it, and slid into the front seat.

"You're the person from the diner." Rain dripped from the curls of hair on his forehead.

"Yes." Maureen pulled her eyes away from the man's face and looked at the rainy road ahead. "I don't make a practice of picking up hitchhikers, but I thought I recognized you, too."

"I wasn't hitchhiking. I was walking."

"I'm pretty sure I saw you hold out your thumb, hitchhiker style."

"I was waving you to go past me. There was no thumb involved."

"Even with the poor visibility, I think I saw you put a thumb out there."

"I don't know what to tell you. It wasn't my intention to take a ride from a stranger, but I'm grateful you stopped, considering the lightning and all."

"It wasn't my intention to offer a ride to a stranger either." Maureen felt herself growing annoyed and a touch angry with the guy. What was his problem?

"Let's start over." He stretched his hand toward Maureen, offering a handshake. "I'm Jeffrey."

Maureen shook the man's hand. "Jeffrey, you said? Like in Jeffrey Dahmer?"

It was a Wisconsin thing, and Maureen hoped she sounded amused, not terrified.

"Exactly." His laugh was deep and contagious. "Except for the last name and the fact I'm not a serial killer. Last name's Bennett."

"I'm Maureen." She didn't mention her last name, uncertain she still wanted David's name, Henderson, the one she had made her own when they married.

"Good enough."

They traveled in silence, windshield wipers dragging as the rain dwindled to a few final drops. Maureen was about to turn on the radio to fill the void, when Jeffrey spoke.

"What's that smell?" He screwed his head around toward the backseat. "It's like something died in here."

"That's my dog. Careful, she doesn't like men."

"Can't say I'm a huge fan of smelly dogs either."

"It's wet-dog smell. Or maybe she needs a rest stop. We should check."

Maureen stopped at the side of the highway and opened the door in the back. The dog crawled to the edge of the seat and jumped out, landing belly-flop-style at the side of the road. It waddled off, the tall grass giving way and rustling as she moved about. Maureen was glad when the dog returned to the car.

They drove on, and Maureen noticed the last clouds fading into the east as stars sprinkled the clear, dark sky. Punctuating the silence was an occasional rumbling snore from the back seat.

"At the restaurant, I thought I saw you by a Jeep. Did something happen to it?"

"Some fuel pump thing broke. The mechanic needed to order a part which will take until tomorrow afternoon or later. I have some place I have to be."

"Where's that?"

"Near Eau Claire. A college buddy of mine lives there and is having a celebration I don't want to miss."

"And you thought walking a couple hundred miles to Eau Claire would get you there in time?"

"I'm a fast walker."

Maureen laughed. She turned on the radio, hoping for something stimulating to help her stay awake. It had been a long, horrible day, and she was exhausted. The radio was mostly static, so she turned it off, opened the window, and leaned out.

"I have gum. Sometimes it helps keep you awake."

Jeffrey held out a pack of Black Jack Gum, its faint, disgusting licorice smell permeating the air. Maureen declined and crinkled her nose. What kind of person chews Black Jack Gum?

"I might have to pull over and sleep for awhile."

"How about I drive and you sleep? I'll keep the car pointed north, and you'll get some much-needed rest."

Maureen was thinking she was nuts to allow a complete stranger to drive her car, going who knows where while she slept, but, at this point, she didn't care about anything. All she wanted was sleep.

The two switched places. Maureen lowered the seat back a little and rested her head against the door as the guy named Jeffrey Bennett pulled onto the road. He seemed to know what he was doing, and Maureen felt herself drifting off.

CHAPTER 6

M aureen awoke when Jeffrey stopped the car.

"I dreamed we were back in Illinois. Where are we?"

"Frank's Fifty-Three Truck Stop. It's on Highway 53 outside Eau Claire."

"You covered some distance. How long did I sleep?" Maureen strained to see the clock on the dashboard.

"Long enough to get us here. While you were sawing logs, I called my buddy. He's going to pick me up in half an hour."

"Will you be in time for the celebration?"

"It's tomorrow, so, yeah, I've time to spare. Let's get something to eat, my treat."

"You don't have to do that." Maureen realized she hadn't eaten anything qualifying as food since yesterday, and Jeffrey did offer to pay. "On second thought, I accept. Thanks."

When they got out of the car, she worried about the dog being left behind, so Jeffrey volunteered to buy takeout and have them eat at the outdoor tables. The food he brought smelled tempting, but Maureen could only manage to choke down a few bites and spent her time tossing bits of burger and bun to the dog, who swallowed everything whole.

Maureen wandered over to the truck stop's convenience store and, with the last bills in her wallet, bought a toothbrush, toothpaste, deodorant, and hairspray. She attempted the ATM to replenish her cash, but the card was rejected again. Feeling defeated and broke and wishing she had the one hundred dollar bill she wasted on the taxi ride that morning, Maureen trudged back to the parking lot.

Next to a beat-up green pickup truck, Jeffrey and the dog were standing with a giant of a man sporting several days' growth of blond stubble and a full head of grayish-blond dreadlocks. He towered over Maureen and reminded her of a lineman on a football team.

"Maureen, I'd like you to meet Dill. Dill and I went to law school together. Dill, this is the woman who got me here. Her name is Maureen."

"Pleasure to meet you." Dill offered a rough hewn hand to Maureen and shook hers with enthusiasm. "Having Jeffrey here will mean the world to Summer."

"Summer is his wife, who, by the way, was my girlfriend until Sasquatch here stole her from me."

Maureen felt she was supposed to laugh at the comment, but considering her recent personal situation, the scenario didn't sound funny to her. She could only manage to give Jeffrey a half-hearted smile. Dill was grinning across his entire face.

"You can't lose something you never had, Jeffrey, my friend." Dill let loose a deep, engaging laugh.

"You two went to law school?" Maureen tried not to sound surprised, but somehow the pieces didn't fit.

"Hard to believe, I know. It's a long story from a different life."

"No time for that right now." Dill motioned for Jeffrey to get into the truck. "It's only a half hour from here to the farm, but the ice cream I bought for Summer will be soup if we don't get going." Dill stepped up into the truck's cab. "See you again, Maureen."

"You'll be all right here?" Jeffrey worried out loud.

Maureen's eyes filled with tears at this near-stranger's genuine concern, something her own husband and sister had not shown.

"I'm good. Besides, I've got my dog to keep me company." She reached down to pat the animal's head, but it ducked and sauntered away towards Maureen's car. "Guess she's anxious to leave."

"Here's my number, in case you need me," Jeff said, handing her a business card, before slamming the truck's rusty passenger door.

The two men drove away, arms extended in farewell waves from the truck windows. Maureen waved in return and allowed a few self-indulgent tears to drip down her face and onto the card Jeffrey had given her, imprinted with his name, Jeffrey L. Bennett, Attorney-at-Law.

She tucked the card down in her pocket, lifted the dog into the back seat, and started the engine. Convenient to the truck stop was a motel located across the highway, and Maureen drove into its parking lot, pulling in near the main entrance. The exterior was clean but shabby and worn, wearing the faded decor of the 1980s.

Walking in, Maureen caught the two-inch heel of her sensible pump in a crack between the cement and the metal threshold, snapping it off in a jagged stump. She hobbled her way across the lobby to the check-in desk, where the manager, sporting a 1980s mullet, was seated.

"I'd like a room." Maureen stood one-footed on the undamaged shoe and leaned against the counter to steady herself.

"Seventy-nine dollars for one night. Includes continental breakfast from 6:00 to 9:00. Firearms are allowed. No pets."

"No problem." Maureen handed him a credit card and stared at her image in the blotchy mirrors covering the wall behind the counter. Her clothing was rumpled and her disheveled hair had sprung from its tie, standing up in wiry corkscrews. It was not a good look.

"Card's no good." The man slapped her Visa onto the cheap laminate surface.

"That can't be. It doesn't expire for at least two years."

"Not according to your credit card company. Wanna try a different card?" It was obvious to Maureen the guy had been down this road before.

Maureen fumbled her wallet open and mumbled to herself. Target? Nieman Marcus? Piggly Wiggly? She ended up handing him a BP card, but it was also denied.

"Sorry, lady. We do accept checks or cash. ATM is outside."

"Thanks. I'll try that."

When the bank machine flashed "Invalid Card" as had occurred before, Maureen pounded the display panel with both fists. What was happening had David written all over it.

CHAPTER 7

Wearing one broken shoe, Maureen tottered to her vehicle. She had no idea what to do about David and her credit cards. Would she have to reinstate them? Wasn't there a law or something? Maybe she could ask Jeffrey, but she hated the idea of involving him in her personal drama. As she neared the car and saw the slobbery face of the road dog pressed against the back window, Maureen laughed in spite of everything. David could wait until tomorrow. Right now her priority was finding a place to spend the night. She looked across at the well-lit truck stop.

"Looks like we're camping tonight."

Maureen left the gloomy motel where the parking lot was dark and empty and returned to the busy, well-lit truck stop, parking away from the main entrance and not far from the truckers. She moved the front seat back as far as possible, halting when the dog released a low growl.

"I don't suppose you'd trade your back seat for the front seat, which, though smaller, has a much better view." The dog rolled over, its backside to Maureen, signaling there would be no deal.

They spent the night in the car, the dog sleeping, and Maureen nodding off for minutes on occasion when she wasn't wrestling with the car seat. Only once did Maureen actually fall asleep, dreaming about the scene she was remembering with Dr. Taylor's help. Maureen could see details she hadn't noticed before, like the blue summer sky, the green of the grassy yard, and the pink of the little girl's ruffled dress, but the characters in the picture were frozen in place, as if someone had pressed the 'Pause' button. When she awoke, the sun had peeked over the Frank's Fifty-Three Truck Stop sign, and Maureen left the car in search of a restroom and coffee.

The facilities in the truck stop were clean, and Maureen did the best she could to make herself more presentable. Using coins she salvaged from the bottom of her purse, she purchased coffee and a bottle of water. In the garbage receptacle outside the restaurant she found a plastic container to use as a water bowl for the dog. It had been a downward spiral from Anson-Chambers' account executive to dumpster diver, she thought as she filled the bowl with water.

"I guess your name is Road Dog." Maureen set the container in front of the dog and watched her slurp at the water. "I know it isn't creative, but that's all I can come up with right now. We can always change it later."

Shoeless, Maureen sipped her coffee as she and Road Dog strolled around the area designated for dog-walking, a grassy space separated from the restaurant by rows of parked trucks, many of them rumbling and ready to roll. Maureen was envious of the truck drivers, heading off with a definite travel route and destination in mind. Not only did she not have a planned route, she had no destination, a car hovering on empty, and no financial means to remedy anything.

"You've hitched yourself to a train wreck." She touched Road Dog's head, and the dog didn't move away. Looks like we're making progress, Maureen told herself.

It wasn't the first time she had started with nothing, Maureen thought. When she and Jasmine moved from their Aunt Toni's, they rented a single room above an old garage downtown. Although advertised as furnished, only a double bed occupied the tiny room, but there was plenty of light from a lightbulb hanging in the center of the ceiling, with heat in the winter, and a window to open when the weather was warmer. It didn't matter to either of them what the place was like, because they were together, and it was the first time in a long time Maureen felt safe for herself and Jasmine.

Road Dog and Maureen passed the day loitering at the truck stop, staying away from the main entrances and trying to look inconspicuous. While the dog snoozed or snuffled about in the shade, Maureen wrestled with her options. As far as she knew, she still had a job with Anson-Chambers, but the prospect of returning filled her with humiliation and dread, as did the idea of facing the David and Jasmine situation. Maureen needed time to heal and to figure out where her life was going, whether it would be back to where she had been, or forward to something, anything else.

Earlier that afternoon, Maureen had noticed a "Waitress Wanted" sign posted in the restaurant window. She squared her shoulders and made the decision to apply. Maureen was certain asking for a job in bare feet would be unacceptable, so she searched under the benches until she found several pliable gobs of discarded gum, secured them to the bottom of her shoe and forced the broken heal into position, held by the gum. If she walked with care and placed minimal weight on that foot, it might work.

It was mid-afternoon with only a few customers in the restaurant, and the man swabbing his way along the length of the lunch counter wore a grease-spattered shirt with the name "Frank" stitched across the pocket. He was over six feet tall, middle-aged with a slight paunch, a patrician nose flanked by piercing dark eyes, and thick, black hair threaded with silver-grey strands. His eyes narrowed when Maureen limped to the counter.

"Is the waitress job still open?"

"Sign's up, so I'm gonna say it is."

"My name's Maureen. I'd like to apply."

"You the one who slept in her car in the back lot? The one hanging around all day with that dog?"

So much for being inconspicuous.

"May I have an application?"

"Ever done any waitressing?"

"I worked as a waitress while putting myself through college."

"How long you gonna be around?"

"For awhile. Until I can get back on my feet."

He studied Maureen for a moment, reached under the counter, and handed her an application.

"Fill this out. Check back with me in a couple of days."

That second night, Maureen and Road Dog slept in the car or rather, Road Dog slept while Maureen spent the night re-positioning herself and her body parts like a game of Twister. The next morning, Maureen was slumped against the steering wheel when someone tapped on the hood of her car.

"You realize this isn't a campground." Frank, the truck stop guy, was bending over, peering into her open window.

"I've grown to love the view and the ambience of the place." Rolling out behind Maureen's vehicle, an eighteen-wheeler, spewing diesel fumes, kicked it into gear, and roared away towards the exit.

"My morning crew is one waitress short. You're here, so you might as well get to work."

Twenty minutes later, Maureen had squeezed herself into a Frank's Fifty-Three uniform, one that had belonged to Frank's much smaller ex-wife. Since Maureen's shoes were not fit for working, or wearing, she was forced to borrow a pair of Frank's sneakers, which fit perfectly, but it was embarrassing nonetheless. She wrestled a hairnet around her hair until it was restrained, the result looking a bit like a large Brillo pad affixed to the back of her head.

There was no time to fret over her appearance, as Frank was barking instructions, breakfast orders were waiting to be delivered, tables needed clearing, and customers stood in line to be seated. Maureen grabbed a coffee pot and jumped into the fray. Waitressing was harder than she remembered, but she had been fifteen years younger the last time she stood on her feet for longer than ten minutes.

"You look like you've done this before." A tough-looking blond waitress with a buzz haircut tipped in neon orange and sporting a pierced nostril and upper lip, plus multiple tattoos, shuffled past, balancing a tray loaded with steaming platters. "I'm Ronnie. Welcome aboard."

"Thanks. Maureen."

"Watch out for Kenny over there. He'll clear your tables in a hurry and help himself to most of your tips if he gets a chance."

"Good to know."

After serving her table, Ronnie maneuvered her way past Maureen again.

"Nice hairdo." She patted Maureen's Brillo pad hair and released a loud, husky laugh. "I'm kidding. With hair like mine, I've got no business poking fun at anyone."

"It's okay. Fixing my hair is the last thing I'm worried about."

"Atta girl." Ronnie flashed Maureen a wide grin across her large, white teeth, revealing a gap between the top two front ones. "Frank's giving me the ole stink-eye, so I'd better boogie."

Ronnie hustled away, turned around, and headed back to Maureen.

"Watch your orders when you do pick-up. Wendy and Deb get their jollies out of rearranging everything, so your food plates might be all screwed up."

By the end of the shift, Maureen was exhausted, and her ankles were swollen so much her legs resembled large, thick parking meter posts. Besides working with Ronnie, the only bright spot in the day came when Frank offered his storage room to Road Dog as a place to hang out during Maureen's shift.

"It's too hot in your car for anything to survive. Long as the health inspector doesn't spot a dog near the kitchen, and as long as the dog doesn't bother anybody, she's welcome to stay here."

After the lunch crowd cleared out, Maureen went to the storage room with a pan of leftovers and meat scraps Frank had given her for Road Dog. She found the dog looking contented, sprawled out on the cool concrete floor. As Road Dog gobbled up the food, Maureen told herself the dog was doing all right.

Sleeping in the car came a bit easier that night, because Maureen was beyond exhaustion and had started earning some much-needed money. After her first two days on the job, Frank, exasperated by Maureen's nights spent in the car and her morning cleanup ritual in his restroom, offered the storage room to her and Road Dog as temporary housing until they could afford something else. He placed a clean cot and some bedding in the room for Maureen along with several old blankets for Road Dog, and beside the cot he added a crate with a small lamp.

"This is one of the nicest things anyone's ever done for me." Maureen was touched at how kind her new boss was. "Thank you, Frank."

"I'm mostly doing it for the dog."

"Road Dog thanks you, too."

"It's just a storage room." Frank turned to go back to the kitchen. "One more thing. Use the truckers' shower. It's only three bucks. You're starting to smell worse than that dog."

CHAPTER 8

....

T hree weeks passed. Maureen never turned down a shift, working six days a week, twelve hours a day. She needed the money and appreciated being busy, with little down time to think about David and Anson-Chambers and her sorry excuse for a life.

Frank was a fair and easygoing boss, and working with Ronnie turned out to be an unexpected pleasure. She made certain Maureen was given first dibs at working the full tables and reserved sections where large tips were guaranteed, and Maureen found herself laughing with Ronnie when she made fun of rude tourists and exchanged jokes and wisecracks with the regulars.

One evening, after serving a boisterous group from a bachelor party, Ronnie handed Maureen a generous stack of bills as her portion of the group's tip.

"Why are you so nice to me?" Maureen was astounded as she thumbed through the stack of bills that must have been over one hundred dollars.

"What? You don't think I am, by nature, a nice person?" Ronnie's face was hard and unsmiling.

"No, I mean, we barely know one another, and I, ah . . ." Maureen stumbled with embarrassment.

"Gotcha!" Ronnie laughed and slapped Maureen on the back. "Relax. I know what you mean, and I know what it's like to be down on your luck. Believe me, I've been there a few times myself."

Ronnie showed Maureen how to use one of the computers in the truck stop's WIFI Guest Area, and her first contact was Andrea, who was in a panic over Maureen's absence. Together, the two concocted a story creating a family emergency which evolved into a family death, a lengthy funeral, a contested will, and anything else that could explain where Maureen was for so long. Andrea expressed her fear that she would not be able to stall Anson-Chambers forever.

"They're going to fire you. I know it!"

Maureen spent her days off investigating what happened to her bank accounts and credit cards, all of which seemed to have disappeared into a financial black hole. The more time she spent online, the more Maureen worried she would somehow alert David regarding her whereabouts. The realization struck her that he would not care where she was or what had happened to her, causing Maureen to drink the rest of the Tito's vodka and cry herself to sleep that night on the canvas cot she shared with Road Dog.

When Maureen arrived at work the next morning, Ronnie held out an enormous mug filled with steaming, black coffee. "No offense, but you look like hell."

"A crying jag and half a bottle of Tito's vodka will do that to any beautiful girl."

"I didn't take you for a drinker."

"It comes and goes, depending on how depressed I'm feeling."

"I hate to break up your little coffee klatsch." Frank opened the kitchen door and gestured the two waitresses into the dining area. "Get to work."

Maureen's section was the east one-fourth of the dining room, comprised of three booths, four small tables for two to four people, and two larger tables seating five to twelve people. The four waitresses on the shift shared handling the counter. It was still early, and most of the booths and small tables were filling with folks who frequented the restaurant on a regular basis, usually for the plentiful breakfast platters served up hot, fast, and cheap.

"Coffee, Dwayne?" Maureen smiled at the burly deputy parked in the booth next to a window.

"From you, beautiful lady, it would be a pleasure." Dwayne's smile stretched across his chiseled, tan face, as the sunlight, streaming through the window, reflected off his shiny bald head.

"The usual?" Maureen asked, pouring his coffee. Dwayne worked the nightshift, 11:00 P.M. to 7:00 A.M., and he stopped for breakfast at the restaurant at least three times a week on his way home from work.

"Yup. Breakfast like a king, right?"

Business was bustling that morning, and Maureen had no chance to visit with Dwayne, something she enjoyed doing. By the time she returned to his table, he'd gone, check payment and tip underneath the empty coffee mug, and, disappointed, Maureen began clearing the booth's dishes.

From outside the restaurant, Maureen heard yelling. Peeking out the window she saw Dwayne engaged in a shouting match with Ronnie.

Dwayne walked around to stand, face to face with Ronnie, and both of them appeared to be yelling at the same time. Then Ronnie's right hand shot up and pushed the deputy backwards.

She's assaulting an officer of the law, Maureen thought. Without hesitation, she hurried outside, hoping to save Ronnie from certain arrest.

"Dwayne, is there a problem?" Maureen maneuvered between the two, and the yelling stopped. "Everyone take a breath and step back."

Maureen stood helpless for a few, agonizing, silent seconds, glancing back and forth from Ronnie to Dwayne, until the two erupted into laughter.

"It's okay, Maureen." Ronnie's chuckling paused, and she held up her hand. "Dwayne's my husband."

"Sorry, about the misunderstanding, Maureen. Ronnie and I were having a disagreement about where to go for dinner tonight." Dwayne was grinning. "Sometimes our discussions get a little heated, that's all."

"I'm so embarrassed." If she could have managed it, Maureen would have slipped between the crack in the concrete. "Ronnie, I thought you were getting yourself into trouble with the law."

"That's sweet, but I'm used to being in trouble with the law, right officer?" Ronnie kissed Dwayne on the lips and pinched his cheek.

"Now get home, lover, and make those reservations at MY favorite restaurant." For emphasis, Ronnie slapped Dwayne's rear end, grabbed Maureen's arm, and strolled the two of them back towards the restaurant.

"You should see your face right now." Ronnie gave Maureen's arm a squeeze. "Really, that was a terrific thing you tried to do. A little off the mark, but nice, all the same."

"Thank you, I think. I'm still trying to get over the fact you're married to a cop."

"I know, right? I mean, with the hair and the tattoos and the piercings, who woulda thought?"

"I think you are both very lucky," Maureen told her as they hurried inside.

Late morning on the following Tuesday, a woman entered Frank's and collapsed into a booth. Her face was scored with deep lines and her straggly, brassy blond hair sprouted from grey roots. She might have been attractive once, Maureen thought, but the years had not been easy and her choices had been unwise. Positioning a pair of bifocal glasses onto her rundown face, the woman studied the sticky menu.

Maureen turned the coffee cup upright and began pouring.

"Good morning. Are you ready . . ." Maureen halted in mid-sentence, the coffee now overflowing onto the table.

"Hey, watch what you're doing."

"Sorry." Maureen grabbed the towel from her waistband and began swabbing the table as she stared into the woman's face. The pool of coffee detoured onto the customer's lap.

"What's your problem?" The woman grabbed the towel from Maureen.

"Hello, Aunt Toni." Maureen's voice was childlike and unsteady.

"You got the wrong lady. I ain't your Aunt Toni." The woman stopped mopping at the coffee in her lap, glancing from Maureen's face to her name tag. "I don't know anybody named Maureen."

"It's me, Darla."

"That can't be right."

"It is. I used to be Darla, and now I'm Maureen."

"So you changed your name." The woman studied Maureen's face, recognition taking root. "It's been twenty years, at least, ain't that right? I kinda thought you were dead or had moved to Timbuktu or somewhere far away like that."

"I was far away, but I'm back."

"I see you've come up in the world." The woman grinned, showing yellow, tobacco-stained teeth.

"As always, you know how to make a girl feel good about herself."

"As always, you're still whining that poor me routine."

"Do you want to order or not?"

Maureen left the booth shaking as she struggled to write Toni's order on her notepad. Seeing her aunt's face and hearing her voice pulled Maureen back to a time she had shut away behind a locked and keyless door.

When the order was up, Maureen placed it in front of Toni, then slid into the booth, facing the woman who glared across the steaming plate at Maureen.

"I'd like to eat in peace."

"This won't take long. I was wondering about my mother's house."

"It's still there, if that's what you're asking."

"I need a place to live for a short time. I was thinking there would be room for me now that your kids are all grown."

"Ain't that a hoot?" Toni spewed out a dry, sarcastic laugh. "When you moved out with Jasmine, you said you wanted to forget you ever had a mother, and that, next to her, I was the worst person on earth. You claimed you hated me and never wanted to see me or your cousins again. Now, you want to live with me?"

"Only until I get back on my feet."

"So you've returned to make our loving family complete again?"

"It never was a loving family, and I can't change the hate I feel for my mother. She is a convicted murderer who deserves to be locked away in prison." Maureen was horrified she had said the words aloud.

"Don't you say that about her. Despite everything, Peggy is still your momma."

"And you're her sister, but I don't hate you. I know you took care of Jasmine and me during that terrible time. Please forgive me for being unappreciative. I was young and scared and selfish." Maureen really needed a place to live and hoped Toni would believe her.

"Not to mention mean and nasty. Plus, you took off with the last twenty bucks I had until my next welfare check."

"I know being sorry doesn't fix what I did, but I am sorry. You did Momma a great favor by taking care of us, and having you live on her farm must have been reassuring to her."

"You're darn right. Peggy gave me the deed to her property, including the house, for safekeeping. That's what I did, kept it safe. Only had to sell off a portion of the land to help pay the taxes and such."

"But you still have the house?"

"It's a rental property. Helps pay the bills, plus a little for me for my trouble." Toni flooded her food with a river of catsup.

"Is it rented now?"

"Yup, a nice young couple with kids. They tend the house and work some of the land. Works out real good." Using a serrated knife, Toni sawed away at her strip steak.

"I need a place to live, Toni."

"Is that so?" The woman shoveled a heaping forkful of hash browns into her mouth, chewing and talking at the same time. "A couple years ago, I bought this little tavern just off the highway. Called it Toni's Tap. Clever, hey?" Using her napkin, she swabbed her mouth.

"It's got a small apartment on the second floor, and that's where I live now. Well, me and Sandy, who's got two kids, no husband, and no job, plus Ricky who's on parole and looking for work." She chewed with her mouth open, a dollop of catsup landing on the front of her wrinkled blouse. "As they say, there's no room in the inn."

"It wouldn't be for long, maybe until the renters leave my mother's house. I could sleep on your couch or wherever."

"Ain't gonna happen." Toni shoved the last of the steak into her mouth. "Maybe next time be more careful about burning your bridges, Maureen or Darla, or whatever your name is."

Her cackling laugh surrounded Maureen, like a murder of crows, flapping and cawing.

CHAPTER 9

....

"Hey, Maureen!"

Approaching the booth where Maureen and Toni sat were Jeffrey and Dill.

"Looks like you've landed on your feet." Jeffrey looked her up and down.

"Yes, landed on my feet, twelve hours a day, six days a week. How about you?"

"I came for Summer and Dill's party, and let's say, I'm the guest who didn't leave."

Toni, purse under her arm, stood to squeeze past the two men surrounding the booth.

"Jeffrey," Maureen said, "this is my, er, this is Toni, one of my regular customers." He reached out a hand, but Toni had moved past him, focusing on Dillon.

"I know this young man." Toni poked a long-nailed finger into Dill's chest.

"Hello neighbor! Good to see you again."

"Dillon, you are handsome as ever. I haven't seen you in my drinking establishment lately." Toni smiled and shook Dill's large, calloused hand. "Now that's a man's hand," she said.

Toni sashayed away, heading toward the cashier, then turned and called out. "Stop in soon, and the drink's on me."

"I think the lady has a thing for you." Jeffrey grinned at Dill, but Maureen was appalled.

"That's no lady." Maureen stood and began clearing the booth. So far Frank hadn't seemed to notice she was sitting down during her shift, and she didn't want there to be any trouble. "You guys want a booth or a table?"

"Table, and bring us each a beer and a couple of Frank's famous chili dogs. Dill's been talking about them for days."

Maureen placed their order and tended to the few other customers on her side of the room. When it was her break time, she walked to where Jeffrey and Dill were seated.

"Mind if I rest here for awhile?" Without waiting for an invitation, Maureen sat, coffee cup in hand.

"Sure, take a load off. Waitressing is a tough way to earn a living," Jeffrey said.

"It's hard, hard work, that's for certain, but I've no other options." She swallowed the last of her coffee. "The worst part is not being able to find a cheap place to live, so I'm sleeping in the storage room here at the truck stop."

"No way!" Dill was grinning. "How's that working out?"

"My dog loves it. Plenty of food, safe place to sleep, lots of new friends." Maureen stared into her empty cup. "I've decided I hate waitressing. More than that, I hate living where I waitress."

"I wish there was something I could do to help, you know, to return the favor you did for me when you thought I was hitchhiking."

"You were hitchhiking. I saw your thumb."

"There was no thumb."

"Let me make a suggestion." Dill took a final gulp of his beer and wiped the foam from his mustache. "Come to work for us at Crooked Creek Farm."

"Summer and I are swamped. Our organic farm has many CSA customers and a weekly booth at several farmers' markets. Plus, we supply local restaurants and grocery stores with lots of produce. It takes many hands to get all of this accomplished, and good help is hard to find." He pointed toward Jeffrey. "I mean, so hard, we hired this guy. He had to be taught which end of the spade to hold."

"Not true, Maureen. At least, not totally true." Jeffrey laughed.

"If you're not afraid of tough work, there's a job for you, Maureen. It's dawn to dusk, six or seven days a week. You get your meals, and we have an extra bedroom across the hall from Farmer Jeffrey, if you don't mind rustic lodging."

"Dill, I'm sleeping in a restaurant storage room. Staying anywhere in a house would be deluxe accommodations."

"Doesn't pay much, but it's honest work."

"I accept." Maureen hesitated. "What about my dog?"

"Summer likes dogs better than most people, so I'm certain your dog is welcome."

"It's settled then." Jeffrey smiled. "Let's get you out of this place."

"I'll need to give Frank some notice. He's been good to my dog and me."

"Of course. Call me to let us know when you can start."

CHAPTER 10

A week later, Maureen and Road Dog said good-bye to Frank and Ronnie and were on their way to Dill and Summer's farm. As they pulled out of Frank's parking lot, Maureen looked back at the two friends who had made the worst weeks of her life tolerable and had helped her survive. Her hand reached to touch the soft scarf tied around her neck, a parting gift from Ronnie who advised her to always watch her back and protect her jugular.

Driving with the windows down, Maureen let her hair blow untethered and wild, as Road Dog occupied the front passenger seat, loose face flapping with the wind. The drive was less than thirty miles, but Maureen could feel the burden of her left-behind life lifting from her shoulders in this green and tranquil place.

Earlier that morning, Maureen received a frantic call from Andrea. The Anson-Chambers Board of Directors was meeting later in the day to discuss what they considered Maureen's irresponsible departure from the company, and, as rumor had it, to fire her with expediency, a term meaning Maureen was done for. If the rumor was true, she would be disqualified from receiving any severance pay, accrued vacation pay, and sick leave pay.

"I'm afraid there's more," Andrea said. "You remember Tyler, the tall guy in auditing? Well, he and I have become semi-close. We were talking about work, and I told him how much I missed working for you and how I wished you would return. He let it slip he doubted you were coming back because you were already making withdrawals from your 401K plan with the company."

"I haven't touched that money." Maureen was shaken at the thought of losing years of savings.

"That's what I figured. Who would be hacking into your account?"

"I'm not sure." Maureen was sure. David was stealing from her.

"You realize the Board views those withdrawals as proof you have no intention of returning. You are coming back, aren't you?"

Maureen couldn't give Andrea an answer because she had no idea what she was planning to do. Believing she still had a well-paying position at Anson-Chambers had been reassuring, even considering the company's recent treatment of her. The fact they would fire Maureen after her fifteen years of loyal service was not unusual in the business world, but it was still hurtful. More cruel than the possibility of Anson-Chambers firing her was David's willingness to commit criminal acts, like cutting her off financially and stealing from her personal retirement savings.

Maureen turned off the main highway onto County Trunk ES. It wound its way into a broad valley strewn with streams, tucked between rolling hills and steep slopes covered with hardwood forests. After a mile or so, Maureen spotted the broken, hand-painted signpost attached to a white fence Jeffrey said was the turnoff to Dill's farm. It read "Go Straight to Crooked." Maureen was reminded of the sign in Winnie the Pooh, "Trespassers Will." Both signs, by their broken brevity, were noticeable, but teetered on the brink of being unhelpful and confusing.

White fencing lead Maureen and Road Dog past fields and gardens, their car tires crackling and bumping along the gravel road. Rattling across a low, stone bridge, Maureen slowed as they approached an impressive, white house, surrounded by oak trees. She parked the car and stood facing the home, hands on her hips, admiring the expansive porch that extended across the entire front and wrapped itself around the corner. A massive front door was painted strawberry red and was flanked by spiral topiary trees in copper urns. White wicker chairs faced the front lawn, and enormous red geraniums in white pots hung above the length of the railings which were anchored with sturdy pillars at the corners. A variety of large colonial and bay windows assured the interior would be filled with sunlight. Maureen loved the house.

Bounding down the side porch steps, headed straight for Maureen, was a mountain of a black dog. A piercing whistle from the porch stopped the animal short of where Maureen stood, frozen in place.

"Samuel, sit. Stay." A tall, slender woman wearing faded jeans, a Crooked Creek Farm tee-shirt, and knee-high barn boots crossed the yard, hand outstretched.

"You must be Maureen. I'm Summer. That's Samuel."

Her hand was calloused and tanned, and she captured Maureen with blue eyes the color of wild chickory. Summer had one of those exquisite faces that would cause everyone, even women, to turn and stare. Her head was smooth, tan, and bald.

"Samuel's friendly. Sometimes he's too friendly." Summer released the dog from its sit/stay, and he met Maureen with exuberance and droplets of slobber.

"I'm glad you like dogs. Jeffrey said you were bringing yours with you?"

"Yes, that's her, hanging out of the passenger window. Her name's Road Dog."

Maureen opened the car door, and Road Dog dropped to the ground with her usual lack of grace. Samuel was there before either Maureen or Summer could stop him, and Road Dog's reaction was immediate. Teeth bared, she lunged, snapping and growling as poor Samuel retreated to hide behind Summer, with his ears down and tail tucked.

Maureen was horrified, while Summer laughed.

"No worries," she said. "Samuel is big and looks intimidating, but he is afraid of his own shadow. Give it time. The two of them will figure it out."

Maureen had serious doubts about Summer's prediction, but figured Road Dog could hold her own, no matter what. Grabbing her sparse belongings from the car, Maureen followed Summer in through the side door to the spacious kitchen. Jars of jam and jelly filled the oversized island in the center of the room. There was an old-fashioned farm sink and a vintage 1960s stove surrounded by pale grey cabinets. The two remaining walls were deconstructed down to the studs, with electrical wiring, heating ducts, and plumbing winding through them.

"As you can see, we're in the midst of remodeling. It'll be finished someday."

"I thought this was a brand new house."

"The exterior, including all of the windows, is new. Most of the inside is almost done."

"What an enormous island!"

"I had to decide between having a new refrigerator and stove or this island." Summer ran her hands over the smooth, granite surface. "We're still using Dill's grandparents' stove and their old Frigidaire limping along in the back hall. Feel free to go in the refrigerator and help yourself to whatever you need."

From outside, a flurry of barks riddled the air, instigated by Samuel with Road Dog joining in. The barking followed Jeffrey into the kitchen.

He greeted Maureen with a quick hug and headed for the refrigerator. "Did you have any trouble finding us?"

"Your directions were excellent." Maureen laughed. "The sign threw me off a little."

Oh, yeah, I always forget about the "Go Straight to Crooked" thing. We gotta fix that."

"No, leave it. I think it's whimsical and draws attention to the farm."

The honking of a horn grabbed Maureen's attention.

"That's Dill," Jeffrey said. " Lots of customers in the berry patch today. I should get back." Hurrying down the steps, Jeffrey turned to say, "Glad you're here, Maureen."

Summer was positioning a baseball cap over her shiny head. "If you're ready, I've a mile-long list of things needing to be done."

For the next three hours, the two women worked thinning, weeding, and hoeing in an enormous vegetable garden near the house. Maureen was introduced to the Dutch push hoe, a long-handled hoe with a T-grip at one end, easy on the hands and back, which required no bending over to make it work. After a late and quick afternoon break, Summer put Maureen to work turning the compost piles.

"Compost is the black gold of gardening. The piles need to be turned on a regular basis to keep the interior temperature consistent and hot."

After some initial directions from Summer, Maureen spent the remainder of the afternoon working the compost piles, each at varying stages of decomposition. Although it was early June, the day was warm and humid, and when Maureen felt she could not lift the pitchfork one more time, Summer called it a day. The two women headed toward the kitchen carrying baskets filled with peas, lettuce, kale, new potatoes, and young beets. Samuel and Road Dog tagged along behind them.

"I hope you like vegetables, Maureen, because they're our dinner tonight. Actually, they're our dinner most nights," Summer said. "Now, if we're lucky, Dill will remember I asked him to save us some strawberries for our dessert."

CHAPTER 11

T he evening meal prepared by Summer was delicious, and despite Maureen's weariness, she ate with gusto. Around the table, the dinner conversation was lively among the three long-time friends, and Maureen, grateful her participation was not required, concentrated on devouring the healthy, scrumptious food.

After dinner, Summer showed Maureen to her bedroom located upstairs in a small section of the house Dill and Summer had not begun to renovate. The wooden door's hinges creaked and complained when Maureen and Road Dog pushed their way inside, and the worn pine floor planks were uneven waves beneath their feet. A single window in the room was open to the evening breeze, setting the pale pink ruffled curtains aflutter.

"The bathroom is at the end of the hall," Summer said. "It's a bit old-fashioned, but the plumbing works fine. I'll put out some extra towels for you."

"You'll share the bath with Jeffrey," she said over her shoulder, "but don't worry. He's a neat freak. His bedroom is across from yours."

"Everything is lovely. Thanks, again, for giving me a place to stay."

"You're welcome, but, believe me, we're not giving you anything. Your hard work will earn it, and then some."

Lucky for Maureen she had few possessions, because the room, tucked into an alcove, was small, with one tall dresser against the east wall, a single bed with a light clamped to its headboard, and a closet no bigger than an over-sized refrigerator. Maureen hung up a few shirts and the clothes from her last day at Anson-Chambers and used the tall dresser for the remainder of her things, tossing a couple items of clothing in each drawer until she ran out of clothes. When she felt settled in, Maureen hurried to take a shower, not wanting to cause Jeffrey any inconvenience by getting in his way on her first day.

By the time Maureen returned to the bedroom, Road Dog was arranging herself on the bottom half of the bed. Maureen had become accustomed to sharing sleeping space with Road Dog when they lived in Frank's storeroom, but she decided being in their new home was an opportune time to establish some ground rules.

"Here's how this is going to go. This is your bottom corner of the bed. I need to straighten my legs, so the rest of the bed, including this part at the end, is mine. Understood?"

Maureen snapped off the headboard light and slid into bed. Road Dog was still sprawled across the bottom half and gave a half-hearted growl as she was pushed aside, but Maureen held her ground for the leg space she needed. It might not last the night, but as she stretched herself out for the full length of the bed, it felt good.

Sometime during the night, Maureen awoke. At first, the room was silent except for Road Dog's purring breaths, but something had dragged her out of a deep sleep, so Maureen held still and listened. There came a different sound, like the back and forth creaking of a swing, a sound so clear Maureen could picture the little girl from her memory, the one wearing the pink dress, swaying high and low, pumping her legs to make her toes touch the sky.

Maureen switched on the light. Road Dog opened one eye, glanced around, and rolled over. Maureen could see there was nothing amiss in the room, still dark around the edges. The curtains at the window hung limp and motionless.

Turning toward the small closet door near the foot of the bed, Maureen heard the odd sound again. There, that was the sound, coming from the other side of the white painted door. A mouse or squirrel perhaps? The wind? The creaking and complaining of an old farmhouse?

She slid her bare feet to the cool floor and stepped to within inches of the closed door. Pressing her ear to the chipped worn surface, Maureen listened, not breathing, palms pressing against the wood. Maybe she should go back to bed and ignore the noise. Maybe the sound would go away on its own. Then, she heard it again. There was nothing to do but open the door and find the source of the noise, so she could forget about it and salvage a few hours of precious sleep. She yanked the metal latch downward, and the door released, drifting open. Maureen's few belongings were hanging as she had left them, clustered together. On the far end of the metal bar, a distance away from her clothing, there was something else. A thin metal hanger was swinging on the bar with a scritch scratch sound. On the hanger was a little girl's pink ruffled dress.

CHAPTER 12

M aureen slammed the closet door and wobbled backwards, pressing her hands over her ears. Somehow, she and Road Dog ended up stowed away in the bathroom, with Maureen sitting on the floor, bleary-eyed and wringing her hands. Was she crazy, or was the dress in the closet identical to the one worn by the girl in Maureen's memory?

"Unless you're dead in there, I'd say your time is up." The words were slow and measured, while the knocking at the door was rapid fire.

When Road Dog added her barking to Jeffrey's insistent thumping, Maureen stood up, stiff from sitting on the floor. How long they were in there, Maureen had no idea, and she said a silent thank you to Jeffrey for unknowingly interrupting her mental breakdown.

"I'll be right out." Her face in the mirror was pale and haggard, surrounded by a halo of wiry, disorderly curls. There was no fixing any of it, so she opened the door and hustled out, head down.

"It's all yours." She and Road Dog were back in the bedroom before Jeffrey had a chance to comment.

Maureen leaned against her room door and fixated on the closet a few feet away. The bedroom was silent and still, except for a delicate breeze now rustling the curtains. With baby steps, she crossed to the closet door, grasped the metal latch and pulled it open. Inside the tiny closet, her clothes remained where she had hung them. The opposite end of the bar was empty.

She reached inside the closet and ran her fingers along the smooth metal bar to where she had seen the dress. She checked underneath and between all the other hanging clothes and dropped to her knees, skimming her hands over the worn and dusty floor. No pink dress was in the closet. Had there ever been one?

When Maureen closed the closet door, Road Dog laid herself in front of it, stretching out her stocky body as she shut her eyes. Sitting on the end of the bed, Maureen searched for an explanation of what seemed to have happened. Perhaps she hadn't been awake at all, but instead had sleepwalked to the bathroom where Jeffrey's knocking had awakened her. Maureen had experienced sleepwalking before. Several times David found her wandering about in the middle of the night engaged in strange behaviors, like rummaging through the kitchen cupboards or standing on their back porch staring into the darkness.

"All finished in the bathroom, in case you need more time." Jeffrey tapped on her door.

Get a grip, Maureen ordered herself as she climbed back into bed. Whatever you thought you saw wasn't real at all.

CHAPTER 13

I t was Maureen's first full day at Crooked Creek Farm, and she soon discovered there was no time to dwell on the closet episode. Organic farming is labor intensive, and a small crew of experienced, tireless laborers began at sunrise and worked until the day's jobs were finished. Besides Dill, Summer, and Jeffrey, Dill employed his long-time friend Loriano and Lo's wife Silvia, both of whom had been working at the farm since Dill's grandparents operated it. Filling out the employee roster were Eric, Lucy, Will and Genna, all of whom planned on majoring in Agri-Business after graduating from high school. This was their second or third season working at Crooked Creek Farm, and that left Maureen last in the pecking order. Not only did she know little about organic farming, she was totally out of shape and definitely the oldest crew member.

As they walked to Dill's truck, Eric told Maureen how the pressure to weed, irrigate, and harvest intensified as the days in June became warmer. Today he, Lucy, and Maureen were to pick the snap peas, spring greens, fennel, radishes, rhubarb, and kale, while Will and Genna were picking boc choi, swiss chard, spinach, leeks, arugula and early carrots. It was not uncommon to harvest as many as twenty different crops in one day, in preparation for the CSA pickups scheduled.

Dill started his old truck and transported the harvesting gang out to the vegetable fields. As the produce was picked, full containers would be placed at the ends of rows, with the pickers working their way down the rows and across the fields, until they arrived back at the produce wash area. After being cleaned and sorted, the vegetables and fruits would be transported by Dill to the barn for preparation and pick-up by their CSA customers.

Maureen had done farm chores as a girl, but the immensity of this operation was impressive and intimidating. She had never shied away from hard work, so she began with enthusiasm, accepting suggestions and tips from Eric and Lucy on what to do and the best way to do it. Determined to keep up with them, Maureen soon figured out that doing so was impossible.

"It's okay to take breaks," Eric told her as he guzzled from a metal water bottle.

"I would, if I could only stand up and straighten my back." Maureen groaned.

"I remember the summer I started at CCF. I could barely move at the end of those first days." Lucy stood up and stretched her slender torso, then twisted left and right. "Yoga helps. And Tylenol. Lots of Tylenol."

Maureen managed to stand erect and stretched her hands over her head, remembering seeing something similar on a yoga program she had recorded by mistake. Swaying her head from side to side, she hoped to loosen her neck muscles. Off in the distance to her left, she noticed an unusual land formation resembling a monster-sized sand dune.

"What's that over there?" Maureen pointed, shielding her eyes from the blinding sunshine. "It reminds me of a sand bar, like on a beach or desert, only it's thirty feet high."

"If only it was a sand bar." Lucy stood in the row next to Maureen and glanced toward the berm. "It's not that romantic. Belongs to a mining operation. The piles are called "overburdens" which is the farmland they move aside to get to what they're mining. It's piled high to try to hide the mine."

"Mining for what?"

"For sand." Lucy wiped the sweat from her neck and tipped her water bottle up to swallow the last drops. "Sand for fracking."

"I've heard of that." Maureen couldn't hide her surprise. "I didn't know Wisconsin had any gas or oil."

"They're not doing the actual fracking here, only mining the sand used in fracking. We have lots of sand up here." Lucy tossed Maureen a water bottle. "Stay hydrated. We'd better catch up."

They started back to work as Eric finished his row and was moving on to the next one. The remainder of the morning was spent bent over the lush vegetables, harvesting them and hauling the large bins to the end of each row for pick-up. Back at the barn, the crew gathered for a quick lunch, then joined Summer in the prep area to wash the produce, remove debris and poor quality vegetables, bunch and bundle like items, and pack boxes for the day's CSA customers.

"The Community Supported Agriculture customers are our bread and butter. There are thirty-five CSA Monday pick-ups," Summer explained to Maureen as they worked. "We do it by the honor system, allowing folks to drive in, find their order, and check themselves off the list."

An ancient John Deere tractor rumbled toward the prep crew, and Jeffrey jumped off, holding something in his hand.

"I stopped at the house and heard this in the kitchen, ringing like crazy." He held out Maureen's cell phone. "I think somebody is anxious to get ahold of you."

"Thanks. I was going to take it with me today, but it needed charging." Maureen studied the phone. "Summer, is it okay if I stop to check this?"

"Go ahead. This is the last box."

Scanning the text messages, Maureen counted nine in a row from Andrea, not to mention her secretary's numerous voicemails. It would be good to hear a familiar voice, even if the news wasn't good.

Andrea answered Maureen's call after one ring.

"Maureen, thank goodness! I've been going crazy trying to reach you."

"I could tell. Sorry, but my phone needed charging, and I was away all day working."

"You forget you're talking to someone who knows you. I am painfully familiar with your technology avoidance tactics."

"Again, I'm sorry. Now, tell me what's happening. Am I fired?"

"The Board called me in, during their meeting. It was intimidating to say the least. I stuck to our story about the funeral and everything, but you've been gone almost a month."

"I know, and I'm sorry. It's just that I'm not sure where my life is headed. How did everything turn out?"

"I'm the one who should be apologizing. As the Board continued to grill me, I panicked. Although they didn't fire you, I'm afraid I may have made things worse."

"Not sure that's possible. Tell me."

"I told them that after the illness and death of your family member and the ugliness of the contested will, you had a sort of a nervous breakdown."

"Believe it or not, you're not far from the truth." Maureen couldn't help herself and began laughing.

"It's not funny, Maureen. The more I talked, the more I panicked."

"I regret that all this landed on your shoulders. Maybe I should send in my resignation and get it over with."

"No, you can't do that." Andrea's voice revealed her desperation. "You've been committed to a mental health facility. Indefinitely."

Maureen became hysterical, laughing until the tears rolled down her cheeks.

"You do seem a little bit crazy, if you want to know the truth."

Maureen pulled herself together. Andrea needed reassurance that her boss and friend was not nuts. Whatever Andrea had done was more than anyone could ask.

"Andrea, it's all right. As a matter of fact, what you told them was perfect. They can't fire me, because it would be discriminatory. Plus, my personal health information is protected under the law."

"I don't think they're going to let this go."

"Neither do I, but you've bought me some time. For that, I am grateful."

"I think everything will be forgiven if you come back soon."

"I doubt that."

"Yeah, you're probably right. One thing I know for sure. If you don't come back, I have to work for Don."

"For that, dear friend, I am truly sorry."

CHAPTER 14

T he workers cleaned the washing area in preparation for the next day and finished the afternoon in the field, pulling weeds and thinning the beets, carrots and radishes. Together, the group walked along a well-worn path, returning to the farmhouse where Summer was lighting the grill. Despite her suntanned complexion, she appeared pale and drawn.

"Grilled veggies for dinner, because I know you haven't seen enough vegetables today!"

There was a collective groan as Jeffrey passed around cold beers.

"Maureen, how are you doing after your first day?"

"Stiff, sore, feeling old."

"After a few days, it'll seem like you've been doing this all your life, your very, very long life."

This time, there was a communal chuckle, and Maureen joined in. It felt good to laugh, even if it was at her own expense.

"I can work a pretty mean grill, Summer," Maureen said, reaching for the tongs. "Why don't you relax, and we'll do the rest."

Summer appeared to be exhausted and accepted Maureen's offer. Dill pulled the chaise lounge nearer to the grilling, and Summer laid back as her husband covered her with a light blanket. Samuel sat at her side, his head resting on Summer's lap.

After dinner, Maureen prodded Road Dog into taking a short walk. The conversation with Andrea was troubling, and Maureen needed time to consider the possibility of resigning from her position at Anson-Chambers and to figure out what to do about her precarious finances.

"Want some company?"

Jeffrey trotted toward Maureen and stopped to pet Road Dog.

"I think she likes me."

"Have you given her any food?"

"Every chance I get."

"Then she likes you."

The three strolled in the direction of the setting sun with Road Dog leading the way. Being with Maureen had been a blessing for the once mistreated and emaciated creature who trotted along with energy and a zest for life. It was amazing what good food and plenty of love could do for living things, Maureen thought.

"Hey, Maureen, I hope I didn't offend you with my remark about you having lived a very long life."

"It's impossible to escape the obvious. No offense taken."

"To tell you the truth, I think you and I are about the same age. Besides, you held you own out there in the field, and that's saying something."

"Thanks. I've never been afraid of hard work."

"That's all it takes." Jeffrey was studying Maureen's face. "Anything you need to talk about?"

"Nope. Residual blowback from my previous life."

"If you need any legal advice, I'd be happy to help."

Maureen hesitated. Her credit cards were unusable, her bank accounts gone, someone had accessed her 401K, her husband was having an affair with her sister, and it was very probable she was about to lose her hard-earned position at Anson-Chambers. She felt deceived, humiliated, and alone, but wasn't sure she was ready to share her painful troubles.

"It's nothing. Since I've been away from home, I've had some problems with my finances."

"What's going on?"

"My money was in joint accounts with another person. When I attempted to use my ATM card or make any online withdrawals, the accounts were closed. The money's gone."

"That's unfortunate. The problem when you have a joint account is that either person has the right to move funds or close the account. You can check your bank agreement to be certain this is the case, but, in general, that's how it works."

Maureen had already surmised what Jeffrey told her, and although she was sick with worry, she tried to make light of the situation.

"Guess I need to be more careful in choosing my banking partner. The bank robber's mask he wore was a definite warning sign I shouldn't have ignored."

"Sometimes it's hard to tell who's the bad guy and who isn't."

Road Dog had turned around and was trotting toward the farm house, so Maureen and Jeffrey followed, walking together in a comfortable silence.

"I think it would be a good idea for you to find a new bank and open an account there," Jeffrey said when they reached the porch. "It will begin to re-establish your financial credibility."

"I'll do that. Thanks for the advice." Maureen wondered if the $237 she saved up from her restaurant tips constituted financial credibility.

CHAPTER 15

It was Saturday, Maureen's day off. She survived the first week as an organic farmhand with a sore back, plenty of blisters, and a sense of accomplishment she hadn't felt in a long time. Taking Jeffrey's advice, she and Road Dog drove toward Chippewa Falls, a nearby town with several banks. Once they entered the city limits, Maureen located the Star Credit Union, and inside, she was directed to a personal banker who would help her set up an account.

"Our checking and savings accounts require no minimum balance and have no fees," the woman told Maureen as she clicked information into her computer.

"That's good."

"You can do your banking online, if that suits you, plus pay any bills using direct pay, right from your accounts." She finished typing and turned to face Maureen. "You look so familiar to me. I could swear I know you from some place."

"I'm new to the area in the last couple of months. Don't know a soul." Maureen could feel the sweat seeping through her shirt, despite the air conditioning.

"You didn't go to high school around here? Maybe you were in sports or 4-H?"

"I'm from Illinois, so, no. Is that all?"

"Yes, of course. Sign in the highlighted areas, and you're all set."

Maureen was almost to the door when the woman called out to her.

"Maureen, wait."

Wanting to run, but needing to avoid suspicious behavior, Maureen stopped.

"You forgot your free checks. They must have fallen out of the folder I gave you."

"Right, thanks." Maureen grabbed them from the woman's hands and fled the building.

In the parking lot, the car was still running, air conditioning on full blast for Road Dog's benefit. Fumbling with the extra key, Maureen opened the door and dropped into the front seat. To placate her paranoia, she locked the doors. Was it possible the bank employee was correct about recognizing Maureen?

It had been a long time since Maureen lived in the area, so the chances of anyone identifying her were slim, especially in a town she visited on only a few occasions when she was young. People do move around and take jobs in neighboring communities, she told herself. It was possible, but doubtful, someone would know her here in Chippewa Falls. Maureen didn't think she recognized the woman, although she did kind of resemble the Norton kids who went to her school. Get over yourself, she thought. The lady was being nice, making conversation. That's all. There was no way this stranger would have identified Maureen as Darla, the girl whose family was in the news all those years ago.

Driving home, instead of turning in the direction of Crooked Creek Farm, Maureen succumbed to her curiosity and veered east, toward the odd berm she had noticed near the far end of Dill and Summer's property. What she saw as she approached the giant formation was something that could only be described as a rural landscape transformed. She parked off the road, leashed Road Dog, and walked through the remnants of a field. Pushing aside some brush, the two emerged at the edge of the mine and peered down at a 20-foot drop into a flat and barren moonscape covering one hundred acres or more. Half of it curved around a slight hill and out of view, and a massive pit was centered inside the operation, the land's bowels ripped open for the sandy treasure buried there. An excavator grunted and puffed as it loaded the silica sand into a dump truck.

Road Dog began a fierce flurry of barks at the machines clattering within the mine, so Maureen hurried the dog away from the disturbing scene. Equally troubling for Maureen was the close proximity of the mine to Dill and Summer's farm.

Rather than turning around and heading west toward Crooked Creek Farm, Maureen and Road Dog continued driving eastward on the road running parallel to the mine's outer boundary. When they had gone about six or seven miles, another enormous berm indicated the end of the operation, in sharp contrast to the lush green fields stretching away from the barren excavation.

"Guess we should go back," Maureen said to a snoozing Road Dog.

Why she didn't turn around, Maureen couldn't say. Something compelled her to follow the road a few miles more, and soon enough, she understood. She had come upon a dilapidated house, squatting in unruly weeds, set back some distance from the road. Like a homing pigeon, Maureen had located the place she called home for eighteen years, a place she had purged from her memory.

The car coasted to a stop, gravel snapping underneath the tires. Maureen stepped out and stood in the weed infested driveway, where there was no wind, no movement of any kind, only the heat and the sun. She stared at the sagging porch, its shingled roof hanging over a pair of windows, tattered curtains limp behind the broken panes. Hanging loose from rusted hinges, the screen was propped open with the remnants of a mailbox. The place appeared to be empty inside. Toni had lied to her.

Something touching Maureen's hand drew her attention away from the house. Road Dog was sitting beside her, licking her hand.

"What do you think of the old "Home Sweet Home?"

Road Dog summoned an indifferent expression and belched.

"I see you are not impressed. Come on, let me show you around."

She approached the shabby porch, devoid of railings and front steps and decided entering there was too risky, and at the rear of the house, the door and windows were boarded shut. Toward the back of what once was the yard, two weathered clothesline poles stood opposite one another, relieved of their lines, with hooks still embedded in their rotting wood. Where the vegetable garden had been, a tangle of burdocks, ragweed, and reed canary grass flourished. Based on her memory of that one particular summer day where the girl moved back and forth on the swing, Maureen was puzzled by what she didn't see in the yard. There was no swing set.

CHAPTER 16

It was late afternoon when Maureen and Road Dog arrived at Crooked Creek Farm and parked in back of the farmhouse. She was grateful no one was around except Samuel, who greeted them in the yard, followed them into the kitchen, and up the stairs, with Maureen carrying a half-full bottle of sauvignon blanc and a wine glass.

With the dogs settled in, Maureen sat on the floor between them, sipped her wine, and contemplated why she was feeling depressed. Seeing the old, run-down house shouldn't affect her, at least not in the negative sense, because years ago she and Jasmine chose to leave and were grateful to be anywhere else. She hated the fact that she wished she could talk to Jazz about seeing the place, but Jasmine was with David. On impulse, Maureen picked up her phone and called a familiar number, certain she wouldn't have to talk to anyone.

"You've reached the office of Dr. Simone Taylor. If this is an emergency . . ." Maureen listened to the rest of the message.

"Hi, uh, this is Maureen. You don't have to call me back, but I wanted to let you know everything is okay. It's possible you've heard some stuff about me . . . on second thought, why would you? Besides, whether you've heard gossip about me or not, rumors of my demise are greatly exaggerated."

"Maureen, hello. This is Dr. Taylor."

"You're supposed to be closed. Why are you answering the phone?"

"When I heard your voice, I made an exception. How is everything?"

"Been better. I left my job and my husband, but not because I wanted to."

"I'm sorry. How are you handling it?"

"Surprisingly well. I have a dog and that helps."

"Anything else I need to know?"

"Nope, that's about it. I won't be back for our little sessions for the foreseeable future."

"I'm glad you've reached out to me. I hope you will continue to stay in touch."

"I probably will." Maureen doubted she would, but she felt compelled to say otherwise. "There is one more thing."

"Tell me."

"It was pink."

"Pink?"

"The dress, on the little girl. It was pink."

Maureen hung up. She wished she hadn't called Dr. Taylor and wondered why in the world she had mentioned the color of the dress. It was a stupid detail, not worthy of being mentioned.

The conversation with Dr. Taylor left Maureen thirsty so she proceeded to finish the bottle of wine before tumbling into bed. When incessant pounding on her bedroom door caused Maureen to drag herself awake, she realized it was already morning and trudged to the door, opening it a sliver.

Jeffrey was in the hallway, wearing blue jeans and pulling a tee shirt over his bare chest, his hair still wet from a recent shower. "You ok?"

"Peachy." Maureen figured she wasn't looking her best, whatever that was.

"I'm sensing you had a little wine last night."

"What makes you think that?"

"Because you smell like wine, you appear to have slept in your clothes, and I know a hangover when I see one."

"Very observant, Detective Bennett. Are you going to arrest me?"

"Nope. Just wanted to let you know I'm making breakfast this morning, and you're invited."

"Great. Thanks."

She closed the door, swallowed three Tylenol, and crawled back into bed. The pounding in her head began to ease as the sun's rays reached through the ruffled curtains and scattered ribbons of light across the floor. Despite the fact it was Sunday and Maureen could sleep in, Jeffrey's invitation to breakfast and the smell of coffee beckoned her downstairs.

She found him in the kitchen, whisking a creamy concoction in a deep bowl.

"What are you making?" Maureen, coffee in hand, sat at the island.

"The answer to all of your problems, possibly all the world's problems."

"That good, huh?"

"Don't believe a word this guy says." Dill entered the room, carrying a colander filled with ruby-red strawberries. "He says that about everything he cooks, and you can see how well it's worked so far."

"Oh ye, of little faith," Jeffrey said, lifting a perfect, round pancake from the sizzling griddle as he reached for a plate. "The first one's for you, Maureen."

"Let me add some strawberries on top to improve the pancake's mediocre flavor." Dill sliced several and fanned them across the golden brown pancake. "Now, enjoy."

Summer shuffled into the kitchen, her gaunt body an apparition floating in a flowing nightshirt.

"Dill, I thought you were bringing my medicine." Summer's voice was shallow and dry, like dead leaves skipping in the wind. "I need it now!"

"I'm sorry. I thought you might be able to eat strawberries today." He held out the bowl of berries like a peace offering.

"How can I eat anything without taking my medicine first?" She swung her feathery hand, knocking the berries to the floor, and left the room.

Dill followed Summer out of the kitchen, while Jeffrey stooped to clean the tossed strawberries from the floor.

"You can't blame Summer. She's had a bad week and is in a lot of pain."

Maureen sat without speaking, chewing what once were delicious pancakes that were now tasteless cardboard.

"Guys, I apologize." Dill lumbered in. "That was all my fault."

He poured himself a half cup of coffee, reached for a bottle in the cupboard, and poured whiskey into the cup, filling it to the top. With Samuel following at his heals, Dill plodded out to the porch, the screen door slamming behind them.

CHAPTER 17

A lthough it was Sunday and not a scheduled work day, Maureen and Jeffrey labored in the gardens all morning, where there was plenty to do. They wanted to help Dill, who normally worked seven days a week, but today he stayed inside taking care of Summer. At noon, Jeffrey called it quits, and Maureen decided to take another drive, this time to visit Aunt Toni and confront her about the rundown condition of her mother's house and the fact it was unoccupied and uninhabitable. There was also the issue of whether the sand mine near or even on Dill's farm could possibly be getting close to her mother's property.

With a sketchy map from Dill, Road Dog and Maureen set out for Toni's Tap, located southeast of the farm on Tainter Lake. The early morning sunshine had disappeared behind a blanket of thick, grey clouds that promised showers, and the two traveled with the windows open, as Road Dog rested her chin on the car door, her nose twitching in the cool breeze.

The tavern was small, with a single door flanked on either side by two windows, each with four panes of glass. It was constructed of logs and chinking, the logs stained a deep, bloody red to contrast with the white filler. The cedar shake roof, aged to a mossy grey, sported an electronic sign planted across the length of the roof ridge. Garish colors flashed "Toni's Tap," punctuated with a pair of puckered red lips. Maureen would not have expected anything less where her aunt was involved.

Maureen leashed Road Dog and the two stepped inside the dark room. An ancient, pine plank bar, scarred and worn smooth, stretched along one wall. Maureen hesitated in the doorway, allowing her eyes to adjust to the dimly lit interior. Road Dog emitted a low growl. The lone man seated at the bar, along with five men playing cards at a table nearby, all turned to stare. When they swiveled back around to the business of cards and drinking, Maureen was satisfied she had not been recognized.

"Well, look what the cat dragged in." Toni stood behind the bar, cigarette dangling from her mouth, makeup layered thick and cheap, her hair teased into a messy french twist. A red satin top revealed Toni's wrinkled chest, and gold disks the size of saucers, hung from her dangling lobes. The smell of cheap perfume met Maureen full force.

"You and I need to have a conversation." Maureen parked herself on a stool, while Road Dog spread out near her feet on the worn linoleum floor.

"I'm working. Stools are for paying customers."

"I'll have a Diet Coke." Maureen tossed a five dollar bill on the bar. "Keep 'em coming."

"What do you want?" Toni snapped open a can and slid it down the bar to Maureen.

"Yesterday, I drove to my mother's house, for old time's sake."

"I'm happy for you."

"Here's some news. The place is empty, abandoned, falling down."

"Guess I lost track of my renters. Could be they moved out."

"Must have been years ago, if there were ever renters at all."

"Not that it's any of your business, but it was costing money to keep up that junk hole, money I didn't have."

"There was nothing wrong with the house when we lived there."

"You were a kid. Easy to overlook what a dump the house was."

"It wasn't that bad."

"Years went by. Things got more and more rundown. After I moved into this bar, there wasn't one soul interested in renting a run-down shack, especially after what happened there."

After what happened there. Maureen felt a shiver ripple over her body.

She stared at her aunt. The house was uninhabitable so there was really nothing to be done about that. Maureen had other questions for Toni, but she doubted her aunt would be forthcoming about anything having to do with the property.

She took another sip of her soda and set the can on the bar. "I think we're done for now."

"I think we're done period."

Outside, Maureen let Road Dog relieve herself before helping her into the car. As Maureen climbed in, she took a long look at the bar. We're not done old lady, not by a long shot.

On Sunday nights, it was a tradition that everyone employed at Crooked Creek Farm was invited to gather around the fire pit in Dill and Summer's backyard to roast marshmallows, eat s'mores, and relax before the work week ahead. It was Maureen's first Sunday on the crew, so she wasn't sure what to expect. Everyone was there, including Summer, and the mood was upbeat and friendly.

"Here's a marshmallow and stick." Jeffrey made his way around the circle of lawn chairs with a bag of marshmallows and a container of two-pronged metal sticks. "First one to drop a marshmallow into the fire buys the beer next Sunday."

Maureen enjoyed being a part of this gregarious group. They laughed easily and often, and no one took themselves too seriously. At first, she had some doubts about eating melted marshmallows washed down with cold beer, but was surprised when she liked the combination.

Summer leaned on Dill's shoulder and stared into the fire with a slight smile on her face. When she lifted a cigarette to her mouth and inhaled, Maureen was taken aback for a moment before she figured out what was happening. Glancing around the group, it was clear others were smoking, too, including Jeffrey. What she was smelling wasn't a sweet wood burning in the fire pit.

When Jeffrey passed his joint to Maureen, she hesitated.

"Sorry. I don't think so."

"No need to apologize. Smoke or pass it along. No worries."

"I've never done it before." Maureen wanted to be part of the group and decided to take a risk. "Will you show me what to do?"

"Sure. To inhale, all you have to do is take a slow deep breath." Jeffrey held the joint between his thumb and pointer finger. "You'll feel the smoke travel down your windpipe and fill your lungs. If you don't feel anything in your lungs, then you're probably not breathing deeply enough. You should be bringing in a little fresh air along with the smoke. Just inhale deeply, give yourself a very short pause, then exhale slowly."

He placed the joint between his lips and proceeded to demonstrate.

"So I don't have to hold my breath?"

"I've never had it make any difference. No need to get yourself all blue in the face."

"Take smaller hits at first," Dill added, "and don't swallow the smoke or you'll get a gut ache."

"Here, you try." Jeffrey placed the joint between Maureen's lips. "Since it's your first time, don't be surprised if you cough when you exhale."

Maureen followed his example, except after exhaling, she coughed, a lot.

"That was perfect. Did you feel it in your lungs?"

"Uh-huh." Maureen had finished coughing, but felt short of breath. "Let me try again."

Jeffrey laughed as Maureen tried again, coughing a bit when she finished. She gazed into the fire and was filled with love for everyone sitting around her.

"This is good stuff, Maureen. I grow it special for Summer. Helps with the nausea and pain." Dill placed his jacket around Summer's shoulders, for despite the warm evening and the roaring fire, Summer was shivering.

"Hey, Maureen, did Jeffrey ever tell you how Dill got his name?" Eric inhaled deeply from a joint, then passed it along to Will.

"I figured it was short for Dillon."

"That's what everybody thinks." Jeffrey switched lawn chairs so he was seated next to Maureen. "In college, Dillon was a master gardener of sorts, except his was a mono-crop called marijuana, with a few other plants thrown in for authenticity. He was famous on campus for his high-quality weed, and the nickname Weed took hold."

"Yeah, that reputation was a huge asset when applying for law school." Dill chuckled, stroking his beard.

"Anyway, to deflect any suggestion of impropriety, out of necessity we started calling him Dill Weed, dill weed being a crop he also grew." Jeffrey took a long drink from his beer.

"May I interject that planting dill weed was not done by accident." Dillon blew on a fiery marshmallow at the end of his stick. "It grows tall and feathery and has a strong fragrance, creating a sort of camouflage for other plants. It also attracts beneficial insects, and, of course, it's absolutely necessary if you want to make dill pickles."

"Interesting, but let me return to my story," Jeffrey said. "The first year in law school, Dill Weed shortened to Dill, a name which makes perfect sense to the grown-up world since his name is Dillon, but his friends know the real story. By the way, he still grows great marijuana."

"Legal marijuana." Dillon held up his hand as a pledge of his honor. "It's classified as a medical necessity for Summer. I'm not responsible for the rest of you stoners."

"Says the guy enjoying a joint of his own." Jeffrey's laughter was infectious and soon the whole group was giggling, including Maureen. She had inhaled several more hits from Jeffrey's joint and ended up feeling dizzy and relaxed.

The group quieted, and individuals drifted off into the evening. When Maureen struggled to get out of her lawn chair, Jeffrey took her hands in his and pulled her toward him until she was standing.

"Would you walk with me? I feel a little unsteady," Maureen said.

"That's what neighbors are for." Jeffrey placed Maureen's hand in the crook of his arm, and the two strolled to the house, Road Dog snuffling ahead of them.

Jeffrey deposited Maureen at her bedroom door and waited until she was inside with the light turned on. Her cell phone, tossed on the bed, was jangling non-stop.

"I'd better get that. Thanks for lending me your arm."

"Good night, Maureen." He ruffled Road Dog's ears before heading across the hall.

"Hello, Andrea. What's up?"

"Maureen, thank heaven. I've been calling you all day."

"Sorry, I was working outside, and then off on an errand."

"There's such a thing as taking your phone with you. That's why the cell phone was invented."

"Sorry. I'm being frugal with my minutes."

"Never mind. Look, you have to contact David."

"No, I don't."

"I told you about Tyler, the guy in auditing. He is certain David is making withdrawals from your 401K account at Anson-Chambers. Substantial withdrawals."

"I can't believe that SOB. It's taken me years to accumulate the money in that account." Maureen could feel the panic tightening her stomach. The 401K money was her security, a contingency plan for her future.

"I'm not sure how to stop him. All the account information and passwords are at home, in David's safe."

"Call him. At least verify that it's David and not some stranger hacking into your stuff."

Other than returning home to the mess she'd left behind, talking to David and Jasmine was the last thing she wanted to do. Did she have any choice?

"All right, I'll call him."

"Thank you. Now I can sleep tonight."

"You're a true friend, Andrea. I'm wondering how I'm doing in the mental health facility."

"Not funny. Last week, Mr. Chambers asked me about your chances of recovery and did I know the name of your medical center so he could send you a card."

"I don't think he can know that. What did you tell him?"

"I told him you are in Wisconsin, nothing more. Anyway, it's all because of Don."

"Ugh, that's right. You're working for Don."

"Yes, and he has a membership at the same fitness club as David. They see each other all the time."

"Oh, that's bad."

"No kidding. Don told me he asked David how you're doing after all that's happened, especially since your mental breakdown. I guess David laughed it off. Said you were fine and taking a break from everything. Don thought David's reaction was suspicious and started asking me all kinds of questions. After I didn't crack, Don ran to tattle to Mr. Chambers."

"I'm guessing both Don and David believe they are the reason I'm gone."

"I know why Don would think that, the weasel. What did David do to drive you away?"

"Let's just say if Don is a weasel, David is a snake in the grass that eats weasels for a snack."

"Ouch! That bad, huh?"

"Yes, and let's leave it at that."

CHAPTER 18

For three days, Maureen avoided phoning David. Early Thursday evening, when she summoned the courage to make the call, her cell phone was dead, as in, out of service dead. Using Jeffrey's laptop, Maureen skimmed through the e-mail notices she received in the last month from her service provider and this time, she read them. Because her bank accounts were closed (thank you, David), any bills handled through direct pay were unpaid and overdue. Despite repeated attempts to contact Maureen, the company had been unsuccessful in reaching her, and, as a result, they terminated her phone contract with them. She chastised herself for ignoring emails, phone calls, texts, messages, tweets, Instagram, and whatever else a normal, modern, responsible adult would handle with ease, and Maureen admitted she needed Andrea to wade through all the electronic garbage for her.

"I'm seeing that worried look again." Jeffrey patted Maureen on the shoulder as he moved toward the refrigerator. "Anything I can do to help?"

"I wish. When my bank accounts were closed, all my direct bill paying stopped. Now my phone service is cancelled."

"You'd think they would at least send you a reminder or offer options for using another payment method."

"They did. All my fault for not keeping up with my emails and other stuff. Without my secretary, I'm technologically helpless."

"You had a secretary?" Jeffrey halted a bologna sandwich halfway to his mouth and stared at Maureen.

"You don't have to look so dumbfounded."

"I apologize."

"Accepted. May I use your cell phone? I need to call my husband."

"You have a husband?"

"Again, not what you expected. What about using your phone?"

Jeffrey pulled a cell phone from his pocket and offered it to Maureen.

"It's not that you shouldn't have a secretary or husband. You just surprised me with unanticipated information." He held out half a sandwich like a peace offering. "Want part of a sandwich?"

"No, just the phone. Thanks for the use of the laptop."

Phone in hand, Maureen walked outside to sit in one of the high-backed chairs on the side porch, now bathed in the golden glow of the setting sun. The western sky was streaked in shades of purple, pink, and apricot, and the calm evening air, sweetened by the fragrances of alyssum and early-blooming roses, hummed with the sounds of insects. Road Dog, wearing a contented smile, flopped beside Maureen's chair, as she tapped in David's phone number.

"Hello." Jasmine answered David's phone.

"I need to speak to David."

"Maureen, is it you?"

"I'm calling to talk to David. Is he there?"

"Maureen, I'm so glad to hear your voice. Are you all right?"

"May I speak with David?" Maureen wanted to scream at Jasmine, call her all kinds of bad names, and then hang up.

"But I want you to talk to me, your sister."

"I couldn't care less what you want. Now get David."

The phone went quiet, and Maureen simmered with anger. She had survived this far without the money in her old bank accounts. She could always apply for new credit cards and find a cell phone service provider. So what if David had taken over all her finances and was depleting her retirement savings? She hated giving him the satisfaction of knowing how much this was hurting her. Hang up and cut your losses, she told herself.

"Maureen." It was that deep voice—masculine, confident, authoritative— the one David used while lecturing his students or when speaking to a group of colleagues, or when he was putting Maureen in her place.

"You closed my bank accounts."

"At first, I didn't know what happened to you. I was protecting your money, our money, so some criminal couldn't access it."

"As it turns out, I can't access it, thanks to you."

"You left me little choice."

"My credit cards are cancelled. I have no way to buy what I need."

"It was a financial precaution, to protect your credit."

"You've been helping yourself to my 401K. That's stealing."

"Maureen, with your mental stability in question, the only thing I could do was to take charge of that account."

"It's not yours to take, and what do you mean, mental stability in question?"

"Until you are evaluated for mental competency, I have control of our assets."

"Control of our assets? How can you do that?"

"When I learned from Don you had a mental breakdown, it became evident to me what has been going on with you."

"What do you mean?"

"You are deranged and mentally incompetent, Maureen, and your actions demonstrate it. The fact that you are currently in a mental health facility confirms your mental instability."

"What actions are you talking about?"

"It's been building for some time, with your increasing use of alcohol, your unfounded accusations and general paranoia, not to mention two years in therapy dredging up forgotten, but more than likely, fabricated memories. Now, with this recent disappearance and the abandonment of your job and marriage, it's crystal clear you are not well."

"None of that proves anything."

"When you're released, let me know. I'm sure we can come to a mutually acceptable solution to the problems you've created." He hung up.

Maureen remained on the porch until the sun disappeared beneath the distant horizon. As Road Dog whimpered and ran dreamy steps in his sleep, Maureen envisioned murdering David, clubbing him over the head with a bottle of Tito's vodka, his shattered skull awash in the crystal clear liquid. She had a perfect and valid insanity defense. She had been seeing a therapist and was now in a mental health facility, albeit it an imaginary one, and, as David, himself, had laid out, she was a bonafide nut case. When she thought about it, Maureen decided murdering David wasn't worth it.

CHAPTER 19

D ill asked the crew to work on Saturday and was driving the five field hands east to pick sugar snap peas, an arduous job that would take the entire morning. If they were up to it, they would spend the afternoon weeding and irrigating.

Maureen rode up in the cab with Dill and used the opportunity to ask him about the mine. "Hey Dill, that earthen berm thing looks like it's close to your fields."

"That's because it's on land I sold."

"Does it bother you, having a sand mining operation there?"

"Why should it?"

"It's sad to see the farmland like that."

"It's not farmland. It's being mined for sand."

"I drove over that way last week. When I saw the size of the mine on your land, I was stunned. It is enormous."

"It's not all on my property. The acres next to ours were also sold, so the mine ended up being sizable."

"Was that the property with the abandoned house, a few miles down the road?"

"Yup. No one's lived there in years. Belongs to Toni, the lady in the restaurant."

No it doesn't, Maureen thought, but that was for another discussion. "The one who owns the bar?"

"That's right. She's a friend of yours, isn't she?"

"Not really. At the restaurant, she was sort of a regular customer. We talked sometimes."

"Doesn't sound as though you liked her all that much."

"I was a waitress. I had to like everybody."

Dill pulled in beside the field of peas where they would work for the morning, and Maureen was relieved their conversation ended. There was no way she wanted anyone to know she and Toni were related and shared a troubling family history.

After working hard all day Saturday, Dill insisted Sunday would be a rest day, despite the amount of field work looming ahead.

"There is virtue in work. There is virtue in rest," Dill said in a philosophical voice.

"Don't be fooled by old Confucius here. He's avoiding paying us time-and-a-half for working on a Sunday, that's all." Jeffrey pulled Dill's beard for emphasis.

"Very true, my son. Now, go, my children, and engage in pleasurable pursuits."

Maureen and Road Dog drove to Chippewa Falls for some shopping, but Maureen's heart wasn't in it. Yesterday's conversation with Dill, where Maureen learned Toni sold land to the sand mining company, distressed her. Toni held the deed to Peggy's property and claimed she had Peggy's blessing in selling some of it, but Maureen wondered if her mother knew who the buyer was and where the money from the sale went. Despite the events of the past, Maureen did not believe her mother would allow the land she inherited from Maureen's father and his parents to be converted into a sand mine. There was no doubt in Maureen's mind Toni used the money from the land sale to purchase the bar. Would her mother ever have agreed that Toni, an alcoholic, should use the money to go into the tavern business?

Although she dreaded seeing Toni again, Maureen needed to have answers to her questions. Tainter's Lake wasn't far, and in no time, the garish "Toni's Tap" sign, with its smacking red lips, flashed in the distance, like a tell-tale red light in front of a brothel.

When Maureen and Road Dog entered the bar, Toni was leaning over a table of poker players, her cleavage bulging from a low-cut blouse, her red-rimmed mouth open and laughing. One glance at Maureen, and Toni, along with the rest of the room's occupants, fell silent.

"Thought I'd seen the last of you." Toni strolled past Maureen without a glance and parked herself on a stool behind the bar.

"This pains me more than it does you," Maureen said, following her.

"Doubt it."

"You said my mother approved of your selling some of her land, to cover taxes and other expenses."

"Yeah, so?"

"Did she know you were selling acreage to a sand mining company?"

"Why?"

"Because my mother, in spite of all her faults, loved that farm. I don't think she would ever allow the land to be anything other than farmland."

"Farming's a dying business up here, especially if the farms are small. One of them sand mining companies bought fifty acres. Paid big money for it, up front. It was a deal that couldn't be turned down."

"I don't imagine sand mining helps to improve the area's environment."

"Environment only matters if you have nothing else to worry about. I had family responsibilities, so get off your high horse."

"You sold my mother's land to buy yourself a tavern."

"Look, the taxes needed to be paid. I needed a place to live and a way to earn money for me and my kids. The property was sitting there, not making a cent for anybody, only costing money. Selling the land was the solution to all of those problems."

"How do you live with yourself?"

"I've long since passed the point of worrying about how I'm living. If you've got a problem with me running the show, take it up with your mother."

Maureen would never take anything up with her mother, and saying "take it up with your mother" was a low blow even for Toni. It seemed Toni believed that having the deed in her possession was as good as owning the land.

When three customers came in and sat at the bar, Toni got up from her stool. As she walked to greet them, she turned towards Maureen and said, "Don't bother coming back."

Driving home to Crooked Creek Farm, Maureen and Road Dog meandered down narrow gravel roads and double letter county highways, like DE, XX, and NM. As they traveled, Maureen noticed more sand mining operations throughout the region, their scoured, damaged tracts in stark contrast to the green vitality of the farms on the brink of being devoured. What she observed told the story of a changing economic and physical landscape in the area.

On a majestic bluff surrounded by encroaching sand mines, Maureen stopped at a vegetable stand set up on the front lawn of a tidy, brick ranch home. The man operating the stand stood up from his lawn chair sitting in the shade and greeted Maureen. He had been tall once, but was bent over from years of hard work. His face was leathery beneath a cap from the local co-op, and he wore bib overalls, clean and washed many times. He reached out a large, rough hand.

"Hello, young lady. What can I help you with?"

"You have lovely produce," Maureen told the man. She selected bunches of lettuce, radishes, scallions, and early carrots, none of which she needed, but she knew when you stopped at a roadside vegetable stand, making a purchase was the polite thing to do.

"Haven't seen you around here before." The man switched his toothpick from one side of his wide mouth to the other.

"I work over at Crooked Creek Farm. Been driving around getting the lay of the land."

"I know Dill and Summer. Good kids. Working hard to make a go of that farm."

"I've noticed not many farms are left around here. Looks like things have been converted to some sort of construction."

"It's sand mining, used in fracking. They're pretty much laying the land blank."

"There sure are lots of trucks, and it's so dusty."

"It's a loud and dirty business."

"How did you manage to end up surrounded by mines, if you don't mind my asking?"

"We had a dairy farm for forty years. Sold it except for this piece of land we kept for a retirement place. Six months after finalizing the deal, the buyer of my farm turned around and sold it to the mining company. He made a boatload of money. The farm is gone, and the land is ruined."

"So the farmers are gone, just like the farmland."

"Well, let's put it this way. Everybody I know around here that sold to the sand mining companies moved out, so that should tell you something."

Maureen thanked the man for his willingness to talk to her. When she and Road Dog pulled away, she waved out the window, and the man gave her a sad thumbs up. A few miles further down the county road, they began passing acres of pastureland enclosed by white fencing. Maureen slowed down when she spotted several horses running to the fence. She pulled over and stopped, leashed Road Dog, and walked through the lush grasses in the ditch to the horses gathered along the fencing.

At first the animals were intimidated by the visiting dog, who was being very polite, but when Maureen produced the fresh greens and carrots, there was a scramble of hooves and noses to grab the vegetables she was offering.

"They'll take your fingers off if you're not careful." A woman in jeans, boots, and a tee-shirt had walked up from somewhere.

"They are so beautiful." Maureen touched one velvety nose after another as she held a carrot in the flat palm of her other hand.

"You have horses?" The woman's face was tanned and etched with lines.

"No, I only have a dog, but who doesn't love horses?"

A large truck rumbled past, surrounded by a choking cloud of dust, sending the horses racing to the other side of the pasture.

"Trucks from the sand mines. They go past all hours of the day and night."

"They are so noisy and everything around here is covered in dust."

"Yeah. In addition, there's the processing plant that runs non-stop, loading railroad cars by the hundreds."

"Sounds awful. Must be hard on your animals."

"Hard on all living things, if there's any left in the vicinity. I've complained to everybody I can think of, but I'm told I'm exaggerating, I'm crazy, or I'm lying."

Maureen left the remainder of her produce with the woman.

"Please accept it as a token of appreciation for allowing me to be meet your horses."

Back on the road, Maureen slowed down and opened the windows so Road Dog's face could flap in the breeze. The fragrance of summer blossoms filled the car. After not seeing any road signs for awhile, it became apparent to Maureen they might be lost. When she saw a woman on the side of the road, emptying mail from a crooked, rusty mailbox, Maureen stopped.

"Excuse me. I seem to have gotten myself lost. I'm headed for Crooked Creek Farm off County ES."

The woman was elderly, but tall and muscular. Her white hair was pulled into a ponytail, and tendrils of curls framed her tanned face. A Jimmy Buffett teeshirt was tucked into her blue jeans, and her leather boots were faded and worn.

"You're not lost by much. If you continue ahead for about two miles, you'll run into Wilkes Road. Turn left and follow Wilkes for about a mile until you hit ES. Turn right until you get to the sign for the farm."

"Thanks. I figured I was close. Is this your farmhouse?" Maureen was drawn to the old, white home set back from the road. It had a wide front porch and narrow windows adorned with elaborate wood carvings. Surrounding the building were gardens filled with flowers and native plants.

"Yup. Lived here for almost seventy years. My grandfather bought the farm in the 1890s."

"It's like something from a magazine."

"I've managed to keep my little piece of what used to be paradise. Not that long ago, my place was surrounded by hills and bluffs. Been replaced with pyramids of sand, stockpiles waiting for shipment to drilling rigs out of state."

"It must be hard to see the disappearance of things that were here for thousands of years."

"That's called progress, I guess." The woman folded her mail under her arm and left.

Maureen followed the woman's directions, and it wasn't long before she and Road Dog passed the "Go Straight to Crooked" sign on the white fence. In the approaching nightfall, the lights in the farmhouse welcomed them home.

Dill, Summer, Samuel, and the entire work crew, were gathered inside for a celebratory dinner. Crepe paper streamers scalloped their way around the kitchen cabinets, and helium balloons bounced along the ceiling. Among the dishes cluttering the island sat a large, lopsided cake with thick frosting and wobbly writing that shouted No More Chemo!

"Let me get you some food, Maureen." Jeffrey sprang into action and was loading a plate with salads and vegetables before Maureen could object.

As the cake was being sliced, Summer, wearing a paisley scarf and flowing caftan, stood and faced the group.

"Thank you for your support and care. It has been a long journey that is now at its end."

She blew kisses to each one of them as they applauded, her eyes filling with tears. Maureen wondered what it was like to have that kind of support during difficult times.

"Now, for the surprise." Dill was halfway through the door, motioning the group to follow. "Everyone outside."

Jeffrey placed a blindfold over Summer's eyes and was leading her to the edge of the porch as the others gathered around her in the growing darkness.

"Lights, please." Dill took Summer's hands and stepped aside, removing the blindfold.

The yard lights illuminated Dill's surprise. There, at the far edge of the yard, was an old-fashioned metal swing set, complete with three swings and a trapeze. Summer clapped her hands and threw her arms around her husband's neck.

"I put this up for Summer," Dill said, holding her close, "because sometimes after chemo we would go to the park near the hospital, where we discovered the swinging motion helped relieve her nausea. Now that she's done with chemo, the nausea will eventually go away, and then the swing will be here for Summer's enjoyment. She never had one as a child, and I know it's something she has always wanted."

Dill took Summer's hand. Through the dewy grass they walked, and when they reached the swings, Summer released Dill's hand, selected a swing and sat down, hands enfolding the metal chains.

"Push me, Dill."

She leaned forward and then back, pumping with her slender legs, as her billowing caftan dress fluttered around her. Everyone applauded and cheered.

CHAPTER 20

E veryone except Maureen. She took a step back, the muscles in her face tense. What was wrong with her? She should be applauding and cheering like everyone else. When they all moved from the porch onto the lawn, Maureen stood frozen in place, watching Jeffrey as he congratulated Dill, while Eric began pushing Lucy on one of the other swings. It was such a happy scene, but to Maureen, the movement of the swings and the creaking sounds they created, were distressing.

"I'm heading in," she yelled to Jeffrey and the others. "Got a splitting headache."

She and Road Dog went up to their bedroom, a place Maureen hated to admit she was avoiding unless they needed to sleep. She told herself it was crazy to believe there ever was a little girl's dress hanging in the closet, but she could still hear the sound of that hanger scratching against the metal bar. It was a sound reminiscent of the one chains make as a swing moves, like when the girl in her memory was swinging. Maureen wondered if Dr. Taylor would say she was giving too much credence to coincidental details. That might be true, or maybe Maureen just didn't like swings.

"Maureen? Are you okay?" Jeffrey tapped on her door a couple of times. "The person you called from my phone has sent a you a text."

"Okay."

"From someone named Jasmine."

"Delete it."

"I don't think I should do that. It sounds important."

"It's not. Delete it."

"At least read it."

"Don't want to."

"I'll wait until you decide otherwise."

Jeffrey wasn't leaving, so Maureen opened the door. He smelled like pot and was sprinkled with confetti from Summer's celebration. It drifted like snowflakes onto the phone as he handed it to Maureen.

She glanced at the text from her younger sister and was overwhelmed by a melancholy feeling of sadness and loss. The message was so like Jazz, dramatic, self-absorbed, and manipulative.

"Maureen, I miss u and beg for ur forgiveness. I was heart-broken when u would not talk to me the other night. I've never been so miserable in my entire life. David and I have discussed it, and I am coming to see u. We r sisters, and I need u to love me again. See u soon. Love, Jazz."

Maureen swore under her breath and handed the phone to Jeffrey, who had stepped inside her room and was petting Road Dog.

"So, this person's coming to visit?"

"You read my message?"

"It was on my phone. It's what one does with a text message on their phone."

"Oh, right. Sorry."

"She's coming to visit?"

"I doubt she'll be able to find me in the mental health facility."

"You're in a mental health facility?"

"Obviously not. She thinks I am, though."

"Why would she think that?"

"Because my secretary told everyone that's what's become of me."

"Your secretary?"

"Yes, my secretary. We've been through this before, Jeffrey."

He had moved outside of Maureen's room and was standing in the hall, looking confused and annoyed.

"Guess I'll see you in the morning, Maureen."

"If I can break out of my straight jacket, muah ha ha ha." She summoned her best crazy laugh.

Jeffrey stared at her, shook his head, and left, muttering to himself.

"You've gotta keep 'em guessing, girlfriend," Maureen told Road Dog who was stretched out on the bed, head centered on Maureen's pillow.

"You can have the pillow. I won't be able to sleep anyway."

Maureen sat on the floor in front of the open window and thought about Jasmine's text. Regardless of what the message said, Maureen wasn't concerned her younger sister would show up to visit her. Jazz was as impulsive as a two-year old and as irresponsible. She pin-balled her way through life, never finishing anything and was as fickle as the wind. When Jazz wrote the message, she might have been missing Maureen and having regrets about David, but Maureen had no doubt within the next ten minutes, Jasmine was helping herself to whatever Maureen had left behind, including David.

When Maureen and Jasmine moved from their Aunt Toni's, Jazz was eight years old and had been without their mother for three years. Maureen, despite working as a waitress and cleaning office buildings while going to night school, made it her mission to provide Jasmine with as normal a childhood as possible. Jazz took dance lessons, joined the Girl Scouts, and played sports. There were sleepovers and birthday parties and visits to the zoo and museums. By age seventeen, beautiful, blond Jasmine was a cheerleader and one of the popular girls in her school. Everyone wanted to be with Jazz.

At the same time, Maureen, at age twenty-seven, was being swept off her feet by the technology professor who taught a night class on computers that Maureen was required to take. Although Maureen believed she lacked the ability to do anything on impulse, six months after she walked into David's classroom, the two were married. David vowed he and Maureen would provide a stable and loving home for Jasmine.

Loving home? You nailed it, David, she thought.

Thinking about Jasmine and David made Maureen feel alone and distrustful, and she glanced suspiciously around the shadowy bedroom. As a safety precaution, and because she was somewhat paranoid about the closet, she opened its door and checked everything, the hanging rod, the clothes, and the floor. She was stepping away when she noticed the closet's back wall.

"What in the world . . . ?" She edged into the tight space for a better look.

The back wall was not smooth, like the others made of plaster. Instead, the surface was ridged, with seven vertical wood planks joined together and painted white to blend in with the rest of the closet. The boards stood about four feet high and were held together with two horizontal wooden cross pieces. There were three rusty hinges on the left edge, and near the top of the right corner of the structure, a metal sliding latch locked the planks to the framework set into the wall.

"An odd place for a door," Maureen told Road Dog, who gave Maureen a glance, closed her eyes, and drifted off to sleep. "I'll ask Summer about it tomorrow."

In her top dresser drawer Maureen found a book Summer had given her for pleasure reading, as Summer called it. The book wasn't too thick, and the picture on the cover featured a dog eating an ice cream cone. Maureen couldn't recall the last time she had read anything for enjoyment.

The book about the dog was entertaining, and Maureen read into the night until she finished the entire thing. It was a compelling story with a happy ending, something Maureen needed to have happen. After the book, she tried stretching out on the floor in corpse pose, some yoga relaxation position Summer had taught her. It involved closed eyes, and Maureen hoped it would bring sleep. It didn't. Before sunrise, she was downstairs, drinking coffee and busying herself around the kitchen.

"Coffee." Dill shuffled into the room, dressed in his work clothes and socks.

Maureen filled Dill's favorite mug and slid it across the counter to where he was standing, peering out the window. He took a long, careful sip before speaking.

"Lots to do today. We've added two more CSA customers, so that's thirty-seven pick-ups, plus the grocery store orders." He grabbed a piece of toast and took a large bite. "Would you do me a favor?"

"Sure. What do you need?"

"I gotta fix something on the tractor before the crew arrives. Could you help Summer shower and dress? Maybe get her to eat something? She's weak and unsteady on her feet lately."

"No problem."

"I know it's not part of your job description. I owe you one."

Before she could reassure Dill that she didn't mind, he was on the porch donning his work boots and baseball cap. He started down the steps, but returned to the kitchen.

"There's a guy stopping over this morning to meet with me. If I'm not back when he gets here, call my cell to let me know he's arrived, and tell him to head down to the barn." He placed Summer's phone on the counter.

Moments later, Jeffrey ambled in, looking as worn and tired as Maureen felt. She served him a plate of eggs and bacon, along with hot coffee, and flashed him what she hoped was a sunny smile.

"Breakfast brings out the waitress in me," she said, hoping last night's text message was forgotten.

"Who are you?" Jeffrey's fork stopped in mid-bite as he stared at Maureen.

She heard Samuel's feet coming down the stairs, a signal Summer was awake.

"Dill asked me to help Summer this morning. Could you get Samuel outside?"

Jeffrey headed outside with the dog, and Maureen hurried upstairs, where she found Summer sitting on the edge of the bed, her boney, pale feet almost touching the floor. Except for the pillow where Summer had laid her head, the tidy bedclothes gave no indication of anyone having slept there.

"I thought I could make it to the shower." Frustrated tears puddled in her blue eyes.

Maureen wasted no time assisting her. When Summer was safely seated in the shower, Maureen took the time to straighten the bedroom and find clothes for her.

"Are shorts and a T-shirt okay to wear?"

"I need something loose and lightweight. Every cell of my body hurts. Sometimes clothes feel like they are bruising me all over."

When they finally walked downstairs, Summer, wearing a soft, cotton knit dress, had color in her cheeks and some make-up on her eyes. She sipped a cup of tea, as Maureen prepared for her a plate of eggs and fruit.

The duet of barking from Samuel and Road Dog snatched Maureen's attention, as a pickup truck pulled into the driveway, horn honking.

"That must be the man coming for the meeting. Would you call Dill to tell him he's here, while I get Samuel and Road Dog?"

As Summer made a quick call to Dill, Maureen stepped out on the porch and yelled for the dogs. Their barking was not welcoming to someone with whom Dill was doing business, and she hustled Samuel and Road Dog onto the porch. The driver of the black pickup, wearing a baseball cap and mirrored aviator sunglasses, rolled down the window and leaned out. On the door, right below his elbow, was the logo for Sandover Mining, LLC.

"That's some welcoming committee you've got there." The man laughed and pointed to the dogs still barking on the porch. "I'm supposed to meet Dillon here this morning."

"Dill's working on a tractor. He said you should head over to the barn." Maureen pointed down the gravel drive.

The man left to meet Dill and waved out the window at Maureen, who managed a half-hearted wave in return. Dill's meeting with the mining company representative could mean he was doing business with them again, selling off more of Crooked Creek Farm, something Maureen hoped wouldn't happen.

CHAPTER 21

I t was approaching mid-July and the farm was in high gear. Crops required constant irrigation, and the watering, in turn, made the job of weeding a never-ending task, since no herbicides were used on the farm. Maureen had been given the additional responsibility of keeping the compost piles rotated and watered, and she found the ideal time for working the compost was after the crew returned from the fields. Although she was fatigued, composting made her feel closer to the soil, which was the lifeblood of the farm, and working to rebuild it had a cathartic effect on her.

She was turning the third and final pile, where the compost was dark, rich, and earthy, when Jeffrey called her name.

"Maureen, look who's here."

Wiping the sweat dripping from the end of her nose, Maureen tipped back her wide-brimmed hat and turned around. Jasmine waved. Her hair was piled high, and she wore tight capris, a skimpy summer top, and stacked sandals. Jeffrey, wearing a lopsided grin, stood beside her.

"It's your sister."

"Yes, I recognize her."

Jasmine rushed to hug Maureen, who stepped away from the attempt.

"I'm too dirty and sweaty to hug."

"You look wonderful. You've lost weight, and I've never seen you with a suntan."

"What are you doing here?"

"We need to talk, but it's so hot out here. Could we find some shade?" She was already walking toward the house and the adirondack chairs beneath the trees.

"Looks like you two have some catching up to do." Jeffrey backed away, gesturing for Maureen to follow Jasmine, and Maureen responded by giving him the finger.

Maureen selected a chair, apart from Jasmine, leaving a buffer zone of a few feet of grass, in case she decided to lunge for her sister's lovely, perfect neck. Removing the sweaty hat she wore every day, Maureen placed it on her lap and studied her dirty fingernails and calloused hands. They were physical proof of how things in her life had changed.

"How did you find me?"

"David has his ways." Jasmine's smile froze. "You know what I mean."

Maureen did not reply.

"This doesn't look like a mental health facility. Is it some sort of outpatient rehab thing?"

"You could call it that."

"That must mean you're getting better. I'm glad."

"Why?"

"Because it was awful to think you were mentally sick, and I felt responsible."

"Get over yourself."

"We, I mean, I, am sorry for everything."

"Good to know."

"Please say you will be able to forgive me one day."

"Can't do that. Is there anything else?"

"Yes." Jasmine hesitated, squared her shoulders, and continued. "I'm going to visit Momma."

"Why would you do that?"

"She's been sick."

"How do you know?"

"We've been writing to each other for awhile."

"Are you kidding me?" Maureen didn't think she could feel more betrayed than when she found Jasmine in bed with David, but knowing her sister would even consider reconnecting with their estranged mother was a stab in the back.

"It's been a long time, Moe. Everyone's allowed to change."

"Not her."

"Come with me. It will be easier if we do it together as sisters."

"You lost the right to call me your sister."

"Don't say that."

"I have to get back to work." Maureen rose from her chair. "If you visit her, you are going to regret it."

"Is that a threat?"

"She will only hurt you."

"I guess I'll find that out for myself."

"Don't say I didn't warn you."

"I'm staying at the Holiday Inn Express in Eau Claire tonight. Tomorrow I'm going to see Momma." Jasmine handed a slip of paper to Maureen. "Here's the motel address in case you change your mind and decide to come with me."

As Jasmine got into her car and drove away, Maureen crumpled the piece of paper and shoved it into her pocket.

CHAPTER 22

The aroma of simmering berries drifted from the kitchen when Maureen and Road Dog arrived downstairs the next morning. It had been a rough few weeks for Summer, and Maureen was relieved to find her making jam, one of her favorite culinary duties.

"Good morning. You're up early." Summer handed Maureen a cup of coffee and scooped scrambled eggs onto a large plate she placed on the floor for Samuel and Road Dog who were waiting with wagging tails.

"It is a great morning," Maureen said. It was especially great for Summer, who was out of bed and looking so much better. "Where is everybody?"

"The guys are fixing the door on the main barn before the crew gets here."

"I noticed it's been harder and harder to shove open."

Maureen wasn't sure this was the appropriate time to ask, but talking about the main door of the barn reminded her of the weird plank door located at the back of her closet.

"Speaking of doors, I discovered a small, white door inside the closet in my room."

"That's the door to the attic. I don't think there's anything stored in there. Dill's gone inside a couple of times to check for critters."

Maureen was forced to leave the conversation at that because Loriano, Silvia, and the others had arrived and were anxious to start the day's work.

"It's getting hot," Loriano yelled. "Let's get going." He began running a sharpening stone along the shovels' edges, as the crew organized the tools, filled water bottles, and loaded everything into Dill's truck.

The main objective that morning was to complete orders for local chefs who offered farm-to-table freshness in their restaurants. Crops were harvested, washed, bagged, labeled, and placed in a makeshift cooler until they could be delivered to customers in the afternoon. Dill supervised every aspect of the work, and he transported the products to the restaurants, met with the chefs, and handled any problems or complaints.

By late afternoon, Maureen and the rest of the workers were on the porch enjoying cold beers, lemonade, and a couple of joints. Eric and Will were launching frisbees for the dogs, who wrangled over every toss, no matter how many frisbees were thrown or how many people were throwing them. From inside the house, voices could be heard.

"No. We can't do it. I won't allow it." Summer's soft voice was forceful.

"We have no choice. There's no other way," Dill said.

"There has to be a better solution."

"If you have any ideas, let me know, 'cause, as far as I can tell, we're out of options."

"Folks, I know this is a hard decision. Why don't you two take your time and look over the figures again. I'll check with you in the next couple days."

It was a voice Maureen did not recognize, and then she noticed the black Sandover Mining truck parked alongside the house.

When Dill and the truck owner walked outside, Dill's face was grim. He offered the Sandover guy a beer, but the man declined, strode to his truck, and sped away.

"Vulture." Dill's eyes followed the truck disappearing into the distance. "Somebody get me a beer."

After an hour of relaxing, a few of the crew, including Maureen, were on their way to being drunk and a little high, so Dill told everyone to go home. Lucy, who was too young to legally drink, insisted on driving everyone. When the others were gone, Maureen and Jeffrey laughed their way into the house and upstairs, as Road Dog dragged behind. Opening her bedroom door, Maureen started inside when the dog padded past her and began giving the room the once-over with her nose, like a beagle on the hunt. Jeffrey leaned in to watch Road Dog playing detective and was so close to Maureen she could see flecks of amber in his blue eyes framed in dark lashes. She placed her hands on his muscular shoulders, pressed her body in close, and kissed him. When she pulled herself away from him, she wondered what in the world had possessed her to do such a thing? The expression on Jeffrey's face said he wondered the same thing. Maureen was sober enough to be embarrassed, and she hurried herself into the bedroom and slammed the door.

Inside the bedroom, Maureen leaned against the closed door and contemplated her options. She could pack her things and disappear into the night, never to face Jeffrey again. She could pretend she had been so inebriated and high she had no recollection of having done anything. She could fake an illness and stay in bed for a few days, hoping he would forget, or she could actually admit herself to a mental health facility.

As she chastised herself and pondered what to do, Road Dog continued to sniff and search the bedroom. Despite their long day, the dog was not settling down, and that was odd. Maureen made a careful visual assessment of the entire room. Earlier that day, in her haste to get downstairs, she had left the bed unmade and the window open, as they remained now. The closet door should have been closed, but now it was open. Maybe, when she shut the closet that morning, the latch hadn't caught, and it had drifted open on its own, or perhaps a breeze from the window had caused it to open. Summer might have come inside the room and opened the closet for some reason. Making such a huge deal out of a closet and its open door was proof the mental health facility could be Maureen's best option.

Road Dog began to settle down as she made a nest of the covers, nudging and fluffing them until they suited her. She dropped into the center of the arranged bedclothes, but kept her head up, eyes focussed on the closet. Maureen figured checking it out was her next move, but she admitted no normal person would consider looking into a closet as such a big deal.

Her clothes were hanging as she had left them, and no other items, like a little pink dress, had been hung there. Shoving the hangers out of the way, Maureen looked behind them at the attic door. Its sliding lock was pushed aside and the door was open a crack, revealing a murky, shadowy interior. She should have locked the door and walked away from the small attic, but, instead, she stepped inside the hot, stuffy room and knocked her head against a bare lightbulb hanging from the attic rafters near the entrance. She pulled the frayed grey string attached to the fixture's chain, fighting against her panic as the walls threatened to close in. The lighted bulb cast a pale yellow wash among the dark grey shadows of boxes, broken lamps, and moth-infested clothes hanging on a metal pipe wired to the wooden beams. From the ceiling, spiders had strung silvery threads criss-crossing in intricate patterns.

Using caution, Maureen moved into the center of the attic, ducking to avoid the low beams overhead. The sturdy, rough-hewn floor was thick with dust, and as she moved, disturbed particles added to the murkiness of the room. Bundles of old newspapers and magazines overspread the floor. Pushed against the far wall was a tattered mattress, piled with boxes of various sizes. One, in particular, caught Maureen's attention, and she stooped to examine the rectangular box, large enough to hold a generous-sized pair of boots. Maureen brushed away the blanket of dust concealing the box's wrapping paper, its original pink color faded. Yellow tape attached a tag to the lid of the box. Maureen bent over to inspect the tag where someone had penciled a message in a thick scrawl, and she leaned in closer to read the words out loud. "Happy Birthday, Love, Daddy."

The box rested on Maureen's lap. Although the attic was stuffy and hot, goosebumps traveled up her arms. Someone long ago had taken the time to wrap the bottom of the box separate from its top, making it convenient to open, and Maureen lifted the fragile cover. Inside was a baby doll. It wore a faded pink dress, and its body was constructed of molded vinyl, with jointed limbs, rounded and plump, and chubby hands and feet, dingy with age. Winking at Maureen was one blue eye that opened and closed, while the other was rolled back into the doll's skull, stuck in place with only the white revealed. The black eyelashes were solid and protruded over the tops of the eyeballs like tiny visors, and the pink mouth pouted around a small hole. A tangled nest of curls extruded through holes punched in the scalp, and someone had bitten off the doll's right ear. Maureen quickly pressed the lid closed and set the box beside her, her heart pounding and her breathing shallow and fast. She recognized this doll.

CHAPTER 23

....

M aureen left the attic, locked its door, and pushed the closet door shut. Using strength she didn't realize she possessed, she muscled the tall dresser across the room and positioned it against the closet. Road Dog watched the performance, her puzzled expression giving way to boredom as she closed her eyes again. Sleep was an impossibility, so Maureen shuffled downstairs to the kitchen. What she wouldn't give for a bottle of Tito's right now.

Instead, she found Dill's whiskey and poured herself a glass. Maureen dismissed the idea she somehow recognized the doll inside the gift box, telling herself the logical explanation was that the doll was a present from long ago, for a daughter from her father, and it merely resembled something Maureen had seen before. If she returned to the attic, would the doll even be there? Maybe it was some sort of apparition. If David were here, he'd say Maureen had experienced a mental lapse and imagined the whole thing. Overcome by uncertainty and apprehension, Maureen slipped the phone from her pocket and called that familiar number, knowing it was late and expecting no one to answer, but feeling more calm at the sound of Dr. Taylor's phone purring its ring into her ear.

"Maureen, this is Dr. Taylor. Is everything all right?"

"You're starting to scare me. How is it you are there and willing to talk to me or anyone at this hour of the night?"

"I'm a night owl." Dr. Taylor laughed. "Besides, I miss our sessions."

"That's a load and you know it."

"Perhaps. I have to admit, you interest me, and the scene you're remembering has a beginning and end, but no middle. I'm a sucker for a well-formed plot."

"So my life has been reduced to plot points on a story line."

"Isn't everyone's?"

"That's just sad."

"Are you calling because you remembered something?"

"Not exactly. My friend has a new swing set, and I'm freaked out by it."

"Does your little friend like her swing?"

"She's a grown woman, and the swing was a gift from her husband."

"Does it freak you out because it's like the swing set in your memory?"

"I don't know. Never mind. That's not why I called you."

"Okay, let's place that aside. Tell me why you called."

"Something I found tonight was oddly similar to details from the day I've been trying to remember. The thing is, I don't know if what I stumbled upon was real or imaginary, if it is pure coincidence, or if I'm losing my marbles."

"Not all of those reasons are mutually exclusive. What did you discover?"

"There's this small attic in the back of my bedroom closet. I found it in there." Maureen's voice grew smaller and hesitant.

"I'm impressed you were willing to step inside a small place like an attic."

"Don't be. I was in panic mode the entire time. I wish I'd never gone in. If I hadn't gone inside, I would not have found the pink box."

"Tell me about that."

"Just an old birthday present wrapped in pink paper. The tag read: "Happy Birthday, Love, Daddy.""

"Did you open the box?"

"There was a doll inside wearing a faded pink dress."

"There could be a logical explanation for what you found, or it could be purely coincidental, don't you agree?"

"Yes, except for one thing. I recognized the doll. A long time ago, her right ear had been bitten off, and I'm the one that did it." Maureen hung up. She couldn't talk about it any more.

She hated whiskey, but started drinking anyway, hoping it would calm her, or, at least, make her numb. Sitting at the island, she leaned her elbows on the granite countertop, and sheltered the glass in both hands. In front of her, yesterday's local newspaper and pieces of unopened mail were scattered about. Separated from the others was a large envelope from Sandover Mining, and Maureen picked it up and turned it over to the place where someone had slid their finger underneath the flap to unseal it. She coaxed the papers inside to slip out.

The offertory letter was official-looking, printed on letterhead stationery, and signed by the CEO of Sandover Mining, LLC. Additional pages spelled out in detail the terms of their business proposal, including the location of the acres the company wanted to purchase and the sizable amount of money they were offering to Crooked Creek Farm. Maureen was stunned when she read the entire contract was contingent on Sandover's success in securing acreage from the land adjacent to Dill's property, the land owned by her mother.

The sand mining company would not buy Dill's property without the land next to it. Maureen considered whether her Aunt Toni could pass up the opportunity to make more money. Was there the chance Toni would somehow become an honorable human being, one with integrity and morals, a person loyal to her sister? The impossibility of that ever happening made Maureen laugh out loud. Toni was incapable of doing the right thing.

Maureen drank until her hands stopped shaking and her thoughts became cloudy. When she felt she might be able to sleep, she stumbled into the living room, laid down on the sofa, and closed her eyes.

The aroma of coffee and the sounds of Dill making breakfast woke Maureen. Sometime during the night, Road Dog located her and curled up at Maureen's feet. Hoping to sneak upstairs unnoticed, Maureen scooted past the kitchen where Dill was working at the stove, his body turned away from the stairway. Head down, Maureen tiptoed with care up the stairs. At the top of the steps, she raised her head to find Jeffrey standing in her pathway, staring down at her.

"Whatcha doing?" Jeffrey was wearing his best poker face.

"Coming upstairs."

"You're still wearing yesterday's clothes."

"Same shirt, different day."

"Okay. Anything you want to talk about?"

"No. You?"

"Nope. See you downstairs."

Ten minutes later, Maureen was having a quick breakfast before joining the crew assembling near the barn, when a car pulled into the driveway. Outside, Samuel and Road Dog performed their usual barking routine, and Summer stepped onto the porch to check out the commotion. Within moments, she and the dogs returned, ushering Jasmine into the kitchen.

"Maureen, you didn't tell me your sister was visiting today."

"That's because I didn't know. What are you doing here, Jazz?"

"Hello to you, too."

"Hello. What are you doing here?"

"I'll give you two some privacy. Nice meeting you, Jasmine." Summer left with the two dogs trailing behind.

"I visited Momma."

"Good for you."

"She's sick."

"Yes, I know. You told me."

"I mean, she's very sick. She has months, maybe weeks, to live."

"Nobody gets out alive."

"I can't believe you are being so cold-hearted."

"I guess you and I don't know one another like we thought we did."

"We're sisters. That's all we need to know."

"What do you want from me, Jazz?"

"Let's have a civil conversation to start."

"All right. What did you and our mother talk about?"

"She wanted to know more about my life, things like that."

"Did you happen to mention how you ruined my marriage?"

"I was trying to keep the mood positive."

"That's you, always considerate of others' feelings."

"She asked about you, too."

"I'm surprised she remembered me at all."

"I know she loves you, loves us both."

"Previous experiences with her prove otherwise."

"We talked some about the past, good memories we shared when we were together. She asked if I'd been out to the farm, to our old house."

"I've seen it. It's dilapidated and rundown."

"That's sad. It's good she doesn't know. She said she wants you to have it, and I'm sure that means me, too."

"Nothing says love like a shabby, falling down dump."

"The whole property will be yours and mine. She wants it to stay in the family."

"That's going to be kind of hard, because Momma gave the property's deed to Aunt Toni, who has been managing it all these years. It's a sure bet Toni considers the whole place hers."

"It's not hers. Can't we get another copy of the deed somewhere?"

"I think so. Let me ask a friend of mine who might be able to help."

"Okay. I could call you in a few days to find out what you've learned."

"No, you can't call me, because, thanks to David, I don't have cell phone service. That's why I've been using my friend's phone. I'll have to contact you."

"I'm sorry for all the trouble David's caused you."

"Think back to how this all started. There's plenty of blame to go around for the both of you."

"I guess you're right."

"Small consolation. You should go. I've got to get to work."

Jasmine and Maureen left the house together. On the porch, Jazz tried to embrace Maureen, but she stepped away to avoid her attempt.

"Tell David I want my credit cards re-instated," Maureen said, poking a finger into Jasmine's chest, "and tell him to keep his greedy hands off my 401K account at Anson-Chambers."

Maureen hurried down the porch steps and walked to the barn where Dill's truck was parked with the crew waiting inside.

CHAPTER 24

A fter working in the dust and hot sun all day, Maureen trudged upstairs to change her clothes and take a much-needed shower. In order to accomplish those tasks, she was forced to return to her room and gain access to the barricaded closet where her meager wardrobe was hanging. Huffing and grunting, Maureen struggled to move the massive dresser, wondering how she had pushed it into place last night with so little effort. Now, it appeared to be immovable. When Road Dog began barking at Maureen's body contortions and guttural noises, the commotion caught someone's attention, and that someone was knocking at Maureen's door.

"Everything okay in there?"

It was Jeffrey. Maureen swore under her breath and pulled Road Dog close to her in an attempt to cease the dog's frantic barking.

"Fine. Changing up the furniture a little, that's all."

"Need any help?"

"No, I'm good."

Once he left, Maureen tried and tried again to move the dresser. It couldn't be done. There was no choice but to ask for Jeffrey's help. When he walked into her room and saw the dresser parked in front of the closet, he laughed.

"Odd choice for placement of the dresser, especially if you need to open the closet door for some reason, like to get to your clothes."

"It was going to go over there," Maureen said, gesturing to the wall where the bed sat, "when I realized the stupid bed wouldn't fit anywhere else but where it is now."

"It's called measuring, Maureen. Next time, measure first."

She gave him an embarrassed grin and together they finished repositioning the dresser, with only a couple more scratches on the floor and a strained back for Maureen.

"Jeffrey, thanks. I couldn't have done it without you."

"The question is: How did you move it in the first place?"

"I know, right? Today, I'm pretty tired after working hard, but, to tell the truth, I think it's because I knew I could call in the calvary, which is you."

When he was gone, Maureen stood face to face with the closet door. You are being ridiculous, she told herself. Open it.

Everything inside was as it should be—clothes still hanging in place, no little pink dress, attic door locked, nothing crazy here, except maybe me, Maureen thought. She stared at the attic door and considered checking inside for the box, then decided she was too exhausted to confront whatever was behind the door, real or imagined.

At dinner that evening, Dill, Summer, and Jeffrey began reminiscing about their years in college and law school.

"Old Dill Weed, the farmer, was lucky to have me as a roommate," Jeffrey said.

"Not true. In fact, it was the other way around. Thanks to me, there was a constant supply of new friends, including girls."

"Only because you were their dealer."

"Say what you will, but my presence on campus was legendary."

"I was the one who introduced you to my friends and then their friends. You were a farmer from up north in Wisconsin."

"Yup, farmer, and proud of it. My grandparents farmed this land for fifty years, and their parents before that."

"But you left the farm for awhile, right?" Maureen asked.

"All I had known while I was growing up was living and working on a farm, and I wanted to experience more of the world. I was majoring in Agri-Business so I guess deep down my plan was to eventually return to farming. Law school was not something I had ever considered, but I have to admit Jeffrey had an influence on me, especially when he reminded me how much an attorney could earn."

"Substantial difference compared to farming," Jeffrey added.

"Not to mention a lot less work, or so I thought. Anyway, by that time Jeffrey had introduced me to Summer, who was also going to attend law school. She was a big city girl, and I understood she wanted to live where there was culture, entertainment, restaurants, and diversity. Becoming a lawyer was an easy decision." Dill touched Summer's hand and flashed a smile at her.

"How did you end up here, farming again?"

"We spent several years in the fast-paced, cut-throat world of corporate law. We both decided the environments in our physical world and our career world were toxic. When Summer was diagnosed with cancer and her treatments weren't working, something had to change."

"You were courageous to take such a drastic step."

"Not really." Summer sipped from a glass of sparkling apple cider. "Dill inherited the farm from his grandparents, and when he left it to attend college,

I think it bothered him a great deal to rent out the farmland and not be there to care for his family's legacy. He went home to the farm as often as he could, and he spent every summer working there, but it wasn't the same."

"What about your parents, Dill? Didn't they want the farm?" Maureen said.

"My mother died when I was very young. I was raised mostly by my maternal grandparents."

"You were so lucky to live with them and to have inherited their way of life." Maureen was envious of a family that stood the test of time.

"I think they'd be proud I decided to take over the farm."

"When Dill and Summer quit at the law firm and told me they were going to move to Wisconsin, I thought they were nuts." Jeffrey helped himself to more honey-glazed carrots. "After being here this summer, working the land and raising this amazing food, I believe Dill and Summer did the right thing."

"Wait, what? Did I hear Jeffrey say I did something right?"

"Well, that, and marrying Summer."

"Except now I'm the reason Dill is being forced to sell the farmland and maybe lose the whole farm." Summer's thin, pale face looked defeated, her eyes filled with despair.

"That's a discussion for another time and place." Dill stood up from the table and began clearing serving dishes and plates, his clattering and clanging filling the embarrassed silence around the table. Maureen joined Dill, lending him a hand clearing the table.

"If there's anything I can do to help, please ask."

"Nothing much anyone can do."

"We can do the dishes and clean up the kitchen for you," Jeffrey said carrying a handful of dirty silverware. "You and Summer go take the dogs for a walk on this perfect summer evening."

While they did the dishes, Maureen and Jeffrey were able to keep their conversation revolving around the farm and work, while avoiding the topic of Crooked Creek Farm's financial difficulties. After a time, the discussion stalled into an uncomfortable silence, and when they both began talking at the same time, Jeffrey insisted Maureen speak first.

"I'd like to apologize for my inappropriate behavior last night." Maureen hoped her voice sounded calm and nonchalant. "I think I was a little drunk or high, or maybe both, and I'm afraid I was caught up in the moment of a group of friends enjoying an evening together. It was just a kiss and didn't mean anything."

"No need to apologize. I think we were both a little surprised." Jeffrey stopped working on the kettle he'd been scrubbing and faced Maureen. "I like you, Maureen, and would hate to jeopardize our friendship."

"That's exactly how I feel. Let's forget it ever happened."

"Done, and done with this kettle, too." He handed it to Maureen. "Like new again, okay?"

Maureen agreed and began drying the kettle, relieved they had cleared the awkwardness from between them. The last thing she needed right now was any kind of personal life, despite how tempting a guy like Jeffrey was. She still wanted to ask him about property ownership and deeds without creating an uncomfortable situation where she implicated herself and unveiled her family issues in the process. Despite the risk, Maureen decided she had to take advantage of the moment.

"Jeffrey, I need some free legal advice."

"Free is not always guaranteed to be the best, but I'll give it a try."

"I know this person who has been incapacitated for a number of years, and . . ."

"Is this someone you met in the mental health facility?"

"Very funny. Anyway, this person owns some land with a house on it. While they've been out of commission, they gave the deed for the property to a relative as a safety precaution."

"Is this in Wisconsin."

"Yes. For years, the holder of the deed has paid the property taxes and managed the rental of the land to other farmers."

"What's the problem?"

"The holder of the deed has begun selling off the land, using some of the money to help pay the taxes and some of the money for personal gain."

"Did your friend give permission for the sale of the property?"

"That's where it becomes a little murky. Permission was given to sell some of the acreage for paying the property taxes. I'm not sure my friend realized the majority of the money from the land sale was taken by the deed holder for personal use."

"If the deed is a Warranty Deed, the owner or grantor, must present written proof of ownership, in this case, the deed, to anyone buying all or part of the property. If the holder of the deed does not have their name on the document, they aren't entitled to any claim of the property or to money gained through the sale of the property."

"In other words, having the deed in your possession means nothing as far as owning or selling land, if your name isn't on it?"

"Yes, however, I'm wondering if the person with the deed misrepresented themselves, pretending to be your friend. The prospective buyer would most likely have been unaware of the deception."

"Doesn't something have to be filed somewhere when land ownership changes hands as a sort of guarantee everything is legal?"

"Yes, the sale should have been recorded with the Register of Deeds through a Real Estate Transfer Return or RETR. It's mostly for tax purposes, but both parties involved have a responsibility to report the sale and sign the documents."

"What if they don't?"

"The property, according to the law, would still be owned by the grantor, your friend."

Maureen found it hard to believe a company like Sandover could be duped into buying land from someone who didn't own it. The company must have had lawyers who verified Toni's identity and checked for liens on the property. After the sale, an RETR would have been filed with the Register of Deeds by Sandover to record the transfer of ownership. In order to finalize their business deal, if Toni was posing as her sister, she would have been forced to forge documents throughout the transaction.

"Can't we get another copy of the deed?"

"Sure, at the County Court House. All you need is the address of the property."

"But this other person still has a copy."

"Yes, and, by the sound of it, is either pretending to be the owner or pretending to have the owner's permission to sell."

"One more question, Jeffrey, if you don't mind."

"Go ahead."

"How does my friend get her deed back from the person holding it?"

"She'll have to ask for it."

CHAPTER 25

After finishing in the kitchen, Maureen was worn out, so she and Road Dog retired upstairs for an early bedtime. The evening was mild and illuminated with the silvery light of a full moon. A breeze drifted in through the partially open window, and Maureen moved to lift the sash higher. From her window, she watched Dill pushing Summer on the swing in the yard below, their bodies casting long, willowy shadows on the grass. The swing's chains creaked with an eerie sound as the metal posts bounced with every push, and Dill and Summer laughed together, her bare feet reaching into the night sky.

Maureen was mesmerized by the scene, until a light tapping at her door drew her attention away from the window.

"Maureen, you up?"

She opened the door to find Jeffrey holding his cell phone.

"You have another text message, this time from someone named Andrea."

"How in the world did Andrea get your cell number?" Maureen thought out loud.

"Does she know your sister? Maybe she got it from her."

"You're probably right. I'm sorry for bothering you with my personal matters. I am planning on getting a new phone and cellular service soon."

"Good thing. I'm starting to feel like your answering machine."

"My apologies. I used to have Andrea for that."

"Right, your secretary." Jeffrey handed her the phone. "I won't be needing my cell tonight, so I'll leave it here with you. You can return it in the morning."

He was out the door and down the hall before Maureen could thank him. She sat on the bed with the phone, hesitating to find out from Andrea the latest bad news. When she typed in Andrea's number, she answered after two rings.

"Thank goodness the text message I sent to this Jeffrey person made it to you."

"Yeah, my phone's been out of commission."

"I know! I was desperate to talk to you, so I ended up calling David. He gave me your friend's number."

"What's so critical you were willing to contact him whose name I will not speak."

"Okay, I get it, he's a bad guy. It was worth it, though, because I found you. You need to come back to Anson-Chambers."

"Now what?"

"You remember the Wexler deal?"

"How could I forget it?"

"Since you left, problems began developing with the company."

"What kind of problems?"

"Certain insider information, including financial projections, was somehow leaked."

"What happened?"

"No one's certain. As information was revealed anonymously, Wexler Global's stock values began to fluctuate in a steady, downward trend."

"What does that have to do with me?"

"It's Don. He's gone to Robert and the Board. He claims there is a link between your hasty departure and the disclosure of the Wexler information."

"That's crazy. How would I do such a thing, and, furthermore, why?"

"The day you left, you were upset and angry. You packed up your briefcase and were gone. Around the same time, some files and flash drives disappeared."

"That doesn't mean I took them. How about checking in Don's office?"

"Don't shoot the messenger, okay? I know you would never do anything illegal like that, but I have to ask. When you were leaving Anson-Chambers, did you remove anything that didn't belong to you by accident?"

"Of course not. Well, maybe the tape dispenser, but that's all." Maureen felt sick, like she'd had too much vodka to drink.

"I hate to see your reputation being dragged through the mud."

"I think that ship has already sailed."

"It could get worse. What if they decide to press criminal charges against you?"

"They have no evidence, only Don's accusations. It's all conjecture and gossip."

"Yes, but Don's here and you're not. Please come home and clear up this mess."

"I'm not coming back, at least not right now, but I will figure out a way to fix this. Thanks, Andrea, for being on my side."

"You can always count on me."

After the phone conversation ended, Maureen made two quick decisions. First, she had to have cell phone service, or Jeffrey would continue to be dragged into the drama of her old life. Second, she needed to find a way to get rid of the Wexler files and flash drives she took from Anson-Chambers before she could be further implicated in Wexler's financial crisis.

CHAPTER 26

On Saturday, Maureen decided to take the day off, and leaving Road Dog snoozing in the shade with Summer and Samuel, she drove to Chippewa Falls to buy herself a cell phone. She wanted the newest generation phone that was reliable but easy to use, with decent photography options and bare-bones service at a cheap price. Finding what she had in mind didn't take long, but she talked the salesperson into giving her a remediation lesson on how to make the most of her phone. Accomplishing that task took a couple more hours.

Maureen used her new phone to call Jasmine.

"My attorney friend says we have to get the deed back from Toni."

"David thought we could get another copy of the deed from the County Court House."

"Yes, we should do that, but as long as Toni has a copy in her possession, she will find a way to use it to her advantage."

"You need to go see Toni. Get the deed back from her."

"That's not as easy as it sounds. You do remember Aunt Toni?"

"I don't recall much about her except that she hollered all the time and never cooked."

"She's not a nice person. Let's put it that way."

"What are you going to do about it?"

"I'm not sure. What are you going to do about getting the deed?"

"Nothing right now. We're in Door County for a long weekend and won't be home until late Monday night. Besides, you're so much better at handling things than I am."

"Sounds like you're pretty good at handling David." Whenever Maureen suggested they visit Door County, David refused, calling it a hand-painted, over-priced, antediluvian fish boil.

"You don't have to be mean." Jazz was using her pouty, little girl voice.

"You realize you're weekending with a married man, who, by the way, happens to be married to your sister, and you're calling me mean."

"He's going to file for a divorce, so it's kind of like the two of you are not married any more."

"Did you say David is filing for a divorce?"

"I thought you knew."

"I know now."

"I'm sorry, Moe. We're not trying to hurt you, but I think this thing between David and me can work."

"Good luck with that." Maureen hung up.

It wasn't like she had any delusions about reconciling with David after all he had done, but his quick decision to divorce Maureen without talking to her was a brutal blow, and hearing about it from her sister was more than painful. Besides being hurt, Maureen was as angry and frustrated with Jazz as she was with Toni. If Jasmine wanted the farm so much, why didn't she find a way to secure it? It was always Maureen's responsibility to put everything in order. Some things never change, Maureen told herself.

She drove back to the farm to check on Road Dog and pack some things.

"Are you okay with Road Dog staying here with you, Summer? I'm meeting up with a couple of old college friends, and if it gets late, I'd like to stay the night."

"Friends, huh?"

"Yes, girlfriends. At any rate, I'll be home either late tonight or by midday tomorrow."

"Sounds good. We'll take care of our pretty girl, won't we Samuel?"

With the Wexler files and flash drives packed in her duffle bag, Maureen drove south onto Highway 53 and headed for the interstate. A couple of miles into her journey, the check engine light started flashing. She considered turning around and abandoning her objective, but she wasn't sure she would again be able to summon the courage to tackle the Wexler problem if she didn't do it now. Besides, with David and Jasmine gone until Monday night, she couldn't afford to waste this opportunity. Another thing she couldn't afford to do was wait while her car was being fixed. Who was she kidding? She couldn't afford to have her car fixed, period.

Frank's Fifty-Three Truck Stop was less than thirty minutes away, and Maureen crossed her fingers hoping her car would make it. When she turned into the bustling oasis, she gave a sigh of relief. Inside, Maureen spotted Frank behind the counter, and when he saw her, he hurried to greet her with a broad smile and warm handshake.

"Coming back to work for me?"

"You're safe. I have a job."

"What do you need?"

"I hate that you knew I was going to ask for your help. I need to borrow a car." Maureen explained she had to take care of some legal matters, and Frank didn't hesitate to offer one of his vehicles.

"Take the Chevy Sonic. It's reliable, cheap on gas, and belonged to my ex-wife, so I hate the thing."

"Once again, you've pulled me from the brink of disaster."

"Don't get all dramatic on me. I'm lending, and I repeat, lending you a car."

Maureen was more than grateful and was headed out the door with keys in hand when someone grabbed her arm, spun her around, and pulled her in for a bearhug.

"Maureen, you are a sight for sore eyes." Ronnie pulled back and grinned into Maureen's face. "I wondered when we would see you again."

"It's good to see you, Ronnie. I can't say I've missed the restaurant, but I have sure missed you."

"Well, who wouldn't?" Ronnie laughed and hugged Maureen again. "Are you going to be around for awhile? We could go for drinks, 'cause I know how much you enjoy that."

"Wish I could. I have some business to handle and a small window of opportunity to get it done. I'm heading there right now. Maybe next time? Let me give you my new cell number."

They exchanged cell numbers, and Maureen told her, "I'll call you when work at the farm slows down, or if I ever get a day off."

"Sounds good. You take care, and give Road Dog a hug for me."

"You give that handsome deputy of yours a hug for me."

Eight hours later, Maureen passed through the private entrance of the subdivision where she and David built the home of their dreams and planned to live for the rest of their lives. The streets meandered through the well-built brick homes settled among remnants of oak forests.

Pulling into their brick-paved driveway, Maureen had a sinking feeling. What if David had changed the locks or reconfigured the pass codes? On the long drive here, she had pictured opening the garage without getting out of the car, and driving in, avoiding the chance someone would see her and recognize her. When she realized she had forgotten to bring the garage door opener from her own car, Maureen had no other choice but to get out of the vehicle and try the old code, praying no one would identify her or notice the car she was driving. The code worked. Maureen drove into the garage, shut the door, and grabbed her duffle bag.

The entry door to the house from the garage was not locked, and Maureen went into the kitchen. She felt like a stranger. Things had been changed, but even if the walls hadn't been painted a new color or the old refrigerator replaced, the room still would have felt foreign to the person Maureen was now.

As she wandered from room to room, Maureen couldn't believe this was the home of sloppy David and disorganized Jasmine. Everything was immaculate and in its place, but in no place was there any evidence of Maureen ever having lived there. In the upstairs hallway, Maureen opened the linen closet where David had installed their safe, bolting it to the floor. The safe was there, still buried beneath piles of tablecloths and old bath sets. Maureen worried David had changed the combination as she moved the dial of the lock, but when she cranked the handle, the safe opened.

Maureen was meticulous about certain things, one of them being record keeping, and the contents of the safe appeared to be as organized as she had left them. Buried deep beneath the folders of important documents was the small notebook she was seeking.

David believed in everything related to technology and stored all of his passwords and vital information in something called The Cloud. Maureen was more comfortable with a written record she could hold in her hands.

"Old-fashioned," he called her, but she had laughed off his criticism. Now she was glad she hadn't let him push her into doing something she didn't want to do.

Using her cell phone, Maureen began taking pictures of every page in her notebook, checking each photograph to be certain it was complete, in focus, and readable. After finishing, she placed the book where she found it and moved the folders back into position to conceal it. Shoving the safe's metal door closed, Maureen moved the handle to the lock position and gave the dial a few random spins. With the safe once again buried beneath piles of linens, Maureen clicked the closet door shut.

"Is someone there?" A woman's voice called up the stairs.

Maureen froze. She could hear the rustle of the person's clothing as she climbed the stairs, one by one, pausing with every step.

"Is that you, Jasmine? It's me, Mrs. Barnes. I brought in the mail for you."

Maureen remembered Mrs. Barnes lived across the street, but, because Maureen had always worked long hours, often seven days a week, she had never met any of the neighbors. Jasmine possessed a knack for connecting with all sorts of people. Leave it to her to not only know the neighbors by name, but know them well enough to have them check on the house and bring in the mail while she was away.

Maureen tiptoed into the master bedroom to hide, remembering the last time she'd seen this room, on the horrible day she found David and Jasmine together. Her hesitant feet were silent on the carpeting, and she dropped to the floor on the side of the bed farthest away from the doorway. With her face pressed to the soft carpet, the smell of David engulfed Maureen. This was his side of the bed, and underneath it were several pairs of smelly running shoes and miscellaneous running gear, along with crumpled papers, empty soda cans, and dishes covered in dried-on food. Still the same old David.

"Anyone in here?" Mrs. Barnes was at the bedroom door. She stepped inside and stopped. It was so quiet, Maureen was afraid to breathe. She heard Mrs. Barnes using her cell phone.

"Jasmine, it's Caroline Barnes. I'm over checking your house."

Pause.

"No, everything's fine. I thought I heard something upstairs, but I've looked into every room and all seems okay."

Pause.

"I could call the local precinct to come over, if you'd like."

Pause.

"All right. I'll do that."

Pause.

"Don't give it another thought. Enjoy the rest of your weekend."

The woman left the bedroom and walked downstairs. If Mrs. Barnes did call the police, it wouldn't take them long to get to the house. Maureen had to find a place to hide the Wexler files and flash drives, and get out of there. It needed to be a place where David was sure to find them, but somewhere obscure, not like her desk or file cabinets, which she was certain he'd already gone through. It had to be somewhere she could manipulate him into looking when the time was right.

Maureen got up, peeked out the bedroom window, and watched Mrs. Barnes cross the street. With no time to waste, she first checked the walk-in closet she and David shared and discovered her clothes had been replaced with Jasmine's trendy wardrobe. Although this didn't surprise her, it hurt. Maureen found her practical, tailored, and, what she liked to call, timeless wardrobe, hanging in the guest room closet. The banished clothes, like the Maureen who wore them, looked dark and matronly. Among the shoes, shoe boxes, and other things tossed beneath the hanging clothes, Maureen noticed a cardboard hatbox she saved from her childhood, one she hadn't opened in a long time.

She knelt down, smoothed the dust from the vintage box, and untied the faded ribbon securing the lid. Inside were photos from long ago, photos neither David or Jasmine would recognize. One picture caught Maureen's eye. It was of her and Momma sitting with Maureen's father in front of the Christmas tree. She pressed her fingertip to the image of her dad's face, one so like her own, it brought tears to her eyes. His dark hair curled around his ears and onto his forehead, and he held Maureen's small hands as she sat upon his knees. Momma's loving face was turned toward her husband as he grinned at their daughter.

Maureen had no memory of her father or the grandparents whose family farm they shared. When she was two years old, both her father and grand-father died in a terrible farm accident. A year later her grandmother died of cancer, leaving her mother with three-year old Maureen and a sizable farm to manage on her own.

Maureen was certain the hatbox would not have been of interest to David, who thought vintage anything was junk and found looking at old family pictures a waste of time. Jasmine ignored anything concerning Maureen's first family because, to Jazz, life began when she herself was born. It was pure luck the two hadn't tossed the box and the rest of Maureen's miscellaneous belongings into the trash.

Crossing her fingers, Maureen placed the Wexler items among the photos, closed the lid, tied the ribbon, and shoved the hatbox underneath the jumbled mess on the floor. If Maureen asked for the hatbox, David might wonder why, of all her possessions, she would want this particular one, and his curiosity might cause him to open the box to examine its contents.

With her duffel bag over her shoulder, Maureen ran to the garage and pressed the button to open the door, threw the bag in the seat behind her, and backed out. When she got out of the car and punched in the code to close the garage door, nothing happened. She tried again, still nothing. Leaving with the door open was not an option. Saying the numbers aloud, Maureen tapped each individual key, and the door began its descent. She stepped into the car and drove away, being careful not to speed. As she exited through the brick pillars of the subdivision entrance, a police squad car turned in. The officer glanced in her direction, and Maureen gave him a casual wave. All the way to the freeway, she continued to check her rearview mirror, expecting to be surrounded at any moment by squad cars, flashing lights, and officers with guns drawn, signaling her to pull over.

CHAPTER 27

Eight hours later, Maureen pulled into Frank's Fifty-Three Truck Stop, its numerous, towering lights brightening the sky and Maureen's mood, like a welcome home sign. Daybreak was still hours away, and Maureen found Frank working the kitchen, the counter, and waiting tables.

"Do you ever get any time off to sleep, Frank?"

"If I would be lucky enough to hire employees who stayed longer than a few weeks, sleep might be a possibility."

"Good point. Thanks for the use of the car. I filled it with gas and parked it where I found it." She handed Frank the Sonic's keys.

"Did you accomplish what you needed to do?"

"Not sure, but thanks to you, I gave it a shot. How about letting me take over for you to return the favor?"

"That sounds like an offer I can't refuse. Charlie will be in at 6:00 to take over. Until then, do you remember what to do?"

"Like riding a bicycle, Frank. Get outta here."

"With pleasure." He started to leave, then came back. "Forgot to tell you. Your car's fixed." Frank tossed her keys on the counter and was gone.

Maureen, relieved about her vehicle, ended up finishing the night shift and staying until almost noon the following day, because Charlie called in sick with the flu. Although she wasn't much of a cook, Maureen could work grill and had a good handle on the simple menu offerings, some of which were provided by a food service distributor. She was disappointed Ronnie wasn't working, but was happy to help Frank.

"Getting some sleep suits you." Maureen offered her apron to Frank, who came in at midday. "You look like a new man."

"One can only dream. How come you're still here?"

"Charlie has the flu," Maureen said. "Now, tell me about my car."

"Something's always wrong with that guy." Frank headed for the grill. "My mechanic buddy checked over the car, fixed the coil pack, and changed a couple of computer things, so it's good to go."

"You didn't need to do that, but I'm so glad you did. What was the bill?"

"Nothing. He owed me a favor."

"I should pay for having my car fixed."

"Fine. How much did you earn in tips since you got here?"

"I think about $28 give or take. Why?"

"As unbelievable as it sounds, that is exactly what you owe. Twenty-eight dollars."

"How convenient. It's gotta be more than that."

"Nope. I'll pass the $28 on to my buddy along with your profound gratitude."

"You're something else, Frank."

When Maureen got back to Crooked Creek Farm, she found Samuel and Road Dog sprawled in the backyard, with Summer watering the nearby garden.

"How was your visit with your friends?" Summer smirked at her own insinuation.

"It was fine." Maureen was cuddling and scratching Road Dog who was attempting to crawl into her lap. "I did miss my girl, who still believes she's a lap dog."

"She sure was lonesome for you. I wouldn't let her sleep upstairs while you were gone, and she wasn't too happy about that."

"Thanks, again, for watching her. Where is everybody?"

"Anyone who was available came in and went with Dill and Jeffrey to the fields along the eastern edge of the property. Something about a water line break at Sandover causing flooding problems."

"I should see if they need more help. Okay if I leave again?"

Maureen fired up the 4-wheeler and drove off across the fields. She spotted the crew at work near the Sandover property. Dill and Jeffrey had set up gasoline-powered pumps, and everyone worked together laying PVC pipes to direct the water away from Dill's land and back onto the sand mine's property. Once the pipe laying was finished, shovels were used to dig channels to keep the water flowing in an easterly direction. If they worked fast enough to remove the water from the field, the crops planted there would survive the brief flooding. It was dirty, sweaty, back-breaking work.

As the crew returned to the farmhouse, night was closing in. The sultry air hummed with the songs of cicadas and twinkled with lightning bugs, and the dusk was filled with fluttering brown bats and nighthawks flying in unpredictable patterns. Summer called everyone inside for sandwiches, garden fresh salads, cucumbers, and watermelon. Because Maureen hadn't slept since Friday night, she and Road Dog were the first ones to leave the table and head upstairs to bed.

It was hot in their room. While Maureen was gone, Summer must have come in to adjust the window, but though it was wide open, it offered no breeze. The unmoving air was oppressive and suggested a storm was building off in the distance. After a cool shower, Maureen dropped into bed beside Road Dog and fell asleep.

In the darkest hours right before dawn, Maureen was awakened by lightning flashes, explosions of thunder, pounding rain, and howling winds. More alarming than the storm was the creaking of chains and thrashing of metal in the yard outside. She bolted to the open window where the wind and rain were rushing in and watched the swings being launched into the gale and flung back, their chains twisting and tangling as the metal supports were ripped from the ground. When Maureen was forcing the window closed, the entire swing set was catapulted into the side of house, smashing beneath Maureen's second story window.

Now wide awake and drenched, she flipped the light switch, but there wasn't any power. Having no idea where her phone with its flashlight might be, she dropped to her hands and knees and began mopping in front of the window with her throw rug and feeling along with her hands until the floor was almost dry. As the storm moved off, moonshine filtered into the now chilly room, and, shivering in her damp pajamas, Maureen padded to the tall dresser in search of a dry pair. Months ago, when she first moved in, the dresser had been orderly, probably because it was almost empty, but over time, Maureen had added a variety of things. She admitted keeping drawers neat wasn't a top priority of hers.

Starting at the top of the dresser, Maureen eased the drawers open, one by one, feeling the contents of each, wishing she was more organized. Why was her underwear tossed in a drawer with flip flops? Did it make sense to store three bags of chicken jerky dog treats in the same place as the only two nice pairs of pants she owned? What normal person housed toothpaste, blue jeans, work shorts, and instant coffee together? Where were the two other pairs of pajamas she was pretty sure she owned? With one bottom drawer left, Maureen felt confident the pajamas were there.

She had to muscle the hesitant drawer open, wriggling it from side to side on its warped wooden glides. As it opened, a moldy smell enveloped Maureen, and she reached down into the dark drawer. Instead of finding pajamas, she touched something smooth and cold. Jerking her hand out, she peered closer, but couldn't see much of anything.

"This is ridiculous," she thought. "Put your hands into the drawer and see what's there."

Slowly, Maureen reached in and pulled out what was inside. It was a life-sized baby doll. She could feel its tangled nest of curls, the smooth, plump vinyl arms and legs, and the jagged place where its right ear had been. Maureen held the thing away from her. The movement caused the doll's eyes to rattle and a whooshing sound to escape from the round hole that was its mouth. It was the doll from the attic box.

CHAPTER 28

As though it was on fire, Maureen flung the doll back into the drawer and used both hands to force it closed. She sat back on her heels and stared at the drawer, half expecting the doll to come crawling out on its own. At that moment, the light in her room flickered on, so she tugged the drawer open again. Her heart pounded and her body shivered as she looked in the drawer and picked up the doll. What was wrong with her? It was doll, not a cadaver or severed horse head.

Maureen was startled by a nudge at her elbow. Road Dog, who had been buried deep in the covers to block out the storm, was sitting next to her. The dog used her nose to give the doll a disinterested once-over and moved to plant herself in front of the room door, an indication it was time to go outside. Maureen shoved the doll under the covers of her unmade bed and was about to follow Road Dog, when her cell phone rang. She answered the call on the way downstairs.

"What do you want, Jasmine?" Maureen's voice was an angry whisper.

"I wondered if you had a chance to contact Aunt Toni?"

"No, I didn't. I have a job and a life."

"This is important, Moe."

"So important you cut your lovers' weekend short to tackle the problem yourself?"

"No, we're leaving for home now." She stopped talking as someone in the background was speaking. "David wants you to know he's sorry he didn't talk to you about the divorce."

"Right."

"He said to tell you if there's anything you want from the house before the divorce settlement, we'll try to get it to you."

"You mean besides all of my money and half of everything we own?"

"I think he means clothes or personal stuff."

"How thoughtful of him." Maureen was seething, but then recognized the opportunity presenting itself. "Now that you mention it, I'd like the picture albums from the years when we were a family, just you and me."

"Oh, Maureen. That makes me so sad."

"I'd like my books from the study. David will know which ones are mine."

"Of course. Is that all?"

"There's an old hat box in the back of our closet, under my shoes and shoe boxes. It's the one with the pictures of my dad and his parents. It's all I have left of them."

"I think I know where it is. Anything else?"

"Not that I can think of right now. You'll need an address." Maureen dictated the mailing address for the farm.

"Be careful with my books and the old hat box, and please don't mess with the pictures inside the box as they are old. You wouldn't know any of the people anyway." Maureen hoped she wasn't overdoing it by mentioning the box with the pictures again.

"All right. Let me know if you talk to Aunt Toni, and I'll do the same for you."

"We both know you have no intention of doing anything."

"You're being so unfair to me. That's very hurtful." Jasmine hung up.

"My apologies. Wouldn't want to be unfair to poor Jasmine!" Maureen said into the vacant phone, then shoved it into her pocket.

The work day was long, and the cool morning following the storm simmered into a sweltering afternoon under a relentless sun. The crews harvested mountains of produce, more than Maureen had ever seen, all headed for the local grocery stores. Tomatoes, green beans, melons and cucumbers were prolific, and summer squash vines formed a tangled web throughout the gardens. It was amazing and exhausting, and everyone was glad when they were finished and drove back to the house.

In the kitchen stood rows of Mason jars filled with colorful vegetables Summer had canned that afternoon. The meal she prepared for the workers was laid out on the island, and they didn't waste any time digging in.

When Maureen finished eating, she planned on taking a quick visit to her aunt's tavern, but even though she hated the idea of seeing that creepy doll in her bedroom, she had to get cleaned up. When she headed toward the stairs, Summer called to her.

"Maureen, I stripped the beds today so the sheets could be hung outside. Hope you don't mind that I went into your room."

"Not at all." Should Maureen mention the doll she'd tossed under the covers of her bed? She decided against it.

Upstairs, her bedroom had been tidied, the bed was clean and neat, and the doll had disappeared. Maureen checked the drawers and the closet. The attic door inside the closet was closed and latched.

It was possible Summer removed the doll after straightening the room. It was also possible the doll was a figment of Maureen's imagination, perhaps brought on by the tumultuous swing set and the stormy night. The doll seemed to be identical to the one in the attic, and it was so real Maureen had held it in her hands, or at least she thought she did.

"You saw it and even sniffed it, didn't you?" Maureen asked Road Dog, rubbing the dog's ears and scratching her belly. "If only you could talk."

When she and Road Dog arrived at Toni's bar, the tawdry sign on the roof was dark and the parking lot was empty. Maureen wondered if the tavern was closed, but the lights were on inside, so she figured Toni must be there.

They walked into the smoky, dismal room where Toni sat alone on the patron side of the bar, staring at a soundless baseball game on the television, an empty glass and a half full bottle of whiskey keeping her company. She turned to give Maureen half a glance.

"This day keeps getting better and better." Toni turned back and filled her glass to the rim with whisky. "Bar's closed on Mondays."

"I'm not here as a customer. I'm here to get the deed to my mother's property."

"I told you to take this up with your mother. Until I hear from her, the deed stays right where she intended it to be."

"Holding that deed does not give you the right to sell the land."

"Never said it did. How many times we gonna go around about this?"

"As many times as it takes to get you to do the right thing."

"Ha, that's laughable coming from you."

"What's that supposed to mean?"

"Nothing. It's too late anyway, so forget it. Now get out."

Maureen and Road Dog walked out, and Toni was not far behind them.

"Closed means closed. Next time, I'll remember to lock up the place." She slammed the door and clicked the deadbolt.

CHAPTER 29

....

Summer was relaxing on the side porch when Maureen and Road Dog arrived back at the farm. The heat of the day had eased, and Maureen joined Summer for awhile, hoping to weave the topic of the missing doll into the conversation without sounding ridiculous.

"That was some storm last night. I'm so sorry about your swing set getting trashed," Maureen said.

"Dill thinks he can fix it." Summer gazed off toward the empty space in the yard where the set used to be. "I do miss the swings."

"I'm sure he'll have them repaired in no time." Maureen accepted the glass of lemonade Summer poured for her "Thanks for washing my sheets today. They smell so good after drying in the sun."

"I know. The sweet smell helps me sleep." Summer sipped from her glass. "Plus, air drying the laundry saves energy."

Maureen took a drink of her lemonade and measured her next words, not wanting to sound paranoid. "When you were in my room this morning, did you notice whether I had left something on the bed?"

"What was it?"

"An old keepsake from when I was little."

"Only thing I found on the bed was dog hair. Was the keepsake important?"

"Not a big deal. You know what a slob I can be. It's probably under the bed or something."

Maureen finished her lemonade, excused herself, and headed inside. She knew the doll wasn't under the bed or something. She was pretty sure where she would find it and was drawn upstairs to her room and the attic. She pictured herself in a horror movie where there's a disturbing noise in the basement, and the entire audience screams, "Don't go down there!" but she goes toward the noise anyway.

With a snap, she opened the latch, and the attic door creaked open. She stepped inside the room and felt the beads of sweat begin to form on her neck. The final rays of the departing sun focused a dusty shaft of light into the dim garret. Despite the light filtering in, Maureen couldn't see much, so she pulled the string of the light above her head. Things appeared as they were the first time she was there—the hanging clothes, broken lamps, the stacks of newspapers and magazines, the ratty mattress piled with boxes, including the pink box. Maureen hoped the doll, if it was in the attic, would be sitting out in the open, but it wasn't. She would have to look inside the box, and the thought filled her with dread.

Instead, she distracted herself by concentrating on the bundles of newspapers piled on the floor. There was a thick layer of dust obscuring the page on the top of the stack, and she brushed it clear. The papers were from the Leader-Telegram, a publication located in the nearby city of Eau Claire. She set aside the first bundle, dated in the 1990s, and worked her way down the piles, until she spotted what she was trying to find. The year was 1982.

In the issue dated Thursday, September 16, 1982, there was a story covering the entire top half of the front page. "A Tragic Farm Accident: Death in a Silo" was the account of how Maureen's father and grandfather were trapped in a silo and died there. The details of the tragedy were difficult to read because the deaths might have been prevented. It was the time of year when all the feed bins had been emptied, and the men were using the remaining silage from the depths of the silo. During feeding that morning, the augers used to pull the corn up from the silo jammed, and the damp feed had clumped along the concrete walls. With no other method to extract what they needed to feed their cows, Maureen's grandfather entered the silo to dislodge the clumps. The unstable grain collapsed, and, within moments, it buried him under twenty feet of corn silage. The escape hatch at the bottom of the silo was broken. Maureen's dad didn't hesitate, entered the silo to rescue his father and was soon engulfed himself. It took four hours to extricate the bodies from underneath the mountain of corn that entombed the two men.

Maureen finished reading the article, the faded newspaper now sprinkled with her tears. She pressed the paper to her heart, wondering how life would have been different for everyone if the feed bins hadn't been empty, if the augers hadn't jammed, if the escape hatch hadn't been broken, and, most of all, if the hasty decisions the two men made that day had not been so deadly.

The daylight had disappeared from the attic, and the bare lightbulb hanging near the door caused objects in the room to cast distorted, macabre shadows along the floor and walls. Maureen wanted to leave, but the appearance and subsequent disappearance of the creepy doll in the drawer plagued her. What bothered her more was that she couldn't deny how the combination of the birthday gift in the attic and the baby doll she found in her room showed a troubling resemblance to her growing recollections from that one particular summer day out of her past. Her inexplicable reaction to the swing set was also worrisome, but seemed to fit as a piece of the puzzle she was putting together.

Tucked against the farthest side of the room, where the beams in the ceiling slanted down to meet the wall, was the gray, tattered mattress piled with boxes. Ducking her head and bending low, Maureen felt her legs weaken and her heart race, so she focussed on the boxes while the darkness closed in around her. Some of the boxes were empty, and the others were filled with junk. As she searched, Maureen's body dripped with sweat. Run away, she told herself, but reason convinced her the doll was inside that box, hidden by the shadows.

Shoving the rest aside, she picked up the one box left, the faded pink birthday present. Something solid and compact was inside, and, with hesitant hands, she untied the frayed, discolored ribbon wrapped around it. Lifting the lid, she found the baby doll there, resting in her tattered pink dress, one blue eye staring up at Maureen and the other rolled back into the eye socket. Pressed between the doll's pudgy fingers was the ragged gift tag. Maureen held the card up to the light and read the same words out loud. "Happy Birthday, Love, Daddy."

CHAPTER 30

For the remainder of the week, Maureen was tormented by the weird happenings she had experienced that would probably be everyday coincidences a normal person could explain by rational thinking. Why these innocuous incidents bothered Maureen was a maddening mystery.

Each day, Maureen avoided going upstairs until the last minute, and she and Road Dog spent as much time as possible either outside or downstairs. Maureen used Jeffrey's laptop and the passcodes she had photographed with her phone to check her 401K account. It was a relief to find there had been no recent withdrawals, and she began the process of changing her passcode and locking down the account. With the log on and password for her credit cards, she was able to reactivate two of them with new numbers. Using the passwords for the closed bank accounts, Maureen initiated a claim for the money removed from them. She felt more in control of her finances than she had in many months.

She had to admit, however, that the weird things she'd been experiencing at the house felt out of her control. She considered asking Jeffrey to switch rooms with her so she could avoid any further incidents, but couldn't think of one sane reason why he should be inconvenienced. After all, she could hardly tell him the truth about the strange things she had been seeing and hearing in her bedroom, in the closet, and in the attic, and that these were identical to details she had been remembering from her past. She couldn't imagine revealing how she felt about the swing set. No, she wasn't crazy at all.

After working long hours for weeks harvesting vegetables and maintaining the fields, Maureen was relieved when Dill said they were caught up enough to enjoy some much needed rest, and he told the crew the following weekend was theirs. Maureen appreciated the time off and was going to use the weekend to travel to the Taycheedah Correctional Institute in Fond Du Lac where her mother was serving a life sentence.

Visiting her in prison was a gut-wrenching decision and something Maureen would never have considered until her recent encounters with Toni. Exasperated and stumped regarding what to do about that situation, Maureen asked Jeffrey for advice as they picked tomatoes in Summer's garden.

"It's clear the property deed is not going to be given back to you." Jeffrey lifted a vine, heavy with ripe, red fruit. "I'd suggest you get a quitclaim."

"What does that do?"

"It will transfer the property over to the person named on the document, in this case, you." Jeffrey stood to wipe the sweat trickling down his temples. "You just need the owner's signature. Voila! Any other deed becomes invalid."

"Voila? Is that a legal term?" Maureen couldn't hide her skepticism. "Seems too easy."

"A quitclaim is pretty straight forward. Doesn't require any title search, but you have to sign before a notary public and file the signed claim with the State and the Register of Deeds."

"I guess it doesn't sound impossible to accomplish."

"Tonight I'll help you find the necessary forms online, and we'll fill them out together." Jeffrey brushed off a tomato the size of a large apple, winked at Maureen, and took an enormous bite. "Gotta have quality control."

In the evening, Maureen and Jeffrey worked on the quitclaim and searched the website for Taycheedah, which indicated a notary public was available on their staff. Maureen learned she was already listed as an approved visitor, thanks to Jasmine, and due to her mother's deteriorating physical condition, the prison approved Maureen's request to visit the following weekend.

The week was filled with sleepless nights as Maureen agonized over her upcoming trip to the prison. When she and Jasmine severed all ties with their mother, the two sisters left the past behind them and started a new life together. Now, David and Jasmine had eliminated Maureen from that life, and she was on her own again. The only things that mattered to her were Road Dog, the people at the farm, and the chance she might one day operate her own farm, an idea percolating since Maureen learned Toni was selling the farm land. Maybe Maureen was crazy enough to make it happen.

In order to outsmart Toni and catch her off guard, Maureen had to visit her mother and get her to sign the quitclaim. She calculated it would take her about eight hours, allowing seven hours for driving and one hour or less inside the prison. The trip was too long for Road Dog, so Maureen told Summer she had some business to do, and she didn't want the dog left sitting in the car while she did it.

Maureen was relieved when Summer agreed to keep Road Dog without any questions asked. The last thing Maureen wanted to do was lie to Summer, but she would have been forced to make up a story to hide the truth from her friends. Maureen smiled at the ease with which she called the people at the farm her friends, but she felt certain the incredible group she toiled with every day were her friends, an experience she hadn't encountered often in her life.

She had looked up some details about the prison. Taycheedah Correctional Institute, a maximum/medium security prison, was spread over acreage in low-slung, formidable buildings, secured by a 12-foot high fence covered in razor wire with additional electronic detection systems, and an armed vehicle perimeter patrol. When she arrived there, Maureen parked near the visitors' entrance, showed her identification, received approval for the papers she carried, including the request for a notary public, and passed through a metal detector. She was a little early, so, with her stomach tied in knots, she waited as other visitors arrived and were escorted away. At Maureen's scheduled appointment time, she was accompanied to the section for inmate patients. Keys rattling at her side, the stone-faced officer was silent, until they reached a restricted area, where she unlocked the heavy doors using one of her many keys and tapped in numbers on a digital key pad.

"Visitation with patients in this area is limited to thirty minutes." The officer ushered Maureen inside and motioned for additional assistance.

Another medical staff member dressed in green scrubs and holding a clipboard, led Maureen down a grey corridor, the woman's rubber-soled shoes squeaking on the tiled floor. They entered a large room labeled Ward B, lined with eight beds separated from one another by retractable room dividers. The antiseptic air was filled with murmurs of conversations drifting from the isolated partitions.

"She's in here, bed number 102B." The divider was slid open, and the staff member leaned in, motioning for Maureen to step inside. "Usually, in the medical unit only two people at a time are allowed to be with the patient, so keep your visit short. Press the call button when you want the notary to come in."

Expecting she would be the only visitor, Maureen was surprised to see Jasmine standing at one side of the hospital bed, while, off in the corner, David was seated. Although it rattled Maureen that they were there, she ignored them both and focused on the person lying in bed.

The frail figure was small, almost childlike, and her boney arms and upper torso were visible above the bed covers tucked along the rest of her body. Her wispy, colorless hair all but disappeared against the pillow, and her translucent skin was an abnormal yellow-grey. The one thing Maureen recognized was the woman's blue eyes, the eyes belonging to her mother.

"Darla, you came."

Maureen's pounding heart was pierced with pain upon hearing the name that once was hers, spoken by the mother she once loved.

"Hello, Momma. It's been a long time."

"I thought you'd never come." Tears lined her mother's eyes.

"Me, too." Maureen turned to glare at her sister and David. "I didn't know you two would be here."

"I guess we could say the same thing about you." David stood and walked the few steps to the hospital bed. "Peggy, it was good to meet you. I'm sorry it didn't happen sooner."

He started toward the opening near the room divider and passed Jasmine, placing a hand on her shoulder.

"We should probably go."

"You don't have to leave on my account. I won't be here long." Maureen pulled the folded legal papers from her inside jacket pocket.

"Momma, I know you are very ill. I also know you loved our farm."

"Those were good years, Darla. We were so happy together."

"When you were leaving us and you gave Toni the deed to the farm, I believe you meant for her to protect it and save it for you. Am I right?"

"Yes, Toni was good to me during those awful times, lived on the farm and took care of you girls."

"In the beginning, that's what she did, but things changed, and Jasmine and I moved out. A few years later, Toni left the farm, even started selling off the land."

"She told me about needing to do that. It had to be done to pay the property taxes."

"With a great deal left over for her. Now, I think she's planning on selling a lot more of the land. She's going to keep selling it until it's gone."

"Toni would never hurt me or steal from me, just like Jasmine would never hurt you or steal from you."

"It's already happened, and it will happen again. Sometimes sisters can't be trusted."

"Jasmine and David said almost the same thing about Toni as you've told me. I guess it's true."

"I promise it is true." Maureen laid the legal document on her mother's bed, pressing the folds of the paper smooth. "In order to stop Toni, I need you to sign this paper."

"But I already signed a paper for Jasmine. She said it will protect the farm from Toni."

"Yes, Momma, you did." Jasmine's face flushed and tiny beads of perspiration dotted her upper lip. "There's no need to sign another."

"Is it a quitclaim deed?"

"Yes." Jasmine would not look Maureen in the eye.

"It has to be signed in front of a notary public."

"It was. I'm a notary." David's voice dripped with smugness, his arms crossed with defiance over his chest. Jasmine stood next to him.

"I didn't know you were a notary."

"Maureen, despite your delusions to the contrary, you don't know much of anything." David sounded pleased with himself.

"Then it's all settled. No more worrying." Maureen's mother's words were whisper soft. Her breathing was hesitant and shallow. "Please sit down, Darla, and talk to me."

"Momma, we'll leave you two to catch up." Jasmine leaned down, pecked her mother's cheek, and patted her hand.

"I'll be back to visit you real soon." With a quick wave, Jasmine and David disappeared from the room.

"I'll be right back, Momma." Maureen was close behind her sister, following her into the grey corridor. She grabbed Jasmine by the arm and forced her to stop.

"What's going on, Jazz?"

"Nothing. You said to take care of the problem, and I did. I thought you'd be pleased."

"Let me see the quitclaim Momma signed."

"It's not necessary to check it over. David is a notary and said it's legal."

"If it's legal, then why don't you want me to look at it?"

With reluctance, Jasmine retrieved the document and passed it to Maureen. Before she had a chance to unfold it, David snatched the paper from her hands.

"It's legal. That's all you need to know."

"Out of curiosity, whose name is listed as the new owner of the property?"

Neither Jazz or David said anything, and Maureen had her answer.

"Here's the form I was going to have Momma sign." Maureen opened up the quitclaim she had brought along and held it for them to see. It listed their mother's name as the current owner or Grantor, and in the space showing the new owners, labeled "Grantee," were Maureen's and Jasmine's names.

"I'm guessing that's not quite how yours looks."

"David said because I prepared the form and delivered it to Momma, only my name could be listed as the one receiving the property."

"You believed him?" Maureen was yelling. "Of course you did."

"I promise, I'll share it with you. Momma would want it that way."

"You are such a fine example of honesty and loyalty, why wouldn't I believe you?" Maureen turned around and walked away.

"Maureen, wait. The things you asked for from the house are in our car. We were going to deliver them to you on our way to Minneapolis, but since you're here . . ."

"You can put everything in my car. It's in the lot, but had to be locked." Maureen handed over the keys. "Leave them with the guard at the entrance."

"We were glad to do this for you."

"Thanks for nothing." Maureen headed toward Ward B, her anger boiling. David hated Minneapolis, called it a long drive to nowhere.

The woman in the green scrubs approached Maureen.

"Was there a problem?"

"No. I was saying good-bye to my sister."

"You're the one visiting 102B, correct?"

"Yes, Peggy Whitcomb is my mother."

"She's sleeping. Not used to having visitors, I guess."

Maureen sensed the woman's disapproval of her, the daughter who, until today, never visited her dying mother, and she was touched by the nurse's discreet display of compassion for an inmate. On some level, Maureen felt sorry for her mother, too.

Pulling the chair closer to the bed, Maureen sat and watched the rise and fall of her mother's breathing. In the quiet room, with the shades drawn, Maureen's mind drifted to a summer afternoon in the yard behind the farmhouse. Her mother was young. She was wearing a sundress that showed her shoulders and slender arms, and she was taking laundry down from the clothesline. There were dark clouds forming in the distance and she was trying to capture a sheet that fluttered and snapped in the breeze. Someone was singing "Happy Birthday" in a little girl voice, and her mother called out to the girl, "Hang on or you're going to fall." The birthday song and the spoken words were so distinct and real, it seemed they were happening there in the hospital room, and Maureen recognized them as part of that memory, the one she and Dr. Taylor had been unveiling for over two years. Now, Maureen was certain the woman she remembered in the yard that day was her mother. Swinging on the swing, the little girl dressed in pink was celebrating her birthday.

Her mother's eyes blinked open, and she reached her papery, veined hand toward Maureen.

"I want you to know everything I did was for you, Darla." She closed her eyes and slept again.

It was clear there would be no discussion with her mother about the memory Maureen had, and there would be no signed quitclaim from her either. She kissed her mother's cheek and wondered if she would ever see her again.

Leaving the prison, Maureen picked up her keys and returned to the car where she found Jasmine and David's delivery for her. Each of the boxes was labeled, one with pictures and albums from the years after they left Toni's, four larger boxes with Maureen's books, and the last one was the hat box. More faded and tattered outside in the daylight, the box was still secured with a ribbon which Maureen untied. She lifted the lid and examined the stacks of pictures. They were all there, but the Wexler items were not. David had taken the bait.

Maureen wasn't quite sure what, if anything, would happen as a result of David having the inside information, but at least she should be off the hook regarding Wexler's financial problems. If she got lucky and David and Don were already conspiring together in the Wexler scheme, they would use her files to expand their crime, and they might get caught.

CHAPTER 31

....

Maureen felt herself relax as she crossed the bridge to Crooked Creek Farm. She survived the day she'd been dreading and was back where she belonged. She and Road Dog were almost to the bedroom when Jeffrey peeked his head out from across the hall.

"How'd it go today at the prison?"

"Not well. It's complicated, but my quitclaim is not signed."

"That's too bad. What are you going to do now?"

"I'm going to bed. It was an exhausting day."

"I'm glad you made it home before the thunderstorm. I know how much you hate driving in the rain." Jeffrey closed his door.

Inside her bedroom, everything seemed normal. Nothing crazy or unusual had happened in the days since Maureen found the doll in the attic, and twice, when she checked there, the doll was still in the gift box where she left it. Despite things settling down in the creepy department, and as exhausted as she was, Maureen tossed and turned, unable to fall asleep, as her anger intensified like the storm outside. She was furious with Jasmine and David for taking the farm. The two people Maureen had loved most in the world conspired against her and shattered her life along with the hope of having a future on her own farm some day.

When Maureen did close her eyes, she saw the image of her mother's frail, withered body and her sunken, sad eyes. How time had changed the young woman hanging laundry on a breezy summer day. Thinking of that afternoon, Maureen attempted to picture the performers in the scene forming in her head. She now knew her mother was a part of it. The man was there, as was the little girl. Behind the swinging child, Maureen thought she could see someone pushing her, and there might have been another figure standing on the porch

After mulling it over, Maureen decided to find out more about what happened on the day the man was killed. In the attic were stacks of old, local newspapers, where she had found the issues from the early 1980s with the story of her father and grandfather. She summoned every bit of courage she could, opened the closet, and slid the attic's latch, the heat drifting out as the door wobbled open. Maureen felt above her head for the string that would turn on the light. Once the light was on, she stood for a few minutes, letting her eyes adjust to the shadowy room. She listened to the rain beginning to drum on the roof and made a mental note to bring her phone and flashlight the next time she was in the attic, if there was a next time.

The newspapers remained on the floor where Maureen last saw them. On the left were the oldest issues, and on the right, the papers were dated in the 1990s, the time she calculated the shooting occurred. She began with the issue on the top of the righthand stack and browsed the headlines and front pages. If the man was killed as she recalled, the story would have been a major one in their area, worthy of front page coverage. What she found instead was the end of the story first, in the newspaper dated September, 1997. The one-paragraph article was on the front page, but occupied only a small portion of its bottom half.

LOCAL WOMAN SENTENCED IN MURDER TRIAL

Area resident Peggy Whitcomb, 37, has been sentenced in the shooting of Stanley Nowak, 39, to a minimum of 30-years to life. Chippewa Falls Circuit Court Judge Richard McCall presided over the three-week jury trial ending in June which found Ms. Whitcomb guilty of the second degree murder of Nowak, her boyfriend, on July 9, 1995. The prosecution asked for the maximum sentence allowable. Following testimony by character witnesses for the defendant, and, after consideration of other mitigating circumstances, the judge ruled Whitcomb could be eligible for parole after twenty-five years. She is expected to serve her sentence at Taycheedah Correctional Institute in Fond du Lac, Wisconsin.

The man in the scene was named Stanley. Maureen had no recollection of her mother ever having a boyfriend, but he was the reason her mother went to prison. It was this Stanley person in her memory who called in a burly and raw voice, "No getting hurt on your special day, birthday girl." The thought of it made Maureen feel sick.

To her, this was a story about strangers, the woman, a convicted murderer, and the man, her victim. With an exact time frame for the trial, Maureen continued leafing through the stack of newspapers until she found those dated from May and June of 1997. The headlines for the trial described the proceedings as though they were written for a tabloid: "Admitted Shooter on Trial for Murder," "I Only Wanted to Scare Him," "When He Turned His Back, I Shot Him," and "Shooter: I Would Do It Again." Maureen glanced through the papers, each day's coverage of the trial sounding more sensational than the previous one, and she was surprised to feel compassion for her mother, who had to endure the humiliating and frightening ordeal by herself.

The information Maureen was most interested in locating was the first coverage of the murder. On July 10, 1995, the day after the shooting, the story she sought was the main feature on the front page of Eau Claire's Leader-Telegram.

SHOOTING OF LOCAL MAN ENDS IN ARREST

Police in Chippewa Falls were called to the farm of local resident Peggy Whitcomb yesterday after a report of a shooting. They found 39-year old Stanley Nowak of Chippewa Falls dead of a gunshot wound to the head. There were no apparent witnesses to the shooting, but the gun retrieved from the crime scene in the backyard of Whitcomb's home belonged to Nathaniel Whitcomb, deceased husband of Peggy. An arrest was made by investigators on the scene after Ms. Whitcomb confessed to killing Nowak. Ballistics testing was used to confirm the .380 caliber pistol belonging to Whitcomb's late husband was the murder weapon. Ms. Whitcomb is being held without bond at the Chippewa Falls County Jail until her arraignment. Minor children found inside the house on the day of the shooting did not witness the incident and are now with relatives. Local Sheriff Jack Peterson told the Leader-Telegram: "Our quiet, rural community is in shock after a tragedy like this one."

Maureen read the story three times and studied the photographs accompanying the article. There was one of a grinning Stanley in a suit, tall and thickset, one of her mother's house in better times, and one of the .380 caliber gun. The largest picture showed Maureen's mother, hands cuffed behind her back and head down, with one uniformed officer on either side, their large hands gripping her slender arms.

Maureen had been fifteen years old at the time of the shooting and knew her mother had killed someone, but despite reading the article and studying the photographs, she couldn't form a complete memory of what happened. This newspaper story explained at least part of what she remembered, placing her mother and Stanley together in the yard. Maureen believed she was one of the minor children in the house at the time of the shooting, and Jasmine was there, too. It was possible their cousins were also in the house, but none were witnesses to Stanley being killed.

A slight rustle drew Maureen's attention toward the entrance into the attic, as the light overhead became dark. With a snap, the latch slid into its chamber, and Maureen was locked in the small, dark room. She fumbled her way to the door and pressed her ear against the rough surface. Was someone on the other side listening to her? Maureen waited for several minutes, frozen in place. In desperation, she yanked hard on the attic door handle but there was no give. She worried about Road Dog, until she heard her plop down outside the locked door and begin to snore. Whoever shut and locked the door was someone Road Dog knew and allowed in the bedroom. Maureen didn't pound the door or scream for help because she didn't want to awaken the entire household. Rummaging around in the attic in the middle of the night might appear to be suspicious, crazy behavior.

On her hands and knees, Maureen crawled to the window with the hope of escaping through it or at least allowing in fresh air. Tracing her hand along the window's edges, Maureen found the window lock was broken off and the entire frame was painted shut. She considered breaking the glass, but was afraid someone would hear her, so she sat on the rough floor, her back leaning against the door, her brain trying not to panic. The window panes rattled as wind gusts threw rain against the house, and lighting flashes from outside scattered flickers of faint light about the room. Despite the warmth of the attic, Maureen shivered and hugged her knees in close.

She distracted herself by contemplating the list of mounting evidence calling into question her sanity. First, there was the appearing and disappearing pink girl's dress in her closet. Across the attic was the box with the familiar-looking doll inside, a gift from "Daddy." That damn doll. Finding it in her bottom dresser drawer, then having it disappear the next day, and finding it back inside the box holding the gift tag, was driving her crazy. Maureen couldn't forget how she reacted to the swing set Dill brought home for Summer. What about the newspaper articles covering her mother's arrest, trial, and conviction for killing Stanley and all the murky details that didn't quite fit? To top it off, she suspected she was being held prisoner in the attic.

Snap out of it, Maureen told herself. You can't possibly think any of this proves or disproves a person's sanity. She began to analyze the same list of happenings, using rational thinking. What was the problem with finding stored in the attic a doll inside an old birthday gift box tagged from a loving father? Maybe that same doll was placed in the bottom drawer by mistake and then put back in the box. So what if it resembled a doll from a memory she thought she had? The swing set represented a husband's love for his wife, not something ominous and threatening. Many people keep old newspapers, especially local ones with news that affects them or their community. Plus, it's not uncommon for the power to go out in a bad storm. Maureen couldn't explain the door closing and latching by itself, but she thought her bedroom window was open, so with the wind and the storm, maybe that explained it.

The more she tried to make sense of everything, however, the more terrified Maureen felt. The pieces didn't quite fit, and instead of feeling comforted, she felt crazier than ever.

CHAPTER 32

· ·

Frantic scratching on the attic door woke Maureen. When had she fallen asleep, she wondered as she sat up and placed her hands on the door.

"Road Dog, I'm in here." The scratching on the door intensified.

"The door is locked." Saying it made no sense, but it justified her presence inside the attic. She tugged hard at the door handle anyway and was surprised when the door flung open, sending Road Dog sprawling belly first onto the attic floor.

"I don't know what happened, but it doesn't matter," Maureen whispered in Road Dog's ear. "It'll be our little secret."

A pale, early morning light filtered in through the open bedroom window, and Maureen absorbed the fresh air, relieved to have escaped her prison. Road Dog needed to go out, so Maureen threw on her work clothes, and the two hurried downstairs. They were standing in the yard when several pieces of heavy equipment rumbled east past the farm. Leading the caravan was the familiar black pickup truck with the logo for Sandover Mining, LLC. The last flatbed truck was loaded with an enormous excavator.

This can't be good, Maureen told herself. If Sandover was bringing in substantial earth moving equipment in addition to what was already on site, chances are they were planning an expansion, and what better place to expand than on property adjacent to the existing operation? Did Dill and Summer sell more land to Sandover? When Dill came out of the house, Maureen had to confront him.

"Looks like you've sold more land to the sand mining operation." Maureen knew it wasn't her place to question how Dill conducted his farm business, but his actions affected what happened to her mother's property.

"Had to be done. Medical bills got to be paid, and the price was right."

"Mind if I ask how many acres you sold?"

"Not that it's any of your business, but I had to sell them sixty acres."

"Had to?"

"Yeah, their plan was to secure at least one hundred additional acres to reach the company expansion target or some darn thing."

"So what about the other forty acres?"

"They bought it from Toni's farm next door."

"Do you know what part of the land Sandover bought?"

"The acres along the road where our two properties meet were the first we sold to them awhile ago. Now, they purchased close to a hundred acres north of that land, plus a couple acres on either side of their current mining operation."

"Toni sold over forty acres to Sandover?"

"Give or take. Why are you so interested?"

"No reason. Just asking." Maureen tried to act nonchalant and turned toward where Jeffrey had driven up in the truck and was honking the horn. She climbed in the cab with Loriano and Jeffrey, while, in the back, sitting among the tools, water containers and empty bins were Silvia, Lucy and Genna on one side of the truck bed and Eric and Will on the other,

It was still early when Jeffrey drove the crew to the eastern fields, where several crops remained to be picked. When they were within a quarter mile of their work location, the Sandover pickup and the empty flatbed trucks were leaving the area. Maureen heard the clanking and rattling sounds of the excavating equipment already in operation, and when the workers arrived at their destination, the noise was deafening. The bulldozer and monstrous excavator rumbled along the ridge next to the planted field, traveling north to where Dill said the newly sold acreage was located.

"What do you think they're doing?" Maureen shielded her eyes as she peered ahead.

"It looks like they're headed for those oak trees." Jeffrey pointed into the distance.

The two mammoth machines were heading straight for a grove of bur oaks standing fifty or more feet tall, sentinels that had endured the icy blast of perhaps 150 winters. The massive trunks, covered in deeply furrowed bark, soared upward, divided into large, spreading branches, and culminated in rugged, rounded crowns. They withstood all life could throw at them, until now. Maureen had to do something.

"Everybody, I need your help. They're going to take down those oak trees. We have to stop them."

Maureen started running. She wasn't sure if anyone would follow her, and she had no idea what she would do once she reached the trees, but she ran anyway, faster than she had ever run in her life. Racing in a beeline for the trees, she stumbled several times on the uneven terrain, but managed to stay on her feet, arriving in time to position herself between the trees and the machinery lumbering toward them. Grasping her knees to catch her breath, she was soon joined by the whole crew, breathing hard and awarding each other with high fives. Jeffrey pulled up beside them in the truck.

"What do we do now?" Lucy sounded excited and almost gleeful.

"We could join hands to form a human barrier," Genna said.

"There aren't enough of us to surround all the trees." Jeffrey sounded doubtful as he surveyed the area. "Everyone, grab a long-handled tool from the back. I'll pull the truck alongside us."

"Spread out and don't move." Maureen rushed to the outer edges of the long grass growing beneath the broad overhang of the trees. "Whatever you do, don't let them get close enough to dig in and start moving the soil."

The group separated and positioned themselves in an arc facing outward, enabling everyone to see whatever was coming at them.

"If they get close, stand your ground," Loriano said. "What they don't need is a lawsuit for injuring someone during a peaceful demonstration."

When Maureen gave him a puzzled look, he shrugged.

"I've been in a few demonstrations in my day. Guess you could call me an activist."

Loriano's voice was drowned out by the rattling tracks of the bulldozer and excavator, both within thirty yards of the stand of oaks. The operator on the dozer flashed his lights and started yelling. Maureen couldn't make out what he was saying, but he continued making motions with his hands for the crew to move out of the way. When the excavator was less than twenty yards off, its massive jointed arm raised upward and the claw-like bucket shifted into digging position.

"Move out, expand the perimeter." Jeffrey was yelling and waving his arms. "If he gets any closer with that thing, he'll be able to start crushing the trees from the top down."

Maureen rushed forward, the dust from the machines and the diesel fumes filling her lungs. She was so close she could see the Sandover logo on the driver's hardhat. Jeffrey and Loriano positioned themselves near Maureen, with the others spread out in both directions, preventing the excavator from getting any closer to the trees.

"The bulldozer is going around to the other side." Maureen was already moving in that direction, with Will and Eric close behind.

They arrived with not a moment to spare, as the bulldozer's blade began its death push toward the base of the trees. Will carried a Dutch push hoe, the longest tool they had, and extended it to Maureen, who grabbed on, joining them together. When Eric ran over, he did the same, using his shovel to connect with Maureen while increasing the distance between them. Jeffrey arrived with the truck and parked alongside Eric.

The attacks by the machines continued as they repositioned themselves and approached from different angles, each time being met by a human barrier linked together by their tools and an old pickup truck. When both the bulldozer and the excavator at last backed away, Maureen thought the onslaught might be over. She could see the bulldozer operator on his cell phone, and she hoped he wasn't calling for more deadly machines to use in the attack.

With a break in the assaults, the defenders had a chance to sit in the shade and regroup for a moment. They'd been on the defensive for a couple of hours.

"I realize we're saving the trees for Mother Earth, a noble endeavor which I support, but is there something you're not telling us?" Jeffrey said.

Maureen looked around the group of people who had followed her without question into this mess. They deserved to know the reason they were putting themselves in harm's way.

"The trees are on land I think was illegally sold to Sandover."

"The guy in the black pickup truck was the same one who came to Dill's house that day." Loriano sounded disgusted. "I didn't care for the guy, and even Dill called him a vulture."

"Not much we can do if the property's been sold to them," Jeffrey said. "They have the right to do what they want with it."

"Remember the friend I told you about who was incapacitated and gave the deed for her property to a relative to hold for her?"

"Yeah, I remember."

"I told you the relative sold some of the land located next to Dill's awhile back, and Sandover was the buyer. Like Dill's land, that property is being mined for sand."

"How does your friend, the owner, feel about that?"

"I don't think she knows about the mining, only about the sale of the land."

"What does this have to do with protecting these oak trees?"

"According to Dill, the same relative sold more land to Sandover. It's the land where the trees are standing."

"In order to expand the mine, the trees have to go." Loriano patted the shoulders of Eric and Will. "Guess we're here for awhile."

"I know it's a lot to ask, because it's exhausting and could be dangerous," Maureen said. "Plus, Dill will be furious with us. The sale of his land to Sandover is contingent on the property next door being part of the expansion deal."

"All of our efforts might save the trees today. You should think about what to do for the long term." Jeffrey looked directly at Maureen. "I'd be willing to represent you if you decide to take the legal route."

"That's an offer I can't turn down." Maureen felt hopeful for the first time since the day's battle began. "What should we do?"

"I'll call an attorney friend of mine ." Jeffrey stepped away, cell phone in hand. "He'll get the online filing going for us."

When he returned to the group, the machines parked off in the distance were running again. It looked like the battle was about to reignite.

"A complaint will be filed on your behalf." Jeffrey was talking fast, watching the equipment. "In addition, there will be a petition for a permanent injunction claiming immediate and irreparable damage to the property. As a quick stop measure to protect the status quo, we're filing for a temporary restraining order to go into effect immediately."

"It sounds like you've thought of everything."

"Almost. Still a few details to iron out. For now, I'm going to the Court House to pick up the order." He ran to the truck and drove away past the rumbling machinery.

CHAPTER 33

"Okay, team. Let's show these guys what we're made of." Maureen hoped her false bravado would bolster her friends. They raised their hands in a "Go Team" cheer as the machines revved their engines.

For two hours the battle continued like a game of chess, the excavator and bulldozer maneuvering to gain ground, with the crew spreading out to block the advance. The machines were relentless, attacking repeatedly, only to stop, and then begin again.

It had been over an hour since the last offensive had ended, and now the crew waited, their nerves frazzled and their bodies exhausted. From beyond the field, a thunderous rumbling erupted, and Maureen stared in dismay at what was coming into view. The black pickup truck had returned along with an enormous grader armed with a front blade over twenty feet wide, a massive front end loader on tracks, and a Sandover dump truck, the kind with multiple rear axles.

"There's no way we can stop or even slow down all of that." Will pointed toward the approaching machines.

"We're screwed." Eric sounded defeated.

Maureen lifted her eyes to look through the crowns of the trees spreading above her. Their majestic presence was a humbling reminder of the stark difference between how nature lives versus how humans live. Nature promotes a sustainable and nurturing existence, without compromising future generations' ability to meet their needs, while humans—in their greed, self-centeredness, and thoughtlessness—did not. In that moment, Maureen was ashamed to be part of the human race.

The line of equipment was almost upon the small group of people when Maureen heard the whooping of a police siren and spotted its red and blue lights flashing. In a cloud of dust, Jeffrey drove up in the truck with a sheriff's squad car right behind him, and the two vehicles parked between the crew and the threatening machinery. Jeffrey jumped out, and Dwayne, Ronnie's deputy husband, stepped out of the squad. The drivers of the excavator and bulldozer bounded from their machines and marched toward Jeffrey and Dwayne.

"This is a temporary restraining order." Jeffrey passed the document to Dwayne, just as the Sandover pickup driver arrived. He barged past his men to where Jeffrey and Dwayne stood.

"You need to remove your equipment," Dwayne said, "and cease and desist from any action on this property for the duration of the restraining order." He held out the paper, and the pickup driver snatched it from him.

"We have every right to be here. This is the private property of Sandover Mining." The man was loud and threatening. "You should be arresting these crazy people, instead, for trespassing."

He took a step toward Jeffrey, and Dwayne intervened.

"Sir, I'm advising you to move back and get this equipment out of the area now. That way, nobody has to be arrested today."

"Our company has invested millions of dollars in this area. You will be hearing from our attorneys and the governor."

"Looking forward to it." Dwayne flashed his wide grin. "In the meantime, all of your machinery needs to be removed now."

"This is far from over." The man crumpled the restraining order Dwayne had handed him. Muttering and signaling the equipment operators, he stormed to his pickup truck and drove away.

As the machines retreated, Maureen and the crew cheered, and then applauded Jeffrey and Dwayne.

"Dwayne, we can't thank you enough."

"Shucks, Ma'am, I was just doing my job. Besides, I'm a sucker for the underdog." Dwayne winked at Maureen as he got into his squad. "Ronnie will be calling you real soon to invite you to the house for dinner."

"That sounds wonderful. Give her a hug for me," Maureen called after him as Dwayne drove away, arm extended out the window in a farewell wave.

"Jeffrey, thank you." Maureen couldn't help herself. She threw her arms around his shoulders and gave him a hug.

"No thanks necessary. My buddy did most of the work." Jeffrey pulled away and headed toward the truck as he waved the others to follow. "Come on everyone. Let's get outta here. Pardon the pun, but we're not out of the woods yet."

On their drive back to the farm, Jeffrey told Maureen about his trip to the Court House.

"I was racing into the building and nearly ran over Dwayne. When I told him about the mining construction out at the farm, he blew up. He's not a fan of Sandover. Thinks they strong-arm folks into selling."

"Dwayne said he and a couple other deputies frequent a local bar called Toni's Tap. Seems the bar's owner, named Toni Radzinski, was bragging about making lots of money by selling land she owns next to Dillon's to Sandover. "

"That's no surprise Sandover is buying up farmland," Maureen said.

"No, but it prompted me to head first into the Register of Deeds Office where I checked for the Real Estate Transfer Return or RETR. Toni had filed the forms, all right, but both times she signed the documents using the name Peggy Whitcomb. I'm guessing that's the name of your incapacitated friend."

"Yes, that's my friend's name."

"The signed RETR is proof there was fraud used in the sale of the land. That illegal sale was about to cause additional damage by the adverse party, Sandover. This supported our petition for a temporary restraining order. Better yet, I amended our initial complaint to hold Toni and Sandover responsible for committing fraud. Toni misrepresented herself as the owner and Sandover was complicit in the cover-up of the facts."

"So you bought us some time."

"Fourteen days. After that, if we are awarded the injunction, it will give us another six months before our case goes to court."

"I cannot believe how much you accomplished in so little time."

"Filing online speeds up the process. It also helped when the criminal bragged about their crime." Jeffrey grinned. "I forgot to tell you. When I was amending our complaint, I also asked for a return of the deed as part of the injunction, which, if granted, could get it from Toni within weeks."

"That is good news. You are a genius!"

"I wouldn't go that far. Brilliant, maybe."

"Bringing along a deputy was also helpful and reassuring."

"Wish I could take credit for Dwayne being here, but he knew you were involved and insisted on helping out."

"What's next?"

"Some legal hoops left to jump through. For now, you can relax."

They were back at the farmhouse, and Maureen thanked her co-workers again for their help. When everyone left for home, Maureen and Jeffrey went inside where there was no trace of Dill and Summer. Maureen figured Dill had every right to be upset because of her interference, but she hoped Sandover wouldn't back out of the deal since the new property Dill sold was already under construction. That way Dill and Summer would be able to keep the money the company paid them.

Maureen took Road Dog for his evening outing into the backyard where pieces of the demolished swing set were laid out. Away from the house, Dill was bent over two of the metal parts, welding them together. He wore safety glasses and a welding helmet, and his hands and arms were encased in heavy gloves. A thick apron covered his torso. Nearby, a welding machine chugged as a shower of fiery drops rained down around him. Like spattering bacon frying in a pan, sparks along a seam sizzled and formed an arc from the metal rod he was using to lay a weld joining the broken pieces of the frame together again. Dill stopped when he noticed Maureen watching him.

"I heard what happened today, and I've got nothing to say to you."

"Dill, I had to stop them."

"What are you, some kind of tree hugging environmentalist? Why do you care so much?"

"Because Toni is a liar. The farm isn't hers."

"I've known Toni for awhile. She's always owned it."

"Toni's always claimed she owned it, and it's always been a lie."

"That's impossible. Sandover Mining would never buy from someone if it wasn't legal."

"They would if Toni impersonated the owner and forged their signature."

"Where are you getting this information, and what does this have to do with you?"

"Let's just say I know the owner, and they would never allow their land to be devastated by a mining company."

"It's a little late for climbing on that high horse. The paperwork is signed."

"Doesn't matter. I have a temporary restraining order to stop Sandover from proceeding."

"A temporary restraining order is just that, temporary."

"Jeffrey thinks he can obtain an injunction to stop the construction indefinitely."

"Oh, Jeffrey thinks he can do that. Good for Jeffrey. You realize if Sandover can't purchase Toni's land, they don't want ours, either. There are plenty of area farmers anxious to sell their land."

"But they've already begun work on the property you sold them."

"Doesn't matter. It's in the contract we signed. Both tracts of land had to be included in the sale, or there is no sale."

"I don't know what to tell you, Dill."

"Let me tell you something. Without the money from the most recent sale of our land, we will lose Crooked Creek Farm. The bills for doctors, hospitals, drugs, treatments, and everything else have a financial stranglehold on us. If we lose the farm, everyone working here will lose their job, not to mention Summer, Samuel, and I will be out on the street."

"I can't undo what I've set in motion."

"We took you in, gave you a job, helped you get back on your feet, and this is how you repay us?"

"I'm more grateful than you can know."

"Those are empty words, considering your actions."

"I'll leave if you want me to."

"And make me short-handed during the busiest part of the year's production?"

"If it's what you want, I'll stay and finish the season."

"It's not what I want, but it's what we need right now for the sake of the farm and our crew. You can stay, but keep out of my way."

CHAPTER 34

U pstairs in their room, Road Dog dropped down near the open window and laid spread eagle for maximum contact with the floor, her mouth dripping with spit strings as she panted. Maureen pushed the sash upward as far as it would go and pulled the curtains aside to allow the air to flow in unobstructed. She sat on the floor next to Road Dog and stroked the animal's silky, cockeyed ears.

"One thing about you, my friend. No matter how I screw up or what damage I leave in my wake, you're always here. No one's ever been as loyal to me as you are."

Especially her disloyal, deceitful sister, Jasmine. A startling thought crossed Maureen's mind. What if Jasmine and Toni were in this together, dismantling the farm piece by piece until it was gone? After all, it was Jasmine who mentioned contacting Toni, and when Jazz visited their mother earlier in the summer, maybe she also paid a visit to Toni. Maureen could picture her younger sister being manipulated by Toni into having their mother sign the quitclaim, naming Jasmine as the owner. Toni would have offered Jasmine money from the sale of the land in exchange for an agreement that no charges would be made against her for the forgery. The two would share in future profits resulting from the sale of any additional property. Toni's fraud would be forgotten, and by collaborating with Jasmine, they would both make a substantial amount of money.

Maureen wondered if she was being paranoid. It didn't seem likely forgery and fraud could simply be forgotten. Perhaps the conspiracy theory she pieced together was another indication she was mentally unstable. She was going to call Jasmine anyway about the most recent developments with the farm property. If Maureen asked the right questions in a subtle manner, the discussion could eliminate or confirm the fears she had about Toni and Jasmine scheming together.

The thought of calling her sister was distressing, and it reminded Maureen, once again, how David betrayed her. She slouched against the bed and looked down at her faded shirt and dirt-caked jeans. Was it any wonder David chose young, beautiful, stylish Jazz over her?

Road Dog dropped her slobbery chin on Maureen's knee and gazed up at her with droopy dog eyes radiating unconditional love.

"You know what, Road Dog? You are the best friend I've ever had, and you're an excellent judge of character. If you think I'm deserving of loyalty and love, maybe I am. David doesn't know anything, and, as far as I can tell, he and Jazz were made for each other."

Maureen tapped in Jasmine's cell number, but the call went to voicemail. She hung up, but before she could set the phone down, it rang. The call wasn't from Jazz, but Andrea.

"Maureen, it's so good to talk to you."

"Hi, Andrea. How's everything?"

"If you're referring to my personal life, it's on a downward spiral."

"Welcome to my world. Want to share?"

"Turns out Tyler, the cute guy from auditing, is gay. I knew he was too good to be true. You know—smart, cultured, honest, well-spoken, awesome body, great dresser."

"I'm so sorry. I know you really liked him."

"I did. Dang, he was handsome, and he spoke Italian."

"Isn't that how it always goes? What's happening at work?"

"Ugh! Working for Don is like working in purgatory. He lies, cheats, and schemes, then manipulates and retaliates. The one thing he never does is work. I am the Midwest Regional Manager in every way except for the title and the salary. I also don't have the big office or any of the perks that go with the position."

"I wish I could be there to help you in some way."

"It's good you're not here. All hell is breaking loose."

"What's happening?"

"Things have escalated into a full-blown police investigation!"

"Are they coming to arrest me?"

"Not that I've heard. I do know there was a search warrant issued for your house."

"That can't be good, especially when they, and I mean, Don, was blaming me from the very beginning."

"I get the sense someone is on their radar."

"I feel like I should say 'Don,' but that is too obvious."

"I hope you're right. I want Don to get everything he deserves, and I don't mean in a good way."

"Me, too. Thanks for keeping me in the loop."

"Maureen, one more thing. I have to ask again. Did you stash anything at your home regarding the Wexler account the authorities could find when they execute their search warrant, something that could cast more suspicion on you?"

"I don't blame you for asking, and the answer is no. There wasn't anything related to the Wexler deal left in my house the day I drove to Wisconsin."

It wasn't a lie. She had taken the files and flash drives with her when she drove to Wisconsin. If David devised a scheme to use the Wexler information to perpetrate something illegal, that was his problem.

Although she was exhausted, after talking to Andrea Maureen was too wired to sleep, so she tiptoed downstairs for a beer or something stronger. She was surprised to find Jeffrey typing on his laptop in the kitchen. There were neat stacks of papers lined up in front of him, and several law books marked with colored paper tabs were pushed aside.

"Thought I'd work on your case." Jeffrey's blond hair curled around the pencil he had stuck behind one ear.

"You look very organized and professional." Maureen was pouring herself a glass of wine. "You want one?"

"Maybe later." Jeffrey stopped typing. "I still believe a civil case is our best bet considering what's happened. However, if you think this Toni person and Sandover should be prosecuted, we'll have to talk to the District Attorney to find out if there is a parallel criminal proceeding he can connect to the civil matter."

Maureen didn't think she wanted anyone criminally prosecuted. "Let's keep it simple and have the property returned to the rightful owner as quickly as possible."

She swallowed the last of her wine and was refilling her glass when her phone rang. It was Jasmine, and Maureen stepped out of the kitchen to take the call.

"Geez, Maureen. When you call, why can't you at least leave a message?"

"That's for me to know and you to find out." Maureen giggled and sipped her wine.

"Why did you call?"

"Do you know what I did today?" Maureen paused for dramatic effect. "I saved a tree, well, a bunch of trees."

"Why are you telling me this?"

"Have you ever done anything simply because it was the right thing to do?"

"Like what?"

"Like anything that didn't benefit you in any way."

"I'm sure I have. It's hard to remember."

"This kind of thing you would never forget, because it is one of the most amazing experiences of your life."

There was a long pause.

"Maureen, are you back at the mental health facility? Is that where the trees are that you saved?"

A loud and crazy-sounding laugh escaped from Maureen. Perhaps she should be at some facility.

"Never mind the trees. Were you being honest when you said you would share the farm with me?"

"Yes. I am not one to lie."

"We'll save that debate for another time." Maureen chugged the last of her wine.

"Why did you call me, Maureen?"

"I told you Toni sold some of Momma's land awhile ago. She's trying to do it again. You don't know anything about that, do you?" So much for asking the right questions in a subtle manner.

"How would I know what Toni is doing?"

"When you filed the quitclaim you became the farm's owner. Let's say Toni sold some more of the property. In order to complete her sale, Toni would have had to forge your name or impersonate you, just like she did to Momma. Or maybe you knew what Toni was going to do, and you authorized the sale."

"I didn't authorize anything."

"Then, if Toni made the land deal, she committed fraud, this time against you."

"No, I don't think so."

"What do you mean?"

"I forgot to file the quitclaim at the Court House."

"You forgot?"

"I've been busy. Besides, I still have Momma's signature naming me as the owner. Filing didn't seem very important."

"Momma technically still owns the farm." Maureen almost laughed out loud. "Even though it was stupid and irresponsible, your forgetfulness has solved my immediate problem."

"Why is that?"

"It simplifies things if Momma is the owner. Whatever you do, for now, don't file that paperwork."

"So, I did a good thing, the right thing, by not filing the quitclaim, and it didn't benefit me in any way. What an amazing feeling. I totally get it!"

Maureen had to hang up. Jasmine left her speechless.

She swallowed the last of her wine and went into the kitchen to refill her glass. Jeffrey looked up from his paperwork.

"Everything all right?"

"It is, at least for the time being."

"That's good." He shuffled some papers and paused. "To be clear, the property is owned by the same person, your incapacitated friend. Would you be willing to share any information about this person?"

"The owner is a relative of mine who is in prison." Hearing the words out loud made Maureen want to bolt from the room, before Jeffrey asked for more information.

"What about Toni?"

"Another relative." Tipping her glass, Maureen guzzled the wine.

"Care to elaborate?"

"No."

"There will be a hearing scheduled where Toni and Sandover can contest the TRO. That should result in a Preliminary Injunction."

"Thank you for doing this. I'm not sure when I'll be able to pay you for your services, but you will be paid."

"Let's call this one a pro bono case. It'll look good on my resume, and it fills up the suspicious gap left by my detour away from the law to spend the season working as a field hand."

"You're a good man, Jeffrey Bennett."

"Keep it to yourself. Wouldn't want to ruin my reputation."

CHAPTER 35

M aureen laid down on her bed and willed the room to stop spinning. Talking to her sister renewed her belief in Jasmine's inability to follow through on anything. Maureen wondered if David realized yet that he would have to be the grown-up in his relationship with Jazz, a role he always delegated to Maureen when they were married. If she didn't loathe them so much, Maureen might have felt sorry for them.

Because of Jasmine's irresponsibility, the farm still technically belonged to their mother. Maureen was desperate to get the deed out of Toni's hands, and she hoped the injunction Jeffrey filed would accomplish that. On the other hand, Maureen hated to think of how her mother would react when Toni was legally forced to give it up. Perhaps if Maureen told her mother in person what was going to happen, she could gloss it over and minimize any damage to her mother's health. Using that as her rationale, the next morning Maureen called Tayheedah and scheduled a visitation for the following Saturday. She tried to ignore the possibility she might actually want to see her mother again.

"Sounds like you're going visiting again," Jeffrey said.

"I want my relative to know about the legal steps I'm taking. I hope I can persuade her to be okay with everything." Whether her mother would understand, Maureen had no idea.

Work days were long, halted only by the setting of the sun. The summer crops, now finished, required clearing and composting, and the harvesting of the fall root crops along with an abundance of winter squash was in full swing. Brilliant shades of orange painted a sea of pumpkins in the vine-covered patch, signaling October was fast approaching. The CSA customers' baskets were full to overflowing, the farmers' markets' sales were steady, and the local grocery stores and restaurants couldn't get enough of the farm's fall produce.

Besides laboring from dawn to dusk every weekday, Dill and Jeffrey had been working weekends to screen in the side porch where Summer loved to read and draw. The fall weather had been warmer than usual, and the insects were relentless, so Summer, Dill, and Samuel often slept on the newly screened-in porch, enjoying the cooler evening air. Some nights, Road Dog abandoned Maureen and slept on the porch, too.

When Maureen came downstairs on Saturday morning, Jeffrey was assembling cooler packs in a plastic tub. On the table were six bottles of water, a bag of granola bars, and six peanut butter sandwiches. Road Dog was seated near the sandwiches.

"I have a big weekend planned for Road Dog," Jeffrey said.

Maureen had initially planned to ask Summer and Dill to take the dog so she could visit her mother, but they were spending time with relatives in Madison. When Jeffrey said he'd take Road Dog, it saved Maureen from having to lie to anyone else about where she was going.

"What's the plan?"

"We're going hiking with Eric and Will on trails in the Chippewa Valley. They're awesome this time of year."

"Are you sure Road Dog can make it on an actual hike?"

"She's stronger and more fit than you think. Plus, we'll take breaks and drink lots of water."

"Still not sure it's a good idea."

"See this backpack? It can hold tons of essentials, but I'll have it empty except for some food and water and a soft pillow at the bottom. If Road Dog gets tired, she'll go in the backpack, sitting on the pillow support, and the guys will carry everything else."

"Wait. You're going to carry Road Dog on your back?"

"I backpacked all over Europe carrying more weight than this pudgy girl." He gave the dog a kiss on the head between her lopsided ears.

"You think you're going to be able to place her, without a fight, into the backpack?"

"Watch and learn."

Jeffrey did some unzipping and laid the pack flat, with the main compartment pulled all the way open. He snuggled Road Dog for a little, placed one arm around her belly and the other underneath her backend. In one slick movement, he hoisted the dog up and slid her into the open pocket until she rested on the pillow with her front legs fitted through openings as she faced forward. Jeffrey zipped up the sides to keep her secure, lifted the pack holding Road Dog, and flung it onto his back. He snapped the chest strap and hip belt. Road Dog's paws rested on Jeffrey's shoulders as she peeked around his head to gaze at an astonished Maureen.

"It's a natural seated position for her body, so don't worry about Road Dog being uncomfortable. Plus, she can scope out everything from up above her usual vantage point." Jeffrey grinned and turned in a circle to demonstrate Road Dog's panoramic view.

"I guess it will be all right. You'll stop and bring her back if she gets too tired or doesn't want to be carried?"

"Absolutely."

"I know you will. I think I'm projecting my nervousness because of my trip today."

"Remember, you are doing everything for the right reasons."

"I hope I can convince my relative of that."

The trip to Taycheedah was uneventful, and on the long drive, Maureen's mind wandered to the dusty newspapers stacked in the attic behind her closet. When she first found those issues reporting on her mother's trial, she skimmed them, but lacked the courage to read the specifics of what happened. The headlines were enough to make her disgusted. As time passed, however, Maureen's need to know the truth began to surpass her fear and dread of what she would learn if she delved deeper into the details.

The prison was as ominous and imposing as Maureen remembered. Once she passed the security checks, she sat in the visitors' area, watching the others waiting there, some serious and others animated and laughing. At last she and another woman were lead down the same grey hallway to the medical unit, but the nurse walked beyond Ward B and opened the door labeled Ward C. Inside there were two partitions, providing privacy for each of the three beds located there. The nurse directed the other visitor to the first bed.

"Your mother is here in the third bed," the nurse said to Maureen as she pulled the curtain aside.

There were fewer machines than in Ward B, and soft music drifted through the room. In the bed, her mother was curled into a fetal position, like a cat tucking itself inward for protection from the world. Her head was wrapped in a scarf of blues and greens, and her yellowish skin was translucent and lined with tiny wrinkles as it hung onto her skeleton.

"Momma, it's me, Darla."

When she didn't respond, Maureen moved a chair to the side of the bed and sat down, leaning in close, to be sure her voice could be heard.

"Hello, Momma."

Her mother's eyes blinked open, those same eyes from long ago, and she turned her head to look into Maureen's face.

"Darla, my pretty little girl."

"I think you're remembering Jasmine."

"You are the image of your daddy, with his curly, dark hair and dark eyes."

"That part you have right."

"Nathaniel loved you so much."

"You loved him, didn't you Momma?"

"He was the love of my life."

"You loved the farm and the land he and his family entrusted to you?"

"It was all I had left of him, except for you."

Her mother's eyes closed. There was only the sound of the music and the steady rhythm of the patients' monitors. When her mother opened her eyes, Maureen continued.

"Toni had to sell some of the land. It must have been painful for you."

"There were bills to pay."

"She did have a choice when she used most of the money to buy a bar."

"She isn't a farmer."

"You knew about the bar?"

"She told me after it was done. There was no undoing it."

Maureen thought about her mother, locked in prison, with everything in her life under someone else's control. What a helpless, abandoned feeling that must have been for her. Now Maureen was doing the same thing to her mother by trying to control what happened to her farm.

"I don't want to upset you, Momma, but I need to tell you in person what I'm doing." Maureen paused. "We have petitioned in court to stop the expansion of the sand mining on the property Toni illegally sold. She needs to give back the deed and stop pretending she's the owner."

"Why don't you let Toni have what she wants?"

"Because it doesn't belong to her. It belongs to you."

"You mean it belongs to Jasmine."

Their mother might have been dying, but mentally, she was very much alive. She knew exactly what she was doing when she signed the farm over to Jasmine and only Jasmine, leaving Maureen out in the cold. Nothing had changed.

"It will belong to Jasmine when she files the quitclaim deed. Until that happens, you're still the owner."

"Then, let Toni have it all."

"You realize the land is being ruined."

"I know it is."

"You say that like it doesn't matter."

"Right now, other things matter more."

"What things?"

"It's complicated. Life will go easier for everyone if Toni gets her way."

"She's selling off the land, piece by piece. Soon, there will be nothing left."

"It's the right thing to do, Darla."

"That's what I told Toni, that she should do the right thing. She said, coming from me, the comment about doing the right thing was laughable. What did she mean?"

"Maybe she thought you want the farm for yourself."

"Would me having the farm be wrong?"

"Of course not. Your dad would have wanted nothing more."

"Why did you sign it over to Jasmine?"

"Because she was here and she asked me to. I had no idea you were ever coming to see me. I wanted the farm to stay in our family."

"If you didn't care what Toni was doing, why did you sign the quitclaim? Why didn't you keep it in your name, so you could let Toni get away with doing whatever she wanted?"

"Jasmine is my family. Yours, too."

"But she's not a Whitcomb. Someone else is her father."

"Yes." Her mother swallowed hard. "Stanley was Jasmine's father."

Stanley. The man in the backyard, holding a birthday present out to the little girl and pressing his long finger to his lips. "Give me a kiss, right here, to show how much you love me."

A shiver rippled through Maureen. The memory was too disturbing, and she could tell by her mother's expression how much pain even speaking his name caused her.

"I'm sorry, Momma. I guess I had forgotten his connection to us, other than, well, you know."

"I know more than anyone. Stan was the worst thing that ever happened to me, to us."

"Why did you put up with him if he was so terrible?"

Instead of answering, her mother coughed a dry, raspy sound that rattled deep in her boney chest. Maureen took the water cup from the bedside table, tucking its straw between her mother's dry, withered lips.

"Take a sip, Momma."

"I can't."

The nurse in charge of the ward appeared with a large cup filled with water and a package of sticks each topped with a small, square sponge. She dipped one into the cup and pressed it against Peggy's lips and onto her dry tongue.

"Swallowing has become difficult for her. The sponges allow the water to trickle down her throat and keep her mouth moist. She can't have too much, though, or she will choke."

Assuming their conversation was over, Maureen rose to leave, when her mother's eyes opened again.

"I'm all right. Stay a little longer."

"I'm sorry I brought Stanley into our conversation."

"We're going to have to talk about what happened."

"I don't think I want to."

"Come again, and maybe I'll be a little stronger."

Considering how her mother had deteriorated since Maureen's last visit, the woman's improvement didn't seem likely, but Maureen would visit again if it gave her a reason to hang on.

"If you promise to get stronger, I will come to see you again."

"That's a deal. Now you promise me something."

"What is it?"

"Stop what you're doing in court. Let Toni sell the land and keep the money."

"It's not the right thing to do, Momma."

"Maybe it is."

CHAPTER 36

On the road headed for home, Maureen contemplated what her next move would be. She promised her mother another visit, and she'd have to plan a time for that. Then there was her mother's request for a commitment from Maureen to allow the land to be sold and the money to be given to Toni. Although Maureen had not agreed to do it, the look on her mother's face signaled she believed the promise would be honored. Maureen wished she had stayed home.

As she approached the farm, light streamed from the porch light into the darkness. It felt lonely coming home to an empty house. Summer and Dill weren't due back until noon tomorrow. On the kitchen table was a note from Jeffrey.

"Hope all went well. We'll talk tomorrow." Maureen wondered if Road Dog was having fun hiking with Jeffrey and the guys.

Although she had not eaten anything all day, Maureen decided a tall glass of wine was what she needed. There was an open bottle of chardonnay, so Maureen helped herself to the bottle and a container of kale chips Summer had baked. She plodded upstairs where the cool evening breeze drifted in through an open window.

Maureen parked herself on the bedroom floor, a habit she had acquired from Road Dog, who liked resting on the cool floor, especially with a breeze blowing in. Tipping the wine bottle, she poured a generous amount, allowing herself to relax for the first time all day.

At the prison, after Maureen made the mistake of opening up the topic of Stanley, her mother said they needed to talk about what happened. Perhaps Maureen wouldn't feel so blindsided when discussing the shooting with her mother if she had more facts.

She glanced at the closet and swallowed the remainder of wine in her glass. Grabbing her cell phone, she tapped the flashlight feature on. When she pushed open the closet door, it moved without a sound, thanks to the WD-40 she had found in the barn. She shoved aside the clothes hanging on the rod and was relieved the girl's pink dress hadn't reappeared. Unlatching the attic door, Maureen took a deep breath, gathered her courage, and stepped into the dark, low-slung room.

After pulling the string for the overhead light, Maureen walked ahead into the stagnant attic, ducking her head and allowing her eyes to adjust to the dimness surrounding her. She directed her flashlight on the floor, where the newspapers were still scattered. From the stack, Maureen located the issues she wanted from May and June, 1997, and she sat down with them on the dusty floor.

Reading the articles about the trial, Maureen learned her mother pleaded "Not Guilty" to the charge of first degree murder after officers obtained a confession without informing her of her rights and without any legal representation. The defense portrayed Peggy as a hard-working widow and a loving, devoted parent. She was a lifetime member of her church who had the respect of her community. Peggy's defense team described Stanley Nowak as a violent, unpredictable drunk who preyed on lonely, defenseless women.

On the day of the shooting, witnesses testified Nowak was drinking in a local tavern, but there was conflicting testimony concerning the length of time he spent in the bar and also about the amount of alcohol he consumed. The District Attorney stated the victim was a respected member of the farming community and a long-time County Farm Board member. Nowak had one son from his first marriage and a daughter from his relationship with the defendant. The two were not married and did not live together, but shared custody of their daughter.

According to her mother's testimony, on the day of the shooting, there was a family gathering at the Whitcomb home. When Stan arrived late in the afternoon, he was belligerent and combative, upsetting the children present. Peggy asked Stan to step outside where the two could talk in private, and before she joined him, she placed the revolver in her pocket. There was no intent to use the weapon, according to Maureen's mother, but when Stan slapped her face, punched the side of her head with his fist, and shoved her down the porch steps, she feared for her safety and that of the children. As he walked away from her, Peggy pulled out the gun and fired what she thought was a warning shot into the air towards the back of the yard. From her position on the ground, the trajectory of the bullet was low enough to strike Stanley in the back of the head. Her attorney claimed the wording of Peggy's testimony was: "When he turned his back, I shot at him," but the prosecution called for the court reporter to read back Peggy's statement, revealing the word "at" was not there. Ending her testimony, Peggy said: "I only wanted to scare him." It made perfect sense to Maureen.

There were no witnesses to refute or corroborate her mother's account of what happened, but Toni was there inside the house. Also there were Toni's four children, Peggy and Stan's young daughter, plus Stan's son and Peggy's daughter from previous marriages. If there were no witnesses, Maureen wondered why her memory placed other people in the yard on that day.

Toni stated the children were inside playing games when Stan barged into the house. When questioned whether Stan had been drinking, Toni replied, "Stanley was always drinking." She stated Peggy had grown afraid of Stanley and didn't want him near her children. Asked if she had witnessed Stanley physically harming Peggy or the children, Toni said she had not. The prosecution asked her if she had seen evidence of physical injuries inflicted on Peggy by Stanley, and Toni said no. She did say, however, that Peggy frequently had bruises and sometimes other injuries but they were attributed to farm duties.

Intriguing to Maureen was the article entitled: "Shooter: I Would Do It Again." The proceedings were nearing their end, and Maureen's mother had been on the stand for most of the morning. From what Maureen could discern, the prosecution had come to believe Peggy had not committed premeditated murder, but rather acted impulsively with an intent and understanding of her actions, thus committing second-degree murder. The defense, however, maintained the shooting was an accident which was plausible, until under cross examination, Peggy was questioned as to her remorse for what happened. Without hesitation, she said, "I would do it again." Although her defense lawyer vehemently attempted to diffuse the statement, the words caused irreparable damage. Peggy was found guilty of second-degree murder.

Maureen tried to picture the woman her mother was before the shooting changed everything. They had been close, the two of them left behind to survive without her dad and grandparents. A memory flooded Maureen's mind as she pictured her mother in the car, beginning to back away as Maureen waved good-bye, her eyes teary. She had the sensation of a strong hand pressing on her shoulder.

"I have to go to work, and you have school. We'll be together at suppertime." Her mother's voice was gentle, and those same eyes were looking deep into Maureen's. "You be a good girl for Stanley. He'll help you get on the bus, and he'll meet you when the day is over."

Maureen must have been little, probably five years old. Now, she remembered Stan being there in the morning and late in the day. She remembered her mother saying Stanley helped with the chores and made sure they wouldn't lose daddy's farm, so Maureen had to be nice to him.

After that recollection Maureen decided she needed another glass of wine, or perhaps many glasses of wine. She piled the newspapers and stood up to leave the attic. The next thing she knew, she was lying face down on the dusty, soiled mattress, the faded fabric rough against her skin, its odor overwhelming her senses. Reaching a hand to her head, she discovered a lump was forming. She must have bumped herself on the low ceiling beam when she stood.

Maureen rubbed the tender spot on her head as she was bombarded with pictures from her childhood, like single pages in a flipbook whose static images become animated with the flip of a finger. In slow motion, Maureen saw herself walking out of school and getting into Stan's truck for the drive to his house. Once inside, they walked upstairs. The steps were wooden and groaned as they climbed together, his rough, leathery hand grasping hers, and his whiskery face smiling. There was a lock on the door.

"Stop!" Maureen screamed. She bolted from the attic and locked the door behind her. Using her fists, she pounded the door until her rage was exhausted.

CHAPTER 37

With her wine bottle and glass in hand, Maureen walked downstairs and out the door to the screened porch. She craved the cool evening air, hoping it would cleanse the troubling images she had pictured. As Maureen sipped her wine, she forced herself to fit the pieces together into a story that made sense.

When Stanley came into their lives, Maureen must have been three or four years old. If her memories were accurate, at age five she was left with Stanley before and after school while her mother went to work. Jasmine was born when Maureen was ten years old. On the day of the shooting, Maureen and Jasmine had been in the house and their mother didn't want Stanley near them. Whatever happened that day was more than Peggy wanting Stanley to stay away from her and her kids. What if it had something to do with Maureen's own memory of going back to Stanley's house after school?

The headlights of a vehicle bounced up the driveway and flashed across the porch where Maureen was sitting. Road Dog and Will jumped out of the Jeep. Jeffrey followed hauling a cooler and backpack he pulled from the rear of the vehicle. Eric limped along behind him.

"I thought you guys were camping out tonight?" Maureen hugged Road Dog and held her close, scratching her ears.

"Eric slipped and twisted his ankle. We've been at Urgent Care for the last three hours."

"Yeah, sorry guys." Eric sounded embarrassed and sat down, propping up his injured ankle and foot encased in a soft, black boot.

"No worries. We had a great time up until you slipped like a girl and twisted your delicate ankle." Will slugged Eric's shoulder, and the two laughed.

"The hiking was fantastic, and Road Dog loved it," Jeffrey said as they finished unloading.

"Except for some of the trails where the sand mines were so close you could hardly hear yourself think." Will was dragging coolers back to the house.

"Plus, there were trails that had been diverted to accommodate the mines, which was a pain." Jeffrey carried the last of their gear inside, and Maureen and Road Dog followed.

"Ravines and cliffs I remember from past hikes are now a flat wasteland," Eric said. "It doesn't take long for people to screw up things."

Before long, the three guys, Maureen, and Road Dog were sitting around the fire pit, drinking beer and roasting marshmallows and hot dogs, all left over from the camping trip. The distraction was welcomed by Maureen as she began to relax, grateful for the company and for Road Dog's return. They were laughing about Eric's rendition of how he managed to slip on what the other guys perceived as "absolutely nothing" when Maureen's cell phone rang. It was Andrea. Maureen excused herself and stepped away from the fire.

"Maureen, hi! I have some good news and some bad news."

"I could use some good news."

"The search warrant was executed and guess what?"

"Oh, I don't know. Let's try: They found nothing."

"Almost. They found nothing that implicates you."

"I feel like I should say "Yay!" but I don't think I have enough information."

"Remember how I told you Don and David both belong to the same health club?"

"Birds of a feather, right?"

"Absolutely. Seems they got pretty tight."

"In the context of this conversation, what does that mean?"

"During the search of your house, the police found files and flash drives with Wexler data, hidden in your ex-husband's desk, along with all kinds of notes with charts, graphs, and projections drawn up by him. They suspect Don, David's new buddy and, apparently, his partner in crime, gave David the information he needed."

"So Don provided the Wexler stuff. What, exactly, did David do with it?"

"The authorities are maintaining David used what Don provided him to hack into Wexler's servers where he obtained additional confidential information."

"I know firsthand David is skilled at hacking into things."

"A person close to the investigation said David and Don timed the leaking of the insider information David hacked, so the two could buy and sell the company's stock to their advantage."

Maureen suspected when David stole the funds from her 401K, he had no plan for what he was going to do with the money. It was an act of pure spite, because the money was Maureen's, and because he knew how to take it. She pictured the smug look on David's face when he realized that money was what he needed to bankroll the Wexler stock scheme. Other than borrowing against the house, Maureen's money was the only other way David could have put his hands on so much cash.

"How is Robert taking all of this?"

"Mr. Chambers distanced himself from Don weeks ago, when it appeared the stock manipulations were an inside job. The Board fired Don."

"You realize none of this would have happened if they named me Midwest Regional Manager way back when."

"I know. Don managed to fool all the good ole boys."

"What happens now?"

"Not sure how it will all play out, but I wanted you to know what's been going on."

"Thank you." Maureen hated to ask, but had to know. "What's the bad news?"

"I heard when David was confronted, he implicated you."

"How does that even make sense?"

"He's saying the insider information he used came from you, not Don."

"But I'm not there, haven't been for months."

"I know. Don's hands are all over this, so try not to worry. I'll contact you if you need to update your passport."

"Okay, that's not funny."

"I'm sure it will all straighten itself out, and the bad guys will get what they deserve."

"Right, because that always happens."

Maureen hung up, not knowing whether to feel relieved or worried. Without question, she was heartbroken all over again. The fact that David would steal money from her was one thing, but then he used information he knew came from her workplace along with the stolen funds to commit a crime more serious than Maureen could ever have anticipated. Worst of all, he laid the blame on her. She wondered whether the David she married was a genuine person or a part David was playing to manipulate her and get what he wanted. It was true her salary was three or four times David's. There were the years when he took sabbaticals to finish his PhD when he earned nothing. Even the two textbooks he authored failed to produce the money and notoriety he envisioned. Whatever they did, like taking a vacation or buying a house, David's opinions and wishes always were the priority. What a sucker she was.

"Everything all right?" Jeffrey was dousing the flames in the fire pit and gathering empty beer bottles. The other guys had gone home.

"Nope, but no way to make it better."

"I forgot to tell you, the hearing to see if Toni and Sandover are going to contest the TRO is scheduled for tomorrow."

"Good. We need this case to move along."

"Right. The sooner we get into court, the sooner we can protect your relative's property."

"Here's the thing. The owner asked me to allow Toni to sell the land. Whatever money the land sales generate, it is supposed to be Toni's."

"What? Why would she change her mind?"

"I'm not sure, but I'm doing some digging. Something's not adding up."

"Do you want me to forget the whole thing?"

"Not yet. Keep going as we planned. Selling the land to be devastated by mining is not right, no matter how much money it makes."

Upstairs in the bedroom, when Maureen's phone rang again, she considered not answering. It was Jasmine calling.

"Jazz, what's up?" Maureen thought she knew what was coming and said a silent thank you to Andrea.

"What's up is you set us up." Jasmine sounded close to hysteria.

"I can't help you if you don't calm down."

"You planted things in the box with the pictures, knowing David would find them."

"What things are you talking about?" Maureen worked to keep her voice steady.

"You know exactly what things I'm talking about."

"What is going on, Jazz? Tell me, step by step."

"Step one, you stole records from work. Step two, you stashed them in the box you asked us to send. Step three, David found the records and kept them. Now he's been arrested."

"Look, I didn't take any files or records when I left Anson-Chambers, and, if I did, why would I put them in a box of old pictures?"

"Because you wanted David to find them and keep them, so he would get into trouble."

"That makes no sense at all. Did you actually see him remove the Wexler items from the box?"

"No, but . . ."

"You know how David lies, Jazz."

"He doesn't lie to me."

"If I wanted David to find something, why would I put it in a place where he would never look?" Maureen hoped to plant a seed of doubt in her sister's mind. "For arguments' sake, let's say I placed files in the box. Even if David did look in such an obscure place and find the files in there, removing them wouldn't get him into trouble, would it?"

"No, I guess not."

"Did he tell you what he did with the information that he found?"

"Not in so many words."

"Allow me to put it into words for you. First, David stole money from my retirement savings. Next, David used Anson-Chambers' company files he acquired somehow to hack into Wexler's mainframe and steal confidential information. At that point, David, along with Don, another employee from Anson-Chambers, who, most likely, did supply the files to David, used the stolen information and my money to run an illegal stock market scheme. In the end, David and Don were arrested."

"He didn't tell me any of those things, except for the arrested part."

"Lies of omission, Jazz, are still lies. David doesn't want you to know what crimes he's committed."

"I don't believe any of it." Jasmine's words couldn't hide the doubt in her voice.

"Believe, don't believe. It makes no difference to me. Don't get me mixed up in David's mess because it's not my problem. It's yours."

Maureen pressed the End Call button. David had taken the bait, and the outcome far exceeded any of Maureen's expectations. She should be ecstatic, but, instead, she didn't feel elated, heck, she didn't even feel good, about how things turned out. Despite his betrayal, deep down, Maureen was sorry for David, not sorry enough to do anything about it, but sorry all the same.

CHAPTER 38

Early Monday morning, Maureen and Road Dog were sharing scrambled eggs and toast at the kitchen island, when Dill and Samuel arrived home. Dill's pale, exhausted face, hunched shoulders, and shuffling steps were the picture of defeat.

"What's happened?" Maureen dropped her toast. Samuel caught it and swallowed it in one gulp.

"Summer wasn't able to come home. She's still at University Hospital in Madison."

"I don't understand. I thought you were visiting relatives."

"She didn't want anyone to know she needed to be in the hospital again."

"What are they doing to help her? Will she receive more chemo? It worked before."

"It didn't work, at least the last rounds didn't. Earlier this summer she made the decision to stop the chemotherapy so her final days would be a little easier."

"Oh, Dill, I'm so sorry." Maureen pictured what she thought was a celebration last summer with crepe paper streamers, balloons, and the cake announcing No More Chemo.

"It's been a long, long fight. I think she deserves to take a rest. We both do."

"Is there anything I can do?"

"Yes. Stop fighting over the sale of the land to Sandover."

"I'm afraid that's not possible." Maureen hated herself for saying the words.

"The money would help pay for Summer's medical bills."

"Won't Sandover honor your part of the contract? After all, they've already spent money in starting expansion of the mine. They won't want to lose their investment."

"It's more complicated than that. The sandstone deposit runs wide and right below the surface. This makes it easy to reach, but also means in order to extract large quantities of sand, mines have to be dug across many acres. For this kind of mine to be worth the effort and investment, both properties have to be part of the deal."

"This is about more than preventing the destruction of land, Dill. A family farm's legacy is at stake."

"Those are pretty words, but worthless to me under the current circumstances. Why do you care so much about this particular farm?"

"I'm a concerned citizen, that's all."

"That's not what Toni says. She claims you two are related."

"Toni lies and can't be trusted."

"Together, she and I have cooperated to get these land deals done. Whenever I sell, she sells, and vice versa. Makes both of our properties more valuable. It's not illegal."

"Toni has no right to sell the land because she doesn't own it, and that is illegal."

"According to you. Toni says something different."

There was no sense arguing the point, so Maureen stopped talking. When Jeffrey came downstairs, the tension in the room must have been noticeable.

"So, what'd I miss?"

"Summer is in the hospital in Madison." Maureen couldn't look at Dill.

"What happened?"

"They are figuring out what palliative care is necessary to make her comfortable." Dill's voice was thick with emotion.

"But that means . . ." Jeffrey looked stricken and did not finish the inevitable sentence.

"Yup. My hope is to bring her home for her final days."

Thunder rumbled and the sunny start of the day disappeared behind dark, threatening clouds rolling in from the west. Road Dog scrambled to hide under the kitchen table, and Samuel joined her. The two dogs laid side-by-side, their heads resting on their outstretched front paws.

"What can we do to help?" Jeffrey was packing his briefcase for court.

"Forget about the injunction and civil case. Let it go."

"Maureen, what do you want me to do?" Jeffrey stopped what he was doing.

"Dill, I want to help you and Summer, I really do, but we have to see this through."

A look of pure contempt flashed over Dill's haggard face. Maureen wished she could do what he was asking. Reaching into the cupboard, Dill retrieved a bottle of whiskey from the top shelf.

"Work's cancelled for today. I gotta call the crew and get back to Madison."

After Dill stormed out, Jeffrey snapped his briefcase closed.

"I can't believe Summer isn't going to beat this." He smoothed his unruly curls and turned his head away. "I was in love with her once upon a time."

Before Maureen said anything more, Jeffrey grabbed his raincoat and hurried from the room. She figured they all needed to deal with saying good-bye to Summer in their own way. Summer was going to die, and Maureen's guilt about stopping the sale of the land to Sandover was overwhelming. With her coffee cup in hand, she sat at the island, staring out the window at the approaching rain. How could she be so selfish? She felt greedy and disloyal and knew her friends' situation was so much more serious and dire than hers. Maureen's remorse engulfed her, but more than that, her affection for her friends pushed her to decide to put them and their needs before her own. All she had to do was allow the land to be sold, and Summer and Dill's final days together would be free from the stress of their debt.

Maureen hurried outside to stop Jeffrey, but he had already disappeared down the road. She hated to bother him as he drove, so she decided to reach him later at the Court House. In the meantime, she was determined to make the house perfect for Summer's homecoming. Starting in the kitchen, she scrubbed and cleaned the rooms from top to bottom. She took particular care to make Summer's bedroom welcoming and cheerful, with fresh sheets and a colorful quilt. From the porch, Maureen brought in several bright red geraniums to sit on the bedroom windowsill, and she propped ruffled red pillows on Summer's bed. Using candles collected from around the house, Maureen assembled all of them into a grouping placed in the center of Summer's dresser. On the antique wash stand, she filled a silver tray with glasses, a water pitcher, and an ice bucket, and she placed an extra fleece blanket on the back of Summer's rocking chair.

Preoccupied with working on the house, Maureen forgot to check the time, and when she tried to contact Jeffrey, she was too late. He must have been in court already and unable to use his cell phone. She chastised herself for not leaving him a text message the first time and thought if she left him one now, by the time Jeffrey read the message he would be out of court. She wondered how he would react when she told him she wanted him to undo the case he just started.

By midmorning, the storm had blown through, but the sky remained grey. Long stretches of dingy clouds continued to scuttle past. Around noon, Maureen was on her way up from the basement with a load of laundry when her phone pinged that she had a voice mail. It was from Jeffrey.

"Sandover's attorney was the only legal representation for both parties. They didn't contest the restraining order, and the judge approved a Preliminary Injunction until our civil case is adjudicated. The paper work has been filed, so that's all there is to do until the court date is set. I'm heading for Madison to be with Dill and Summer. Hope we can bring her home tomorrow."

Around 9:00 P.M. Maureen was satisfied with the house and her preparations for Summer's return. She fed the dogs, gave them a break outside, and put the two on the porch to dry off. Upstairs, she took a quick shower and was finishing dressing when the electricity went out.

If there was one sure thing Maureen had learned from living in the country it was that electric service was susceptible to power outages on a regular basis. She supposed it was the price to pay for the miles of county roads lined with trees and the countryside covered with forests.

Maureen wished she had her phone and figured it was somewhere in the bedroom, but she was tired and didn't have the energy to stumble around in the dark searching for it. Feeling her way to the bed, she laid down to rest her eyes and wait for the lights to come back on.

Maureen felt a presence pressing on the bed, and a large, calloused hand covered her mouth. She struggled to breathe. The attacker pulled something over her eyes. Maureen tried to kick herself free, but the man's body forced her down onto the mattress. He bound her wrists together, stretched them above her head, and tethered her to the spindle of the metal headboard.

Maureen was unable to move, her breathing smothered by the hand that pressed her lips into her teeth. As she struggled, he released a deep laugh.

"Darla, my little Darla. Why do you fight me? You know this is what you want."

She recognized that voice.

"I'm only doing what your Momma asked me to do. I'm taking care of you."

Maureen slowed her thoughts and focussed on details she recognized. Large, calloused hands, athletic to heavy body build, much taller than Maureen, clothing of a rough fabric like denim or canvas. He wore a smell, like the outdoors, and there was something else, when he spoke. His breath smelled like licorice. His hand began moving over her body and underneath her clothes. She fought with a fury she did not know she had, and he punched her hard in the head.

Maureen opened her eyes. Reaching a hand to her head, she felt for a bump or tender spot, but there wasn't one. She had fallen asleep, but what happened was real. Maureen stumbled into the bathroom and threw up in the toilet.

CHAPTER 39

Maureen had felt the weight of him pressing her into the mattress, his rough hands on her mouth and body. His voice and laugh were not new to her, nor was the feel of the fabric of his clothing, and the smell of his breath. It all reminded her of another time. She was walking up those steps as they groaned, Stanley's leathery hand holding hers. When the lock snapped open, he lead her inside the small dark room and removed her school shoes. Resting on the mattress was a gift box, wrapped in pink paper and tied with a satiny pink ribbon.

"This is a present for you, my little Darla," Stanley said. "Go ahead. Open it."

She pulled the end of the ribbon, and it dropped from around the box. Lifting the lid, she folded back the crinkly tissue paper to find a pink, ruffled dress inside. Stanley held it up to her body.

"It's a perfect fit for a perfect little girl."

He undressed her, neatly folded her clothes, and stacked them on the floor.

"Raise your arms high, like you are trying to touch the sun." He dropped the dress over her head, turned her around and buttoned the back. Then, he spun her to look at him and leaned in, his face close to hers.

"Give me a kiss, right here," he said, touching his long finger to his own lips, "to show how much you love me."

Stanley's mouth was large and rough, and smelled of licorice.

"Now, twirl around and make the dress flutter." He gave her a spin and she whirled until she felt dizzy. Stanley was laughing.

"Sit here before you topple over, my dizzy little Darla." He placed her on the mattress and sat next to her. He slid his hand up her leg and pressed his own thick leg against hers.

Maureen leaned over the toilet and threw up again, retching until her throat and belly throbbed. The tile floor was cold, and she laid down next to the toilet, pressing her burning cheek into the coldness. Sobs erupted from a place buried inside her, and she allowed them to explode and spread. The room was filled with her wails and moans until she was empty.

Frantic barking broke through Maureen's catatonic state as she lay curled up on the bathroom floor, and she remembered Road Dog and Samuel were still on the porch. Not certain if she could walk or even stand, Maureen pulled herself to a kneeling position next to the toilet and willed her legs to be steady as she became upright. Moving one foot in front of the other, Maureen wobbled down the stairs, both hands gripping the rail.

As she opened the door to let Road Dog and Samuel inside, their relief and joy when they saw her moved her to tears. Pulling both dogs in close, Maureen held onto them like a lifeline.

After awhile, Maureen opened a bottle of wine and settled on the living room floor, one quilt spread for the dogs and another wrapped around her shoulders. The night was cool, and she felt chilled to her core. With a dog on either side of her, Maureen drank from the bottle, stared into the blackness, and started piecing together her past.

The little girl on the swing wore a pink ruffled dress, the same kind of dress Maureen received from Stanley. Maureen's dress had come in a pink gift box like the gift the man gave the girl on the swing. Even the way the man asked for a kiss was the same. Maureen tried to remember swinging in the yard on her fifth birthday and whether she had received a baby doll from Stanley, but those memories continued to be jumbled with the shooting of Stan by her mother.

There was breathing close to her cheek, and she opened one eye to find Road Dog's smiling face close to hers. Maureen sat up. Her head pounded and her entire body ached. Next time she decided to drink an entire bottle of wine in one sitting, she'd sit somewhere softer than the floor.

Maureen thought about what happened the previous night. Even though it had felt real, she knew she had not been attacked. Instead, she must have reconstructed a memory so strong she relived it as if it was in real time. It made her shudder.

She found her phone in the kitchen and checked for a message from Jeffrey. Nothing. There was a message from Dr. Taylor asking if Maureen was doing all right and to call her any time if she wanted to talk. Maureen's finger hovered over the call back button several seconds before she pushed it.

The phone rang four times, and then there was the message: "You've reached the office of Dr. Simone Taylor. . . ." Maureen tuned out, heard the tone, and hesitated.

"Uh, this is Maureen. Doing okay. Maybe I'll call some other time."

"Hello, Maureen. Don't hang up."

"Are you serious? How is it possible you are at your office this early? Do you live there?"

"It feels like it sometimes." Dr. Taylor laughed. "I'm glad to hear you are doing okay, but you didn't call to tell me that."

"You got me. I visited my mother in prison. She's dying."

"That must have been difficult for you. How are you handling it?"

"I guess I feel sorry for her, being in prison and everything. She called me Darla."

"Did she not recognize you after all these years?"

"No, Darla was my name when I was young. I changed it legally when I was nineteen."

"I would have liked to have known young Darla."

"No, you wouldn't. She was ugly and did shameful, terrible, ugly things. It's better she's gone. Let's leave it at that."

Dr. Taylor was quiet for what seemed like an eternity, and Maureen almost hung up.

"Do you want to talk about your mother?"

"Not much to say. She killed someone and has been in prison ever since."

"Having that happen must have been hard for you."

"Not really. She deserved to be incarcerated, even though the man she shot deserved to die."

"Was this the shooting you remembered on the day of the birthday present?"

"Yes. His name was Stanley."

"Did you know him?"

"Not really. He was Momma's boyfriend." Maureen's head pounded, and her gut lurched.

"I'm proud of you, Maureen. You are putting in the work, and it's paying off in the recollection of more details."

"Gotta fill in those plot points, right Doc? I have to get going." Maureen hung up.

She straightened the living room, washed the dishes, and buried the empty wine bottle deep inside the recycling bin. She contemplated showering, but the crew was expected soon to welcome Summer home, so she pulled her hair into a ponytail and splashed cold water on her face. Maureen baked Summer's favorite cinnamon rolls, sliced fresh fruit, and had the coffee perking as the crew arrived. Not long afterward, Dill and Jeffrey drove into the yard.

The image of Summer and Dill walking hand-in-hand toward their house was one Maureen would remember always. Summer wore a white peasant dress that concealed her thin, frail body. Barefoot, she seemed to float rather than walk through grass still sprinkled with morning dew. Lifting her eyes, Summer stared up at the home she and Dill had built together, and she smiled. Everyone gathered around her and took turns gently embracing Summer. Tears flowed without embarrassment and no one said a word. Summer held Samuel for the longest time and whispered into his ear. Dill urged her to go straight to bed, because the drive had been exhausting for her, but Summer had other ideas.

"I smell coffee and cinnamon rolls. I want to sit at our beautiful kitchen island and have breakfast with all of you."

Inside, the coffee was poured and butter slathered on the still-warm rolls. Summer sat surrounded by the important people of her everyday life. Maureen loved the stories they shared of working together, and she was touched to be part of their world. When Summer no longer had the strength to lift her cup, Dill insisted she needed to rest.

"Thank you for being my dear friends." She appeared too exhausted to say another word.

Two days later, Maureen came downstairs to find Dill sitting in the kitchen. It looked like he hadn't slept all night. There was an open bottle on the table and his hands were wrapped around a water glass filled with whiskey.

"Summer's gone." He took a long drink. "Samuel and I were beside her when she passed away in her sleep."

CHAPTER 40

....

D ill would not allow any talk of a funeral for Summer. Instead, he
planned a picnic and celebration for the second Saturday in September
and invited relatives, friends, neighbors, old classmates, former co-workers,
and anyone else who had known Summer at any point in her life. People were
encouraged to bring their children, significant others, and especially their
pets. With Eric and Lucy's help, a video of Summer's life was created, along
with a photo collage filling four enormous panels that accordioned across
a table filled with memorabilia. Silvia, who was a skilled designer of floral
arrangements, filled Summer's wicker laundry basket with the end of the
season blooms and ornamental grasses. The basket represented Summer's
remains, which had already been spread over the gardens and fields of
Crooked Creek Farm, and it was the centerpiece of the table where guests
signed their names and wrote messages on the linen tablecloth. Donations
to the local animal shelter were accepted in lieu of any other gifts, as Summer
had requested.

It was a perfect day to celebrate Summer. The aspen shimmered in brilliant yellow, and the sugar maples were dressed in red-orange, standing
against the backdrop of a sunny, azure sky. Cars filled the driveway and lined

both sides of the road leading to the farm, and groups of people congregated inside and outside the house. Maureen, Lucy, and Genna took charge of the buffet tables, while Jeffrey, Eric, and Will drank beer and manned the grills. Dogs and kids played frisbee and tag, and a game of bocce ball worked its way around the yard. The swing set Dill repaired was busy all during the celebration, with a line of kids waiting for their turn. Maureen thought it was the most excellent way to honor Summer.

By late afternoon, many of the visitors had gone home, and the field crew went to work cleaning up. They insisted Dill spend his time with the remaining guests, some of whom were a little bit drunk. One person still there, guzzling free beer, was Toni, whom Dill had invited despite the contentious relationship he knew existed between Maureen and Toni. Maureen had done her best to steer clear of the woman all afternoon, which wasn't difficult when there was a crowd. Now, however, she was hard to avoid.

"Dill, how come she's still working for you?" Toni gestured in Maureen's direction with her open beer bottle, speaking so everyone would hear.

"I'd rather not get into that today, Toni."

"I mean, she's gonna cost you and me lots of money."

"Like I said, a topic for another time."

"And what a buttinsky. Like any of this land business is her business."

"Guess she's got her reasons."

"That does not sound like the Dillon Nowak I know."

Maureen dropped the pile of plastic plates she was carrying and turned to stare at Toni.

"You're drunk, Toni." Dill's voice was loud. "You don't know what you're saying."

"Hell, I don't. The Dillon Nowak I know would never give in or give up."

Dill grabbed Toni underneath her arm and hoisted her from the lawn chair she had occupied all afternoon.

"You need to leave."

"What'd I do?"

"You talk too much."

"You got a problem with the truth?"

Toni continued yammering while Dill escorted her out of the yard and down the road to her car. Maureen was struggling to process what she heard, and as soon as Dill returned, she approached him.

"Why did Toni call you Dillon Nowak?"

"Toni is a drunk. She says lots of stupid things."

"Not that long ago, you were bragging about your business partnership with Toni. Now she's a stupid drunk?"

"Sometimes she is. I don't know what you want me to say."

"I want you to say the truth."

"The truth is my name is Dillon Hagen."

"Why did she call you Dillon Nowak?"

"Because, I used to be Dillon Nowak."

"Were you related to Stanley Nowak?"

"Yes, related, but not close. After he died, I didn't want my name associated with someone like him, even at a distance, especially later on when I decided to attend college and law school. I took my grandparents' last name instead, but I guess people around here forget sometimes and revert to my old name."

"You knew what happened to Stanley?"

"Everybody around here knew. Hard not to."

"Of course." Maureen felt embarrassed. "I shouldn't have interrogated you like that."

"No, you shouldn't have. You have no right to say anything to me." Dill trudged toward the house, Samuel trailing behind.

"It's been a rough week." Jeffrey stooped down to help pick up the plates Maureen had dropped. "You two okay?"

"Probably not." Maureen took the plates from his hands. "I found out Dill changed his last name. How come you never told me that?"

"Conveying his personal information is not my business. Besides, the topic never came up. Plus, it's not a secret. He wanted to move on, and folks accepted that."

"Right." Maureen understood the motivation to move on.

"You can't blame a guy for wanting to distance himself from a father like Stanley Nowak."

"Did you say father?"

"Yes, why?"

"No reason." Maureen was dumbfounded by Jeffrey's revelation, but she managed to change the subject. "Must have been hard for Dill growing up."

"Mostly, he was raised by his grandparents. His dad was killed when Dill was thirteen or fourteen, I think."

"I lost my mother when I was young."

"I'm so sorry. How did she die?"

"She didn't. She was sent to prison." Maureen realized where this was headed, but decided it was time for Jeffrey to learn the truth.

"Wait a minute. Don't tell me your mother in prison is the relative who owns the property you are trying to save."

"Yes, that's right. Toni is my mother's sister."

"Things are beginning to make a whole lot more sense now."

"I'm glad you think so. As of my last conversation with my mother, Toni now has free rein to sell as much land as she wants, to whomever she wants. To top it off, the money from the sale is Toni's to keep, no questions asked."

"Sounds like our civil case against Toni and Sandover should be dropped."

"The day you went to court for the case, I tried to stop you, but I couldn't reach you. That same morning, Dill had gone back to Madison to bring Summer home, and I was feeling so guilty about how much money they were going to lose because of me."

"Since you never mentioned withdrawing the case, I'm assuming you have changed your mind about doing so."

"After lots of soul searching, I had decided we should abandon the case because Summer and Dill needed the money more than I needed to save the farm. Sandover won't honor their deal with Dill without my mother's land. Even knowing that, I hate the idea of giving in to Toni, especially since my mother is so adamant about letting her do whatever she wants."

"Are you thinking your mother's decision has some underlying motive?"

"I don't know. I'm having trouble understanding why all of this is acceptable to her. I believe she wants her daughters to have the farm one day, but at the rate Toni is going, there won't be anything left to inherit."

"If it's their family farm, maybe your mother thinks Toni is entitled to a share of it."

"That's not the case. The place belonged to my dad's family, and when he passed away, Momma inherited it. Toni has no claim to any of it."

It was the same old discussion Maureen had been having with herself and others for months. Sometime soon, she would need to pressure her mother into talking about what was going on with Toni, or she was going to be forced to allow the whole issue to drop. Either way, Maureen figured the farm was lost, and so was her future.

CHAPTER 41

W hen the celebration of Summer's life was over and the clean-up completed, it was already dark, and Maureen was the last one to go into the house. As she walked up the porch steps, she thought about how things were when she first moved in with Summer and Dill and what it was like now, with Summer gone, and Maureen living in the house where she was unwelcome and probably even hated. Dill told Maureen he was only distantly related to Stanley Nowak, but Jeffrey said Stanley was Dill's father. Maureen believed Jeffrey, but couldn't place Dillon in her past. The truth about Dill made it hard for her to continue to live at Crooked Creek Farm. In addition, being in the room where her most secret nightmare had been revealed made it almost impossible for Maureen to remain living there. She wasn't sure where she and Road Dog would go, but she knew they would have to leave, sooner rather than later.

Maureen needed the money for whatever she and Road Dog would face next, so she stayed at the farm, toiling hard every day, hoping for exhaustion every night. Preparations had begun for the opening of the pumpkin patch, and as the hours of daylight shortened, the crew harvested produce five or more days a week. Thousands of pounds of root crops were picked to be sold to restaurants and grocery stores over the winter. The CSA pick-ups were scheduled to end in mid-October. After that, there would be time for the planting of shallots and garlic. Enormous amounts of cleanup and composting waited to be finished. Plastic mulch and drip lines had to be pulled and stored, and the irrigation system needed to be blown out. All the tools and equipment would be repaired and cleaned. Dill thought they might be finished by early November.

Maureen managed to avoid Dill. When she wasn't working, she and Road Dog stayed upstairs, spending time with Jeffrey in his room. He was fond of chess and mahjong and was willing and patient enough to teach Maureen the rudimentary rules for both games. They acknowledged playing was a good distraction for them after everything that happened. When Jeffrey wasn't around, he was okay with Maureen hanging out there. She liked to practice the chess moves Jeffrey taught her, and sometimes she just relaxed and read his books. She felt comfortable in his room which was neat and organized and didn't have an attic. The longer she stayed there, the less time she needed to spend in her own room.

On the Monday following the celebration for Summer, Maureen was in the garden closest to the house, the one Summer had always tended. Maureen felt as though she was trespassing on hallowed ground, but the plants had to be pulled and composted, the irrigation lines needed to be removed, and a protective cover crop would be planted. As she tied up the irrigation lines for storage, Maureen heard a vehicle approaching long before it coughed to a stop alongside the garden where she was working. It was Toni. Samuel and Road Dog barked up a storm, but Toni barged from the vehicle without giving them a glance. She marched straight up to Maureen.

"You know you gotta drop the injunction and court case against me."

"It's been sort of busy around here."

"Not my problem. Your momma promised me everything was straightened out."

"Maybe in her mind, but I'm not so sure."

"What's not straight? She owns the farm and gave me permission to sell it."

"Do you have her permission in writing?"

"I don't need it in writing."

"According to my lawyer, you do."

"Okay, I'll get written permission."

"You forged her signature on official documents."

"She's in prison, not living down the street. It's not easy getting all that legal mumbo jumbo done."

"That legal mumbo jumbo is necessary, otherwise it's called fraud. Fraud is punishable in a court of law."

"Here's what we're gonna do. You and I are gonna go visit your momma at the same time. We're gonna sit down and have her sign everything she needs to sign, giving me the legal rights she promised. You can even bring your fancy lawyer to be a witness. How's that sound?"

One way or another, Maureen realized she and Toni would have to settle the disagreement between them, and as reluctant as she was to do it, visiting her mother with Toni was the most efficient solution. Once they were all together, everything would be out in the open and what needed to be said, would be said. If he'd be willing, having Jeffrey there to oversee whatever occurred would be reassuring.

"My bar don't run itself, so the day that works best for me is Monday, when it's closed."

Maureen dreaded asking Dill for a day off from work, but it was the end of the season, and their work days were growing shorter. Maureen and Toni agreed they would meet the following Monday afternoon at 3:00, provided the prison approved their visit.

When Jeffrey rumbled in from the fields on the beat-up four-wheeler, sundown was approaching, and a chill had moved in. Maureen was finished with the garden cleanup and thought Summer would be pleased.

"Looks good." Jeffrey was covered in mud, an indicator he'd been working on the irrigation system.

"I tried to do what Summer would have done. She's a hard act to follow."

"You would've made her proud. What a long way you've come from the city slicker who picked me up along a rainy highway one night."

"Thanks." Maureen felt a little choked up. It was hard to admit how much Jeffrey's opinion mattered to her, and Maureen felt herself blushing at her emotional reaction. She abruptly changed the subject.

"My mother's sister, Toni, came for a visit. She's not too pleased with our injunction and pending civil suit."

"Most people wouldn't be pleased."

"Toni maintains she has had, and still has, permission to sell the property, which is true, but there was no way I was going to agree with her. She wants me to join her in meeting with my mother to straighten out everything."

"Are you going to do it?"

"Other than hashing this all out in court, meeting together is one way for everyone to have their say. Besides, if we wait too long, my mother won't be there to tell her side of the story."

"I know this sounds heartless, but if your mother is gone, the problem resolves itself legally. Unless she signs the deed over to someone else, with her passing, it will go to whomever is named in her will."

"She's already signed a quitclaim naming my younger sister as the owner."

"When did that happen? I thought you said she refused to sign your quitclaim."

"That's true, because she had already signed Jasmine's."

"If your mother isn't the owner, this changes everything." Jeffrey frowned.

"No, Momma is still the owner, because Jasmine did not file the claim."

"That's good. Any more surprises?" Jeffrey took a deep breath. "Is there a will?"

"No more surprises, and I'm sorry I didn't tell you sooner," Maureen said. "I don't know if there is a will of any kind."

"Sounds like meeting together with Toni, your mother, Jasmine, and anyone else involved would be the way to come to a consensus, unless you are prepared to continue pursuing the issue in a legal manner."

"I'm ready to have this settled in the most expeditious way possible. Would you be willing to come with me to the meeting at the prison on Monday?"

"Sure."

"You're a good man, Jeffrey Bennett."

"Again, keep that between us. Mahjong tonight?"

"I'm too exhausted to concentrate. How about tomorrow?"

"Victory works for me any day of the week."

CHAPTER 42

A fter the crew finished work on Friday, Dill asked everyone to stop at the house for a beer and a short get-together. Maureen waited until the others were inside before entering and parked herself behind Jeffrey, who always stood in the back because he towered over everyone else.

Beers were opened and toasts were made, bottles clinking together. Maureen felt a lump form in her throat, knowing this might be one of the last times she would gather with this group of people she had come to think of as her family. She swallowed hard and blinked away her tears.

"I guess I don't have to tell you how great you have been, as a work crew and as friends."

Dill's voice cracked a bit, and he paused to collect himself.

"It's been one of the toughest years of my life, and I don't think I could have made it without each and every one of you. Here's to the best people I know, dirty fingernails and all." Dill raised his bottle in a toast, and the others did as well.

"When Summer and I came here to run this place nine years ago, we left two lucrative law careers. We hoped living on a farm where the air was clean, the earth was close, and the stress was less, would help Summer beat her cancer." He gave the group a knowing look, and heads nodded in agreement.

"We got the part right about the air and the earth anyway." Everyone laughed.

"This farm belonged to my grandparents, and I was privileged to have the opportunity to operate it. You all know farming can be rewarding and sometimes it might even make a little money, but it's also non-stop hard work, unpredictable and merciless." He gazed at the puzzled faces of the crew watching him.

"I'll get to the point, 'cause I know how you hate sermons. I came back to farming for Summer, and now that she's gone, I can't find a reason to continue. Without her, none of this backbreaking work makes any sense, so I've decided to sell Crooked Creek Farm."

Dill cleared his throat before continuing.

"I wanted you to hear it from me instead of someone else. Those of you who are seasonal employees will receive two weeks' severance pay beyond your last paycheck. For Lo and Silvia, I can afford to have you work until the end of the year plus four weeks' severance pay. I know this puts a burden on all of you, but I'll do everything I can to help you find another job, and, yes, Jeffrey, I do know how to write a reference."

"Does this mean you've already sold the farm?" Jeffrey asked.

"No, but it's officially for sale, and I have every reason to believe it will be snatched up quickly. After the property is sold, I'll have an auction to recoup some of my investments in equipment and vehicles."

"Crooked Creek Farm is not going to be functioning as an organic farm?" Eric said.

"No."

"Not a farm at all?" Lucy's voice was quiet.

"Probably not."

"May I ask who you have in mind as a buyer?" Jeffrey stepped forward towards Dill.

"Not that it's any of your business, Jeffrey, but I guess you'll know soon enough. I'm going to offer it to Sandover."

"What will happen to the buildings and the house you and Summer remodeled?" Will said.

"I'm hoping they will move the house. The barn and other buildings will most likely be torn down."

Genna was the first to react, walking to Dill and placing her arms around him in a hug. The others followed her example, except for Maureen, who was certain Dill would think a show of support from her as disingenuous considering recent events. No one said anything as the crew turned to leave.

"Thank you, everyone, for being understanding. You have to know I didn't come to this decision easily." Dill walked to the door with them. "Weather's going to be decent tomorrow, so anyone who wants to clock some hours, come on in."

Maureen walked upstairs with Road Dog, and Jeffrey was close behind her. He peeked his head into her open door.

"Wow, didn't see that coming, did you?" Jeffrey stepped inside the room.

"No, but I guess I can't blame him. Lots of memories here."

"I'm surprised Dill would even consider selling his family's farm."

"It was evident he's struggled with the decision. He's been drinking a lot lately."

"You're right. It must have been tough. I shouldn't judge him."

"I think knowing all of us will be out of a job has made it even harder on him."

"Decent jobs around here are hard to find."

"At least you can return to a real career. I bet your old law firm would jump at the chance to have you back with them."

"Doubt it." Jeffrey hesitated. "Let's just say we didn't part company on the best of terms."

"I'm sorry. I didn't mean to pry."

"I don't mind talking about it. I wish I could say it was something scintillating, like a love triangle gone wrong." Jeffrey laughed. "It wasn't. I lost a very important case, thanks to the advice of one of my senior colleagues, a guy I considered a friend and mentor. After that, I was passed over for being made partner in the firm, something I had been promised."

"I've been there. It's enough to make a person run away and work on an organic farm."

"Exactly. I'm taking it one day at a time, and, at some point, I'll know what I want to do."

"That's a healthy and positive attitude."

"What about you? Do you have any plans?"

"I don't know. I won't be inheriting my mother's farm, so there's nothing keeping me here."

"That's not a done deal, yet."

"I don't see how it can turn out any other way."

The sound of Dill's truck departing caught Maureen's attention. She hadn't eaten anything since breakfast and was hoping for a chance to raid the refrigerator.

"You hungry?" Jeffrey was out the door and down the hall before Maureen could answer him.

They fed the dogs, and then scrounged up peanut butter sandwiches and a bottle of wine for themselves. Maureen didn't realize how hungry she was.

"I'm taking the entire day off on Monday," Jeffrey said, "so before we leave, I'll have some time to check out a couple of things at the Court House. We should depart by 11:00, and, if it's okay with you, I'd like to take my car. No offense, but I am a better driver than some people I know."

"Fine, you can drive."

"I'm hoping everyone you contacted to come to the prison shows up. When we get into the meeting, let me do all the talking, other than niceties to your mother and relatives."

"There won't be much of that."

Maureen and Jeffrey decided to finish going over the details for the meeting on the drive to the prison.

"I'm beat. You working Monday morning before we head out?" Jeffrey asked.

"Yes, I need the money, but I'll be ready to leave at 11:00."

Maureen grabbed the bottle of wine and settled herself and the dogs into the living room, a room Summer had often used. Maureen didn't think Summer would mind if her soft couch, cozy pillows, and beautiful books were enjoyed by someone again. After a couple glasses of good wine, Maureen managed to relax a bit, listening to the soothing snores of Road Dog and Samuel. She closed her eyes and let her thoughts drift away.

When Maureen awoke, Dill was sitting at the other end of the couch, staring at her.

"What are you doing?" Maureen bolted upright.

"Watching you."

"That's not creepy or anything."

"I used to watch you all the time."

"What? When?

"I was about five years old when I first saw you. You were with Stanley."

"Your father."

"You knew he was my father. How did you figure that out?"

"It doesn't matter. Where were we that you saw us together?"

"He used to pick you up from school."

"Did the two of us ride home together with Stanley? I don't remember that."

"My dad made me take the bus. One day, my friend's brother gave me a ride home. I wasn't supposed to, but I took a ride anyway."

"Good story." Maureen wanted Dill to stop talking.

"When I snuck into the house, you were already here."

"I've never been inside this house until this summer."

"It might not look the same as back then, but remember, Summer and I remodeled the entire house, except for a couple of rooms upstairs."

"I think I'd remember if I was here, no matter what."

"Let me finish my story. Maybe then you'll remember. Where was I? Oh, yeah, I hid and watched him walk you up the stairs to the first bedroom on the left, the one you have now."

"You're making this up." Maureen wanted his words to be fiction.

"I followed the two of you. He opened the closet and took you into the attic and closed the door."

"Why are you saying all of this?" She didn't want to hear her memories said out loud.

"He called you his little Darla, his dizzy little Darla."

Maureen started to tremble all over. She wrapped her arms around herself to stop the shaking.

"How do you know that?" Her voice wavered.

"I was listening at the door. From that day on, whenever I came home early from school, I always checked to see if you were upstairs with him."

"I don't believe you."

"When I was older, maybe nine or ten, sometimes he waited for the bus to drop me off and would bring me into the attic, too. There was a mattress on the floor, and a baby doll propped up in one of the corners. He made you wear this goofy pink dress."

The wine lurched upward toward Maureen's mouth. She gagged and swallowed hard.

"He said I needed to watch, so I would know what to do when it was my turn."

Maureen began retching and clamped her hand over her mouth.

"You never made a sound. One time, I thought you were dead, because you didn't move and you were barely breathing."

"I was dead, or at least I wished I was." Maureen saw Darla in that room, laid out on the mattress, her dress pushed up, the dusty air thick around her. The smell of black licorice was as real now as it had been when Stanley pressed close to Darla. The thought of what he did to her while he forced his son to watch, made Maureen want to crawl inside herself until she vanished.

"I remember Stan slugging you on the head when you fought him or wouldn't do what he wanted. He told me to always aim for the head, because it hurt real bad, but never left a visible mark."

"He was sick and perverted, a degenerate monster devoid of feeling and compassion."

"I can't dispute that."

"You're just as bad. Why didn't you help me, or at least tell someone?"

"I was a kid, and he terrified me. Besides, you never told anyone either."

"I tried. No one would listen."

"His plan was flawless, every detail considered. It would have been your word against his, and there were no witnesses. Except for me."

"Why are you telling me this now? Why not when I first showed up at the farm?"

"The last time I saw Darla, I was about fourteen and you were young, too, maybe fifteen. You look like a different person now. You are a different person. Besides, you said your name was Maureen."

"How did you figure out who I was?"

"I didn't. Toni told me."

"Why would she do that?"

"She was at the farm buying strawberries and saw you the day you started working here. She couldn't believe I hired you, and since the two of you seemed to know one another at the restaurant, I asked her to tell me what she knew about you. That's when she blabbed about your true identity and how you changed your name."

Maureen felt dizzy. "It was you."

"What do you mean?"

"The pink dress hanging in the closet, the box with the tag, and the baby doll in the drawer and the box. You snuck into my room and placed those hateful memories for me to find."

"I admit it was me. I only wanted to scare you."

"Did you lock me in the attic that night?

"I'm not proud of it, but there was a method to my madness."

"Nothing could make what you did acceptable."

"I didn't say what I did was acceptable, but there was a reason for my behavior."

"You realize I thought I was going crazy."

"I figured if you were frightened enough and worried you were going off the deep end, you might pack up and go back home to Chicago."

"I wasn't hurting you."

"Yes, your being here dredged up painful, disgusting memories. I couldn't stand the sight of you. When you began interfering with selling the land, I had to make you leave."

"As it turned out, I didn't go off the deep end, at least, not all the way, and I didn't leave."

"Doesn't matter now. Summer is gone, and soon everyone else will leave, too. Maybe it's better that way." He dragged himself off the couch and left Maureen alone, staring into the darkness.

Dill's sickening revelation forced Maureen to peer into the scene she had been constructing. Now she remembered that the little girl on the swing had soft, flowing curls that were blond, almost white. Maureen replayed the girl's lines over and over until the voice became recognizable. She had not been the girl on the swing that day. It was five-year old Jasmine.

As Jasmine swung back and forth, Maureen studied the person standing behind the swing, giving it movement. The face was blurred and impossible to identify. Maureen thought it might have been one of her cousins, but it was hard to tell.

There was a grainy image of someone standing on the back porch, leaning against the railing. It was a woman. Her thick fingers were punctuated with pointed, ruby-colored nails, and she held a tall, brown bottle in one of her hands, tipping the bottle high as she drank. The shorts she wore were skimpy and tight. Maureen wished the person would turn around so her face was visible, but the figure continued to look out into the yard where the child was swinging.

"Enough pushing for today," the woman said.

It was Toni on the porch, and Darla was peering through the screen of the kitchen window, watching the scene unfold. The day was Jasmine's fifth birthday. On the table behind Darla was a large layer cake Momma baked and decorated. On the top of the cake Darla had made a deep dent messing up the word 'Happy' written in pink letters. Several presents were piled on the table, too, along with pink napkins and matching plates. Pink and white balloons floated above the table. No one was in the house with her, and Darla was free to scowl and be angry, and it would go unnoticed, like everything Darla did.

Movement across the lawn caught Darla's attention. Stanley was walking towards the swing set, holding a present done up in pink wrapping paper. Jasmine jumped off the swing and ran toward Stanley. Their arms outstretched toward one another, and she threw herself into his embrace, her little girl hands reaching to hug him around the neck. Darla wanted to call to her sister to run away, but she could only watch as Jasmine picked up the present, pulled the ribbon, and opened the lid. She lifted a doll from inside. Darla stepped closer to the window for a better look and opened her eyes wide. Except for the wear and tear of the years gone by, the doll was identical to the one Maureen had found in the drawer that stormy night not long ago. The new doll's pink dress was not faded or threadbare, and her jointed limbs and chubby hands and feet were cream-colored and unblemished. Brilliant blue eyes winked in tandem and the thick blond hair formed tidy curls that swirled around two perfect ears. The doll was like the one that Darla knew well, the one on the mattress, soiled and used, propped up in the corner of the attic.

The plot points Dr. Taylor talked about were beginning to align.

From these memories and Dill's confessions, Maureen now had a pretty good idea of what she had been trying to suppress. Stanley had been abusing her from the time she was about five years old until she was thirteen. The trauma of that thought was beyond painful.

Maureen held Road Dog for reassurance, until the dog rolled over and went to sleep. For Maureen, sleep was elusive, and her mind returned to the little girl, Darla, and the horror she was forced to live. Maureen wondered how her mother had missed the signs of what was going on. Why wasn't she worried about Darla retreating until she was the shadow of a person, not talking or smiling? At some point Maureen figured her mother did become concerned, because Toni testified at the trial that Peggy had grown afraid of Stanley and didn't want him near her children. In fact, her mother was so concerned, she had shot and killed Stanley. What had changed?

CHAPTER 43

In the morning, an exhausted Maureen joined Jeffrey, Eric, and Will to work on the remaining tools and equipment and harvest root crops for the area restaurants. Dill and Loriano were in the barn for the day doing maintenance on the tractors and larger implements and getting them in proper working order, in preparation for the upcoming auction. Lucy, Genna, and Silvia managed the pumpkin patch, bustling with customers.

"You were quiet today." Jeffrey and Maureen were cleaning up at the dented metal sink in the old milk house. "I don't think you said ten words all day."

"I didn't get any sleep last night. Maybe a little too much wine."

"Wine usually has the opposite effect on me. Puts me out like that." Jeffrey snapped his fingers for emphasis.

Maureen grabbed a towel and moved away from the sink as Dill was approaching. He was the last person she wanted to see. Road Dog and Samuel met her as she was walking toward the house.

"How about a car ride for a juicy burger?" Maureen never did tell the two dogs the burgers they loved so much were veggie burgers.

Maureen had settled the dogs in the back seat of the car when her cell phone rang. It was Jasmine, and Maureen cringed at the thought of talking to her sister.

"Maureen. It's Jazz."

"What do you want?"

"I filed the quitclaim yesterday."

"I told you to hold off filing until we figure this thing out with Toni."

"I couldn't wait any longer. The farm belongs to me now."

"That's just great. You realize this complicates the situation with Toni."

"It couldn't be helped."

"Momma wants Toni to have the land now, so she can sell it and keep the money."

"That's crazy. Momma gave me the land. It says so on the quitclaim."

"Momma and I both thought you would keep your word and not file. If Momma doesn't own the land, giving her permission to Toni to sell it is pointless."

"That's right. Now I'm the one who is going to sell it."

"I thought you wanted to keep the farm in our family."

"I need the money to get the best lawyer possible for David."

"Are you kidding me? You're going to squander the valuable property earned by my family on that lying, cheating fraud?"

"He's my lying, cheating fraud, and I have to help him."

"What a mess you've created." Maureen could not keep the disgust from her voice. "At least show up at the prison on Monday as we planned. We need to find a solution everyone can live with."

"All right, I'll be there, but I've already made my decision, and it's the only solution I can live with."

After she hung up, Maureen got into the car with the two dogs who had been waiting in the back seat, licking the windows and flinging slobber all over the inside of the car. Pulling onto the highway, Maureen thought, nothing ever changes.

Like with Jasmine. What she did was typical Jazz. Everything was always about her and her own life, and if she could use someone to her advantage, that's what she did, which was exactly what David would do, too. David did not deserve the money obtained from the sale of the farm, and, despite all her flaws, it wasn't right for him to use Jasmine. Pretty little Jasmine.

Pretty little Jasmine. It hit Maureen so hard she had to pull over and stop the car. Little Darla wasn't little any longer. Pretty little Jasmine was. Stanley had given Jasmine a dress and a doll, like the pieces of the plan he used for Darla.

Maureen opened her door and staggered out of the car, leaning against the vehicle as cars sped past, honking at her. For a moment, she thought about walking into the frantic, oncoming traffic, relinquishing all of her torment and ugliness to the crushing steel and shattering glass. Then, Road Dog barked and whimpered from inside the car, so Maureen opened the door and slid in before she did something stupid. Road Dog and Samuel needed her.

CHAPTER 44

It was Monday, the day they were driving to the prison, and Maureen was standing in front of the full-length mirror in the upstairs hallway. She had put on the outfit from her last day at Anson-Chambers, thinking it would be appropriate to wear, but it was so large she looked like she was wearing a giant sack. Jeffrey was supposed to pick her up in thirty minutes, and Maureen was out of options for something to wear. She decided to do the unthinkable. With the entire crew still working in the barn, Maureen tiptoed downstairs to Summer and Dill's bedroom.

The room remained as it was when Summer was alive—robe hung on the door, reading glasses folded alongside a pile of books on the nightstand. The walnut jewelry case Dill made for her sat open on the pale oak dresser, and scarves in a myriad of colors and patterns draped the top of the dresser mirror.

On her way to the closet, Maureen stubbed her toe on a plastic bin next to the dresser. The bin was labeled "Hagen Farm - Legal Info." She snapped open the lid and rifled through manila folders with titles like "Taxes Paid" and "Insurances." What she hoped to find was something on the deals with Sandover that would help today and give her a frame of reference for what Toni might have received in payment from the mining company. She had almost given up on finding anything important when she came across a file labeled "Last Will & Testament." It was the will of Paulette and Henry Hagen, Dill's grandparents. In the document, the Hagen's daughter, Nora Hagen Nowak, was named as the primary beneficiary, and Stanley Nowak was named as the contingent beneficiary. Dillon was not named because the will was signed well before he was born, which contradicted Dill's claim that he had inherited the farm from his grandparents. Maureen tucked the files away in the bin and decided she didn't have any more time to waste.

In the closet, none of Summer's things had been removed, and Maureen searched until she found a simple, pale blue dress that looked like it had never been worn. She slipped out of her damp work clothes and slid the dress over her head. It fit. She grabbed her clothes and headed out the door.

Maureen stood on the porch waiting for Jeffrey. Outside it was chilly and grey, with rain-filled clouds scurrying overhead. Because it was cool, Maureen had thought about bringing Road Dog with them on the trip, especially when the dog fretted as Maureen prepared to go away. In the end, Maureen decided to leave Road Dog home. It was going to be a very long and difficult day, and Jeffrey didn't need the added distraction.

As Jeffrey drove in, a misty rain began, and Maureen hurried to get into his car before her hair became an out-of-control frizz fest. He was wearing a dark navy suit, with a pale blue shirt the same color as his eyes, and a distinctive, navy blue, polka-dotted tie.

"Everything go okay this morning?" Jeffrey said. The wipers flopped back and forth against the windshield, as the rain intensified, and he adjusted their tempo.

"We finished up sanding and oiling all the wooden handles, sharpened some blades, cleaned up the back shed. They were cleaning up in the barn when I left. I don't think they'll do much more today with all the rain, so we're not missing anything."

"How was Dill?"

"Only saw him once. He was tinkering with that old tractor to get it running before the sale. How'd it go at the Court House?"

"I didn't file to revoke the injunction or cancel our civil case, which is what I had considered doing. Then I reasoned, we're not sure who owns what at this point, or who will end up owning what after our meeting, so I didn't do anything."

"What do you suppose is going to happen today?" Maureen hoped for some reassurance from Jeffrey.

"I should be asking you that question."

"Jasmine owns the land, but now my mother wants Toni to have it. Someone will win and someone will lose."

"Where are you in all this?"

"If Jasmine stands her ground, our injunction and civil suit are not credible, so I'm out of the equation. If Toni ends up winning, I'm still out."

"Would you consider going back to being business executive Maureen with a secretary and a big office?"

"I'm not the person I was six months ago, so I don't think I could go back, and, to clarify, my office wasn't that big."

Jeffrey laughed and began to talk about the legal aspects of their upcoming meeting and what outcomes were possible, as well as what to expect from the parties involved.

"The act of discovery is important, and we're looking for some sort of resolution of the land ownership and money issues. For the most part, nothing that transpires today will be admissible in court, if it goes in that direction. My hope is to conduct this similar to a deposition except without the parties being required to take an oath. I'll ask questions, with the expectation they will be answered truthfully."

"Good luck getting the truth out of Toni."

"I think everyone knows enough of the background of what has happened that she will be compelled to stick to the facts, not to mention the paper trail she and Sandover left in conducting their business transactions."

"I hope you're right."

"Remember, everyone has their own version of the facts. Keep quiet, stay under control, and listen to identify the misstatements, so we can undermine anyone not being truthful."

After awhile, their conversation veered off into other topics, and eventually they fell into a comfortable silence. As the prison came into view, Jeffrey slowed the car.

"I'd forgotten how gloomy and sinister prisons look," he said.

"Not a place you'd want to book for an extended stay."

"How long has your mother been in here?"

"Over twenty years."

"If you don't mind my asking, what did she do?"

"It's okay. The secret's out. She shot and killed her boyfriend."

"That's rough. You must have been pretty young when it happened."

"Yeah, I don't remember much about it."

"That's not always a bad thing."

Although the lot was crowded, Jeffrey found a parking spot near the visitors' entrance. Once they were inside and their identifications were checked, Jeffrey presented additional documentation, and the papers the two of them brought were approved. After passing through the metal detectors, Maureen and Jeffrey were accompanied to the visitors' waiting area. Since they were early and their check-in was quick, they still had thirty minutes until their scheduled appointment time.

The longer they waited, the more tense and insecure Maureen felt about the meeting. When 3:00 arrived, she was relieved as the prison staff began assembling visitors by their inmate's module number and groups departed to their designated visitation room. Maureen and Jeffrey were the last to leave the waiting area. As they followed the guard down a long hall, Jeffrey's phone rang and they stopped for him to take the call.

The door behind them opened and Toni sauntered in with the man Maureen had seen in the Sandover truck and another distinguished-looking man Maureen figured was the Sandover attorney. Walking close behind the three was Dill, minus his scruffy beard and blondish dreadlocks. His resemblance to the picture of Stanley was so striking Maureen was speechless. To add to her dismay, not far behind Dill, Jasmine and David were walking, hand-in-hand.

Jeffrey acknowledged Dill with a slight nod as he walked past them, and Jasmine waved to Maureen, who didn't return the greeting.

"Did you know Dill was going to be here?" Maureen said under her breath as the group moved down the hall.

"I'm as surprised as you are. Who's the guy with your sister?"

"My soon-to-be ex-husband, David."

"Are those two together?"

"Yes, they're together." Maureen laughed at the look of disbelief on Jeffrey's face. "You can't make this stuff up."

Maureen and Jeffrey caught up with the others as they entered the grey corridor leading to the medical wards, and the prison guard stopped the visitors with a flat-handed halt signal.

"Because this is a larger than normal group size, we've made special allowances for your meeting. Your family member has been moved into the Ancillary Unit where you'll have some privacy. Keep it down and do not leave the

Unit." She motioned them to follow her with another hand signal, making it clear they were to stay behind her at all times.

Maureen felt guilty for the white lie she told in reserving an appointment time. It wasn't a total lie. They were meeting to finalize her mother's end-of-life decisions, but she failed to mention the main reason for the gathering was to determine the person or persons who would inherit the Whitcomb family farm.

The Ancillary Unit was one large room with a wall of windows. Maureen glanced at the treeless landscape outside, its yellowing grass mowed low. Against the pale blue wall facing the windows was a single hospital bed sitting beside a machine monitoring Peggy's vital signs.

"She's been napping most of the day, saving her energy for your visit." The guard patted Peggy's bed and left.

Maureen walked to her mother's side and stared at the delicate figure propped upright in the bed. A pillow tucked on either side of her body kept Peggy from falling over sideways, and the white bedclothes were stretched across her chest and shoulders, holding her close, with her hands and arms secured underneath. A turquoise scarf dotted with sunny yellow flowers covered her head and framed her tiny, pale face, cracked with intricate lines like an old porcelain teacup. Those same blue eyes Maureen remembered from her childhood blinked out of sunken, dark-rimmed sockets.

"Momma, can you hear me?" Maureen sat down on the chair Jeffrey found for her.

"Darla, I'm glad you came back."

"I promised I would. I've brought some other people with me." She motioned for Jeffrey to approach.

"This is my friend, Jeffrey. He's an attorney from Chicago." Maureen didn't think it would hurt to mention his credentials.

"Mrs. Whitcomb, it's my pleasure to meet you." Jeffrey took a position standing behind Maureen.

Jasmine and David pushed their way to the front of the group, and Jasmine pulled up a chair on the opposite side of the bed.

"Momma, it's me, Jasmine. I brought David back to visit you."

"I can see that. He's starting to lose his hair."

"Good to see you again, Peggy." David stood behind Jazz, running his fingers through his thinning hair before resting his hands on Jasmine's shoulders.

Toni, wearing three-inch heels, clattered to the end of Peggy's bed and coughed a rumbling smokers' cough.

"Hey, Sis, look at you. Sitting up and everything. You might pull out of this yet."

"Who's that with you, Toni?"

"The handsome fellow here is Cal Derksen, and this fancy guy all dolled up to impress you is Lyle Grayson. He's a big shot lawyer from Madison."

Both men nodded, said their hellos, and stayed in the background.

"Who's that other fellow, the one hiding in the back?"

Dill came forward and stood next to Toni at the end of the bed, facing Peggy, who gasped.

"Dear Blessed Jesus. It's Stanley." Peggy tried to lift her head off the pillow.

"I'm sorry to alarm you, Mrs. Whitcomb. I know you haven't seen me in quite awhile, but it's me, Dillon."

"Now I recognize you. You look so much like your daddy. For a second, I thought I'd met my maker and gone to hell." Peggy laughed a little. "Still, it's good to see you and talk to you in person after all these years."

"I want to thank you for everything you've done for me."

"No need. Things worked out for both of us. Some day soon, we'll sit and have a good talk together."

Maureen was puzzled by their conversation, but when Jeffrey began speaking, she let it go. They had important business to finish.

"Mrs. Whitcomb, we've all gathered here today to visit you and to see if there is anything you need." Jeffrey stepped out from his position behind Maureen to establish himself as the overseer of the discussion.

"If you could make me twenty years old again, I'd like that."

"It is unfortunate I don't posses the power to work miracles." Jeffrey smiled at Peggy.

"Getting my two daughters and my sister here together is a miracle."

"Then, I guess, sometimes miracles do happen."

"Wishful thinking. I know why everyone's here today, and it's not because of the miracle of family love." Peggy was looking straight ahead at her sister, Toni.

"There are a few things your daughters and sister think need resolving, if you're up for it." Jeffrey glanced sideways at Maureen, sitting next to him.

"Better late than not at all, but you should hurry. I'm not getting any younger." Peggy managed to lift her thin lips into a slight smile.

"First, I'd like everyone here to know I'm recording these informal proceedings, for the sake of accuracy in recounting what is said and by whom. Anyone have a problem with that?"

Attorney Grayson held up his cell phone, indicating he was also recording.

"Because we are having a simple discussion for the purposes of discovery only, and not pledged under oath, it is still expected the information you impart will be the truth insofar as you know it." Jeffrey cast a quick glance into each individual's face for emphasis.

"Momma, we're here to learn what your wishes are and to fulfill them." Maureen had nothing to offer, but if she could give her mother peace of mind, it might be enough.

"Long time since anyone cared about what I want."

"Over twenty years ago you wanted me to take care of your farm, and that's what I did." Toni sounded belligerent and argumentative. "It's nobody's business . . ."

"No one is disputing the agreement between you and Peggy." Jeffrey cut her off before things escalated. "You did what she asked by keeping the property taxes paid."

"You're darn right, I did. It wasn't easy, and the taxes went up every year."

"How many acres, would you estimate, were rented out to other farmers on an annual basis?" Sandover's Attorney Grayson walked forward to stand near Toni and address her.

"It started out small, maybe twenty or thirty acres, depending what neighboring farms needed. At the most, about 300 acres were being rented, but that was a few years ago."

"To what would you attribute the decline in land rentals by other farmers?" Attorney Grayson spoke to Toni, but kept his focus on Peggy and Maureen, sitting near her bed.

"There's fewer farmers around here, and the ones that are left don't need extra land for crops or can't afford to rent land."

"With less land being rented, how did you manage to continue to pay the property taxes for Peggy?"

"It was tough. I'm not a farmer, so running the place myself wasn't going to happen. When my neighbor, Dill, told me about the sand mining company's offer, I couldn't pass it up."

"Ms. Radzinski, if you hadn't sold the land to Sandover, what would have happened to it?"

"I'd guess the county would have foreclosed on it for the taxes I couldn't pay."

"In essence, you saved the majority of the farm by sacrificing a few acres?"

"That's right." Toni flashed a victorious smile in Maureen's direction.

"Did your sister, Peggy, have any knowledge of the transaction?"

"I told her about it. She said to do what needed to be done in order to save the farm for her girls."

"How much money did Sandover pay for the acres you sold them in that first transaction?"

"About $4500 an acre, so over $200,000."

Maureen was shocked the land was worth so much to the mining companies. Never had she imagined the value of her mother's property and all of the property in the area. No wonder Toni and Dill were determined to sell.

"That's a large sum of money. Where is the money now?" Jeffrey re-entered the discussion and worked his way closer to Toni to ask his question.

"Most of it I put into the bank to use to pay the property taxes."

"How much is 'most of it'?"

"About $30,000."

"Not sure $30,000 qualifies as most of the money, but let's move on. Where is the rest of the money?"

"I bought a small business with living quarters included. It was a way for me to support myself."

"The small business you purchased is called Toni's Tap, isn't that correct?"

"Yup, it's a little tavern, plus we serve some food. I live in the apartment above the bar."

"Based on the current assessment for your sister's property, how many years of property taxes will the $30,000 cover?"

"A few, maybe three or four."

"Even if that were accurate, what is your plan for the years beyond those three or four?"

"I'm taking it one year at a time."

"Isn't it true, if you hadn't spent the majority of the money from the land sale on yourself and your interests, there would be enough to cover at least the next fifteen years, give or take?"

"I don't know about that. Besides, Peggy was glad for me to have somewhere to live and a way to earn a living. I'm her sister, and she was helping me like I had helped her all these years."

"I don't suppose you ever considered getting a job instead of using most of the money to buy a bar," Maureen said.

"Let's go back to the first sales transaction with Sandover." Jeffrey gave Maureen a stern glance. "It's the deal you said you couldn't pass up. When you signed the papers to sell the property and filed the RETR as required by law, whose name did you use?"

Toni's expression hardened, and she looked to Dill and the men from Sandover for help, but none was forthcoming.

"Since my name wasn't on the deed, I had to sign Peggy's name. She told me she was okay with that."

"You do realize when you use an assumed name for a fraudulent purpose, in other words, you sign someone else's name to a binding legal document, it's called forgery?"

"I didn't give it much thought."

"Attorney Grayson, were you and your client aware you were not dealing with the owner of the property?"

"I'll take this one, Lyle." Cal, the Sandover representative, stepped forward. "At the time, we were not aware this woman was misrepresenting herself."

"At what point did you become aware Toni Radzinski was not Peggy Whitcomb, the owner whose name was on the deed and other documents?"

"Not until months later, when the money was paid and the site was already in operation. It was too late to do anything about it."

"Here's where I'm having a problem with all of this." Jeffrey walked closer to Cal Derksen and Attorney Grayson. "A second deal was recently made between Sandover and the two parties involved in selling their land, Dillon Hagen and Toni Radzinski. That deal was halted by a temporary restraining order filed by Peggy Whitcomb's daughter, Maureen. On the legal documents related to this sale, Toni Radzinski once again fraudulently signed her sister's name. Again, Sandover offered no objection to her forgery."

Jeffrey pulled several papers from his files and handed them to Grayson and Derksen. "These are copies from the second sale as filed with the County and the State. Is that your signature, Mr. Derksen, next to the signature of Peggy Whitcomb?"

There was no denying what was in front of them. They handed the papers back to Jeffrey.

"Let's all agree this second sales transaction is null and void because of the fraud involved." Jeffrey directed his words at Attorney Grayson.

"Agreed." The attorney looked at Cal Derksen. "It would be in everyone's best interests if this deal disappeared, don't you agree, Cal?"

"I agree," Derksen said.

"You're saying the deal is cancelled, just like that? What about the money you were supposed to pay me?" Toni's voice was loud and angry.

"The initial money Sandover paid to me for the deal is gone, and there's no way I can repay it," Dill said. "How is that going to be worked out, and what about the construction for the mine that's already been started on my land?"

"I'm sure we can figure out an arrangement that is satisfactory to all parties involved." Jeffrey kept his voice calm. "This is not the time or the place to hammer out the details of dismantling the deal, but I think we can all agree settling this out of court will be beneficial to everyone."

"As long as I get something for my trouble," Toni said.

"I think you should be relieved we're dropping our civil case. That would have been real trouble for you." Jeffrey checked the time. "We do need to hear from Peggy, the owner, to learn what her concerns are."

"I guess this is when I need to speak up." Jasmine stood and faced the group. "Momma signed a quitclaim naming me as the new owner of the Whitcomb farm and the document has been filed. There's no need to worry her about what's happening with the property because it doesn't belong to her any more. It belongs to me."

"Momma, I know you said Toni could sell the farmland, so I see no reason to object to my selling it instead." Jasmine was sounding pleased with herself. "In that way, your sister will be off the hook for doing something illegal, and Dill's agreement with Sandover will still be valid."

"Is it all right with you that Jasmine sells the farm, Momma?" Maureen was concerned her mother was too ill to comprehend what had happened.

"Only if she gives the money to Toni."

"I don't think she's going to do that, are you, Jasmine?"

"Why should I? Right now, David needs the money more than anyone else."

"You have to give the money to Toni, or else," Peggy said.

"Or else what?"

"I think what Peggy is trying to tell all of you is she wants to give me the money, because I'm her sister, and that's what sisters do, ain't that right, Peg?" Toni had walked around to stand at the side of the bed, next to Maureen.

"No, that's not right."

"What are you trying to tell us, Momma?"

CHAPTER 45

T he room was silent, as Maureen's mother glanced at the people gathered in front of her. Her eyes found Maureen's face and lingered there
for a long while. Peggy swallowed hard, cleared her throat, her next words
distinct and determined.

"I want to speak to Darla, Jasmine, and Toni. Everyone else, please leave."

"I'll check with the guard to see where we can wait." Jeffrey exited the
room and returned with the guard, who escorted the men out. As he left,
Jeffrey gave Maureen a thumbs up sign and smiled. She didn't smile back.

"All right, they are out of the room. Now, what's this about, Momma?"
Maureen said.

"Toni, tell them. Tell them why I was insisting the money had to be yours."

"Nothing to tell. It's sisterly love, and that's all."

"I'm not going to hide this secret any longer."

"What does that mean, Momma?" Maureen asked.

"Toni knows a terrible secret of mine. She threatened to tell you if I didn't
do what she wanted."

"That's not true. She's starting to lose her marbles," Toni said. "It's the cancer and drugs getting to her."

"Come closer, Darla. You, too, Jasmine."

The two sisters sat down on either side of the bed and pulled close to their mother.

"Hold my hands, please."

Maureen and Jasmine folded the blankets back. Each carefully lifted an arm and placed it on Peggy's chest. Maureen took her mother's right hand, light as a sparrow, into her two hands, and Jasmine held her left hand. They leaned in as close to their mother as they could.

"Darla, there are things I should have told you years ago, but I was never sure if it was the right thing to do. I didn't want to dredge up the past and hurt you more than you'd already been hurt."

"It's all right , Momma."

"No, it's not all right. We must clear the air, get everything out in the open." Her mother paused and took a shallow breath. "I didn't know Stanley was hurting you."

"We don't have to talk about this." Maureen was crumbling inside.

"I need to. Before Stanley came into our lives, you were a happy child. When you became so full of despair, I thought it was because your daddy and grandparents had died, and I went to work and had to leave you."

"None of those things were your fault."

"But it was my fault I left you with Stan. He was supposed to be taking care of you, but, instead, he was hurting you. When you turned thirteen, he told me he thought you could handle riding the bus and being alone after school."

She stopped and closed her eyes. Maureen thought she'd drifted back to sleep.

"Momma?"

"Toni was taking care of Jasmine for me," her mother continued, "but you insisted you didn't need a baby-sitter. You wanted to be left alone."

"I blamed you for not helping me. How could you not know?" Maureen was trying not to shout the words at her mother.

"I swear, I didn't know. Not once, ever, was there any sign. I thought he was a perfect father to you."

Maureen could feel herself screaming inside, wanting to spew out all the words she had caged within her, recalling what her life had been.

"I thought you were just being moody." Peggy turned her head towards her youngest daughter and smiled. "Jasmine was like you, Darla, when you were little, so happy and full of life."

"I think I was happy, Momma," Jasmine said. "You and daddy gave me lots of love."

"Everything changed on the day of your fifth birthday." Peggy's voice was almost a whisper. "Stan brought you presents."

"Jasmine wore the pink, ruffled dress he had given her." Maureen choked on the words. "There was box with a pink ribbon. Jasmine tore off the wrapping paper, opened the box and squealed. A baby doll was inside."

"Momma, what does this have to do with anything? So what if my daddy gave me gifts on my fifth birthday? Isn't that what's supposed to happen?" Jasmine was almost pleading, as if she wanted to end the story before it became unthinkable.

"I saw you standing in the window, Darla, as Stanley gave Jasmine the gift and hugged her."

"Is that when you realized what he had planned?" Maureen said.

"The look on your face as you watched him with Jasmine told me everything. That's when it all came together. I understood what had happened. He hurt you and would do the same to Jasmine."

"That's why you shot him." Maureen couldn't control the hysteria from inside her. "You wanted to protect Jasmine, even though you never protected me. I was the sacrificial lamb. You wouldn't let the same thing happen to perfect little Jasmine."

"No, I couldn't let it happen to Jasmine. Because of me it happened to you. For that, I will never forgive myself."

"What're you two talking about? How did he hurt Maureen?" Jasmine's hands flew to her mouth as she realized what was being said. "I don't believe it. He was a good person."

"No. He was evil, the most heinous kind of evil." Maureen spat out the words.

"You're making up lies because you were jealous of me."

"I am telling the truth." Maureen spoke slowly. "I can prove it."

Maureen left the room. She walked down the corridor until she found a guard. Shortly after Maureen returned to her mother's room, the guard escorted Dillon in. Maureen wasted no time.

"Tell them what you witnessed. Tell them what Stan did to me. They need to hear the truth in your words."

"I was there in the house. I saw Stanley take Darla up the stairs." Dill's voice was without emotion. "Sometimes Stanley brought me in the attic to watch. It went on for years."

"How could he do something like that?" Jasmine began sobbing.

"Jasmine, he was a terrible man," Peggy said. "He deserved to die."

"I suppose you thought shooting Stanley would be your penance for not loving me as much as you loved Jasmine." Maureen was shaking with anger.

"You have no idea what you're saying." Peggy's voice sounded weak and wounded.

"Blah, blah, blah. Stanley's dead, everyone's glad, the price has been paid. It's over. Let's all move on." Toni walked closer to her sister.

"Toni, this conversation doesn't involve you," Maureen said.

"That's where you're wrong. I was there that day, on the porch. I can verify what happened." Toni began rummaging in her oversized purse. "I don't suppose a lady can smoke in here."

"All of us were there. Doesn't change a thing." Maureen had no patience for Toni or anything she had to say.

"That's right, doesn't change a thing, so let's move on." Toni was fingering a cigarette, twirling it between her fingers like a baton.

"I have to accept my mother did nothing to help me." Maureen stood and pushed her chair away from her mother's bedside.

"That's where you're wrong," Dill said. "She did do something to help you."

"Dillon, you don't know anything." Toni was shoving him toward the door. "Get out."

"Maureen, I was there, on the day of the party." Dill was not leaving.

Maureen looked at Dill and tried to picture him as a thirteen-year old. Jasmine was on the swing. Someone was pushing her.

"It was you, pushing Jasmine on the swing." Maureen could see him standing there.

"That's right. Stanley wanted me at the party to get to know Jasmine better."

"I think I'm going to be sick." Jasmine pressed her hands to her stomach.

"You said I was wrong, Dill, and that Momma did do something to help me. How am I wrong?"

"Dillon, please, let me." Her mother focused on Maureen. "I wanted him to die, I really did. I would have killed Stanley, but . . ."

"What do you mean?"

"Before I could react, the back door flew open. It all happened so fast."

"What happened so fast? Who flew out of the door? Who killed Stanley?" Maureen was frantic.

A suffocating silence enveloped the room as Maureen sorted through the possible suspects. If it wasn't her mother, perhaps it was Toni. No, she was already outside, standing on the porch. It couldn't have been Dill. He was in the yard by the swings.

"Maureen." Dill almost whispered her name, as Peggy nodded in agreement. "It was you. You shot Stanley."

Maureen released a moan and stumbled backwards, landing hard on the chair behind her. The words echoed in her mind, bouncing off her bones, bruising her brain.

"No, that's not right. Momma, the police said you did it. You confessed. I read about it in the newspaper." Maureen was crying and pleading for the truth she thought existed.

"You were traumatized, wounded. I took the gun from your hands, and the deed became mine." Maureen's mother summoned the strength to lift her hand and touch Maureen's face.

"While I was in jail awaiting trial, Toni realized you had blocked out what happened." Peggy stopped, closed her eyes, then began again. "Toni told me the only thing you girls ever said was that I was in jail because I killed someone."

"What actually happened that day disappeared," Toni said. "One time Jasmine started talking about it. I told her she had a bad dream and to forget it. I was like one of those psychiatrists or something. I knew you didn't remember. That's what I told your momma."

"Knowing you had no recollection of the shooting was such a relief for me and gave me great consolation over the years." Peggy managed a smile. "I vowed to take the secret to my grave and made Toni promise the same."

"I am so sorry, Momma." Maureen was almost whispering. "I didn't remember what I had done. I still don't. Never would I have let you go to prison for something you didn't do."

"I was the one responsible. What I did gave you the chance to go forward and live your life."

"Guess I'll be heading out." Toni was halfway to the door, unlit cigarette dangling from her lips. "You folks need some time together."

"Toni, stop!" Maureen said.

When Toni kept walking, Dill stepped in front of the door, blocking her from leaving. She turned around to face Maureen.

"I've got nothing more to say to you." She took the cigarette out of her mouth.

"Say the truth. You witnessed the shooting, but you didn't want Momma to tell me what really happened, and not because of any promise."

"I thought it would be better for you if you didn't know. Besides, we had vowed to never tell you. I always keep my word."

"You're lying, Toni." Peggy's voice was faint but harsh. "As long as Darla didn't remember what she'd done, you could continue to threaten to tell her the truth. That way you could do what you wanted."

"I was only taking what I deserved."

"You bought a business and a place to live. That's more than you deserved."

"Your blackmailing days are over." Maureen pointed toward the door. "Get out, Toni."

Toni turned in a huff and clattered out of the room as the guard approached the doorway with Jeffrey, who peeked into the room.

"I think they want us to wrap this up. Is it okay for us to come back?"

Maureen could only nod her head yes. Jasmine, her eyes red and her face blotchy, stared across the bed at Maureen.

The men shuffled into the room. Maureen managed to give them a shortened version of what happened, ending with how Toni had been blackmailing Peggy. Maureen left out the part about who really shot Stanley and why.

"Toni was blackmailing you? Blackmailing and committing crimes against someone are not the signs of a loving and loyal sister." Jeffrey was glaring at Jasmine and David.

The nurse in charge of the Ancillary Unit returned. She checked Peggy's vitals and indicated it was time for them to leave. They agreed to meet that night at Dill's house to work out the details for voiding their business deal.

Jeffrey and Maureen were the last to depart. She glanced over her shoulder at her mother, whose face wore a peaceful, ethereal expression. Maureen hoped she herself would be released someday from the anguish and guilt of what she had done and would be able to find peace.

The drive home to the farm was long and dismal, inside the car and out. Thoughts of the day's revelation wracked Maureen's mind, as she attempted to remember shooting Stanley. It was unimaginable that, for years, Peggy, Toni, and Dillon, kept quiet about what they witnessed, while she and Jasmine buried their memories of that horrible day.

Jeffrey was solemn and quiet. By his demeanor, she knew he could sense something significant had happened, and she appreciated the courtesy he showed by not pressing her to talk about it. He drove, hands tight on the wheel, as the rain continued, and the daylight disappeared. Maureen stared ahead into the coming night, the windshield wipers flapping back and forth like a hypnotist's watch, as the plot points in her memory connected together to form a complete story about that Saturday when she was fifteen years old.

CHAPTER 46

Maureen pictured herself standing in the kitchen, watching through the window as Stanley pressed his finger to his lips and leaned towards Jasmine.

"Give me a big kiss, right here, to show how much you love me."

Darla wanted to scream to Jasmine "Don't do it. Run away." Instead, she opened the cupboard and reached for the revolver stored on the top shelf. On several previous occasions, she had taken the gun from the cupboard and held it in her hands, feeling its cool, smooth weight. She would place it near her face and gaze down its metal barrel, aligning the front site with things around the house, pretending to fire at random. It was kept loaded for emergencies, Stanley said, and she decided this was an emergency.

Darla hurried onto the porch with the gun in her hand and stood firm. Raising her arm straight in front of her, she positioned the revolver and focussed her eyes ahead. She began to engage the mechanism, and the hammer clicked back into place. With a gentle finger, like Stanley touching his lips, she squeezed the trigger. The shot flashed across the yard and entered Stanley's head through the back of his skull, throwing him forward, his body falling like cut timber. For a moment, there was an eerie silence. Jasmine, clutching the baby doll and spattered in blood, started screaming.

Lowering the heavy revolver to her side, Darla watched as her mother sprinted past Jasmine and Stanley's body and ran to the porch. Peggy bounded up the steps and snatched the pistol from her daughter's hand, snapping orders to her and the others outside.

"Get in the house. You were never out here, do you hear me?" She pointed her oldest daughter toward the door.

Darla's ears were ringing and her legs were too wobbly to move. Why was her mother yelling?

"Dillon, this was an accident. I'll call an ambulance." She placed her hand on the boy's shoulder and walked him to the porch steps.

"Go on inside, Dillon. Everything's going to be all right."

"Toni, take Jasmine in the house. Give her and the doll a quick bath. Bring the birthday dress and the doll's clothes outside. I'll burn them and the gift box in the burn barrel."

"Everyone, turn around and look at me!" Peggy screamed the words. "This was an accident, but you didn't see it. None of you were outside. You saw nothing. Understand? Nothing."

Maureen looked at Jeffrey, his brow tight as he stared into the oncoming traffic lights, magnified and reflected by the unrelenting rain.

"Where are we?" She had lost track of time and distance.

"Maybe thirty minutes from the farm. Are you all right?"

"I think I will be. Today, I was struck by a bolt of lightning, and I survived."

"I'm a good listener, if you feel like unloading on someone."

Maureen hesitated. How would he feel about her after learning she was abused as a child, and she had shot and killed someone? Worse than that, her mother had gone to prison for the crime.

"It's quite a heavy load. Are you sure you want to hear it?"

"That's what friends are for, and don't forget, I'm also your attorney. Whatever you say is protected under the attorney/client privilege."

Maureen began talking and didn't finish until they pulled up at the farmhouse. Jeffrey turned off the car. He hadn't said anything during her monologue, but now he leaned over and touched her hand.

"No one should ever have to endure what you did. None of this was your fault."

Dill had arrived ahead of them and was already drinking in the kitchen. Road Dog and Samuel were elated to have Maureen and Jeffrey home, and Jeffrey took them both outside, giving Maureen a chance to speak with Dill alone.

"I want to thank you for what you did." Maureen began filling the coffee maker. "You kept quiet about what happened for a very long time."

"Don't get all warm and fuzzy. I didn't do it for you. If people knew you shot my father, I was certain everything else would have been uncovered by the police. The shame of what he did to you in my grandparents' house, right under their noses, would have cut them to pieces had they known. What Stanley did would have ruined our family's reputation and my grandparents' legacy. I couldn't let that happen."

"Still, it must have been traumatic for you to witness your father being killed and then keep that secret bottled up inside you."

"I hate to let you off the hook, but I was glad he was dead. My life was better without him."

Jeffrey and the dogs came in from outside, followed by Cal Derksen and Lyle Grayson. Dill directed everyone to find a seat around the island and offered the men drinks, but before they were settled and ready for business, Jasmine and David arrived.

"Glad you didn't start without us. Do you have any decent wine?" Jasmine was checking her mirror for smudged mascara and any hair out of place.

"This shouldn't take long. Cal, if Sandover is interested, my entire farm is for sale."

"This is good news, Dillon." Cal was slapping Dill on the back. "How many acres we talking about?"

"Over nine hundred. You'd need to buy it all, the barn, the outbuildings and the house, too."

"I'll have our engineering and geological specialists take a broad look at what's here. Not sure we'd want the immediate acreage with the buildings."

"It's all or none. If your company's not interested, then I'll make the same offer to somebody else."

"Hold on. Don't get ahead of yourself. Give us ten days. I'm sure we can get this deal done. Besides, if you make your offer to someone else, they'll still have to do the research. At least with us, you have the wheels in motion."

"Where does that leave my property, the land you insisted you needed in order to buy Dillon's land?" Jasmine's face had flushed an unattractive and angry red.

"As we discussed at the prison, the entire deal is null and void and the civil case will be dropped." Attorney Grayson's voice sounded dismissive and annoyed with Jasmine. "Did I understand that correctly, Mr. Bennett?"

"Due to illegal irregularities, it was agreed the deal should disappear." Jeffrey had his yellow legal pad ready. "Tonight, we'll do the paperwork to make that happen."

Before Jasmine could react, her cell phone rang. As Jazz declined the call, Maureen's cell phone also rang. Stepping away from the group around the island, Maureen walked to the porch to take the call and returned a short time later.

"That was the warden calling from Taycheedah. Momma died peacefully in her sleep."

Jasmine reached for David and buried her face into his chest. Maureen felt empty and alone, awash with regret for the estrangement between herself and her mother for so many years. Picturing her mother's peaceful face when they said good-bye, Maureen allowed herself to be content with the fact they had spoken the truth and forgiven one another.

The next day, Maureen arrived at the prison before the people from the Hansen Funeral Home came to claim Peggy's body to transfer it back to Chippewa Falls. It was their mother's wish to be buried in the Whitcomb family plot next to Maureen's father, Nathaniel Whitcomb. The funeral director assured Maureen the funeral arrangements would be ready the following afternoon, which suited Maureen, who wanted the ordeal to be over.

Inside the prison, Maureen viewed her mother's remains and signed papers accepting responsibility for the transport and burial of the body and acknowledged she was given the prisoner's remaining possessions.

"This box contains personal things Peggy kept locked in her locker." A prison staffer handed Maureen a cardboard box with her mother's name, birthdate, and date of death. "She did have some clothes and a few other things, but after she was hospitalized this last time, Peggy asked to have the items distributed to other prisoners in her module."

When all the details were ironed out, Maureen waited in the Ancillary Unit for the arrival of the hearse. She was curious about the box and opened it with care. Its contents transported her into the past, when her mother was a child, a young girl, and, later, a beautiful woman. There were old photographs of family gatherings and special events, yellowed greeting cards, and love letters from Nathaniel. Maureen picked up a fragile wrist corsage of dried rosebuds and baby's breath, tied with a silver ribbon. Inside a tiny velvet box, she found two golden bands that must have been her parent's wedding rings. Maureen wept knowing the tragic path this smiling, hopeful woman's life was doomed to take.

The hearse was scheduled to arrive within the next few minutes, and Maureen knew she wanted more time to go through the contents of the box. Gathering up everything she had scattered on the bed, Maureen noticed some official-looking envelopes, labeled "Save for Darla" in shaky cursive penmanship, and bundled together with string. Tossing them into the box with the other items, she promised herself to spend more time reminiscing with her mother's keepsakes.

Returning to the farm was bittersweet for Maureen. She loved the people at Crooked Creek Farm and the time she spent there, but now the field workers were finished, and Dill would be glad to be rid of her. Once her mother was buried, no reason existed for Maureen to remain in the area. Jasmine would sell their mother's property, and Maureen's ties to everything she had come to call home would be severed.

On Wednesday afternoon the funeral home was prepared for her mother's memorial. In tall urns flanking a silver coffin, sprays of white lilies stood nodding above pink roses, sprinkled with baby's breath. A blanket of pink rosebuds covered the casket, and there were floral arrangements from Maureen, Jasmine and David, Jeffrey, and Toni. Maureen had no expectation there would be anyone at the visitation, but a few of Peggy's old classmates, former neighbors, and church members came to pay their respects. When Toni strutted in, she seemed to know everyone.

"You're lucky I showed up," she told Maureen. "This joint was as gloomy as a funeral parlor." Toni laughed as she sauntered off to shake hands and crack jokes around the room.

When Jasmine and David walked in, Maureen was surprised that her sister, looking stunning in a slender black dress, had made the effort.

"Momma would have been happy you came, Jasmine."

"Maureen, we're all grieving. This has been so hard for me. I lost Momma when I was a little girl. Now I've lost her again." Jasmine patted a tear from the corner of her eye. "Then, we found out those horrible things about you. It's all too much for me."

"I can see how you are suffering."

Maureen felt someone behind her and turned to find Jeffrey. He reached for her hand.

"This is a beautiful tribute to your mother. How are you holding up?"

"I'm doing okay and . . ." Maureen stopped mid-sentence when she noticed Dill standing behind Jeffrey.

Jeffrey leaned in close to Maureen's ear. "I hope it's all right I brought Dill along."

"After everything that's happened, I think it took real strength for him to come here."

"I came to pay my respects," Dill said as he walked past Maureen. "Your mother was good to me."

Peggy was buried following the visitation. The Whitcomb family plot sat along the edge of woods that surrounded the Woodlawn Cemetery. Almost void of their leaves, the aspens and maples cast broken shadows among the rows of markers. Maureen was touched to see the black granite gravestones for her father and grandparents, solid and steadfast, and she was grateful there was also a marker for her mother with the words "Beloved Wife and Mother" arching across the top. Below, on the left was Peggy's date of birth, while the place on the right for her date of death was undone. In the center, a pair of fluttering wings was etched.

The funeral director said a few words and read the Twenty-Third Psalm, and, although she hadn't planned to speak, Maureen stepped forward and pressed her hand to the cool silver coffin.

"Long ago, I knew you and loved you. Although I was lost from you for a time, you kept me always in your heart. How fortunate we found our way back to each other before it was too late. That has made all the difference."

The funeral director lead the group in the Lord's Prayer, and Jasmine and Maureen each tossed a pink rose onto the casket as it was lowered on velvet ropes into the ground. Jeffrey took Maureen's hand and lead her to the car.

CHAPTER 47

· ·

They had been gone for hours, and Maureen was anxious to return to Road Dog and Samuel who were left behind at the farm. When they arrived, the windows were dark, and Dill's truck was not there. As Maureen opened the door of the house, the two dogs raced outside. It had been a long day for everyone.

"How about I whip up some scrambled eggs for us and the kids here? You go in and get comfortable." Jeffrey was tossing the tennis balls as fast as the dogs retrieved them. "First, I'll tire them out a little."

Maureen accepted Jeffrey's offer and plodded upstairs, turning into his bedroom where she and Road Dog had been sleeping since Jeffrey graciously traded rooms with her, no questions asked. After changing, she reached for her phone and called Dr. Taylor's office.

"Hello, Maureen. Isn't Caller ID amazing?" The doctor sounded upbeat and pleased with herself.

"Life altering." Maureen flinched. Why did her mouth always get the better of her when she was talking to the doctor?

"Apparently, I agree." Dr. Taylor chuckled. "What's going on, Maureen?"

"There's good news, and there's bad news. First the good news. I have filled in all the plot points and now have a beginning, middle, and ending to my personal narrative."

"How does that make you feel?"

"Knowing everything that happened explains so much about who I am and how I am. Does that make sense?"

"Perfect sense. What's the bad news?"

"Knowing everything that happened. It's all pretty terrible."

"Tell me."

After Maureen explained what she'd learned, Dr. Taylor was silent for so long, Maureen couldn't stand it any longer.

"Well?" Maureen said.

"You know none of this was your fault. You were a child, a victim."

"That's what Momma said, that it was her fault, because she didn't know about Stanley, and she needed to take responsibility."

"A caring and selfless action. She must love you very much."

"I swear, I did not remember what I had done. Momma went to prison for me and died there. Her funeral was today."

"I am sorry your mother passed away in prison," the doctor said. "You know her incarceration was not your doing. She made that decision."

"I guess, except if I'd remembered sooner, maybe things would have been different."

"Maybe, maybe not. Some things are better left forgotten, until we are strong enough to deal with them. It's how people survive something like that."

"I guess I did survive, after all."

"Yes, Maureen, yours is a story of survival."

"Thank you, Dr. Taylor, for all of your help. I don't think I'll be calling again."

After Maureen hung up, she lifted the box with her mother's things, placed it on the bed, and reached inside. Holding the photos and mementoes her mother had saved was comforting and helped Maureen feel reconnected with the young woman her mother was before their lives fell apart.

At the bottom of the box, Maureen found the bundle with the handwritten label, untied the string, and leafed through the five envelopes. One was her mother's end-of-life advance directives. Another envelope, yellow with age, held the last will and testament of Maureen's grandparents, naming their son Nathaniel, as the primary beneficiary, her mother, Peggy as the alternate beneficiary, and any children of Nathaniel and Peggy as second level beneficiaries. The third envelope contained copies of deeds to the family's property going back to the original deed from the late 1800s. Maureen was about to open the fourth envelope when Jeffrey yelled up the stairs.

"Eggs are ready. Oh, and your sister and David are here."

The last thing she wanted to deal with was David and Jasmine, but the smell of bacon and eggs drew her downstairs. In the kitchen, they were sitting by the island as Jeffrey worked at the stove.

"Didn't think I'd be seeing you two again, as in, ever again." Maureen sat across from them, and Jeffrey placed a plate of steaming eggs in front of her.

"We're here because we need to talk." David frowned at Maureen.

"Not sure what we have to talk about." She dug into the food, savoring each bite.

"Jeffrey, if I haven't told you before, you are a great cook. Best scrambled eggs ever."

When Jeffrey sat down next to Maureen with a plate of his own and began eating, he seemed unaffected by the unwelcome visitors watching the food being consumed. There was an odd silence, except for the scraping of forks against plates and the noisy chomping and slurping of the two dogs enjoying scrambled eggs.

"No, really, please continue eating. Don't mind us. It's a perfect display of impeccable manners." David made no attempt to disguise his annoyance at being ignored.

"You two arrived here, uninvited, at dinnertime. How's that for a display of manners?" Maureen hoped the couple would get the hint. "You might as well leave, because, like I said, I have nothing to say to either of you."

"That's too bad, because I have things to say to you." David pointed an accusatory finger at Maureen. "You planted those records and files from Wexler Global in the old hat box, knowing I would look through the box before turning it over to you."

"You said I don't know anything, so how could I possibly know what you would do?"

"You took a chance I'd be curious about what was inside, and that I'd keep what you planted, because it was from the deal I knew you worked on for a year."

"Supposing all of what you said was true, how could I predict you would be willing to use the information I 'planted' for illegal purposes?"

"Because you know me too well."

"Yes, I do know you, or I thought I did. Now, I know you took my house, my bank accounts, and my credit cards, and you withdrew money from my 401K account with Anson-Chambers, all without my permission. You stole from me, your own wife. In theory, it would not be a stretch to believe you would be willing to defraud a meaningless corporation like Wexler."

"Maureen, I am facing real jail time here. If you would at least admit to being responsible for taking the information from your office and leaving it in our home, a few of the charges against me might be dropped or at least reduced."

"David, there is nothing I can do to help you. Whatever you did, you alone must face the consequences of your actions."

"I told you, David. Maureen will never admit to having responsibility for any of this." Jasmine placed a hand on David's arm. "I guess it's payback time."

Payback was something Maureen felt she deserved, like having David's actions earn him prison time, and Jasmine being left behind, alone and penniless. As a result, Maureen might be vindicated, but what would she have gained? She recalled something about the best way to get revenge was to be successful and considered what success for her would look like.

"Unlike you two, I am not heartless and selfish." Maureen pushed her half-eaten meal away and looked at Jasmine. "I'm going to make you an offer. You need money, probably lots of money, for David's legal battles."

"Yes, the only reason I would sell the farm is for David."

"So you've said. My 401K account still holds a good sum of money, even after David stole from it. My offer has two parts. First, I will give you the remainder of what's still in the account. It should be enough to cover most of David's legal fees. In exchange, I want to buy Momma's farm. If you sell to me, you won't have to waste time searching for a buyer or lose a commission to a realtor. You'll have the cash immediately, and the farm will remain in the family."

"What do you consider a good sum of money?" David asked.

"About $350,000."

"What's the second part of the offer?" he asked.

"Admit to stealing from my 401K account and you can also keep whatever is left of the money you stole."

"I'm not admitting to anything."

"David, we need as much money as we can get." Jasmine was using her pouty voice as she stroked David's arm. "Just say you took the money."

"I think we should wait to see if we can get more for the land. Maureen's offer is plain old robbery."

"Speaking of robbery, what if we have the authorities add to the list of charges against you the illegal withdrawals you made from my retirement funds? You remember, it was the money you used to finance your stock market crimes."

"You can't prove I did any such thing."

"Yes, I can." Maureen was bluffing, but hoped David, being backed into a corner, would believe her. "Mine is an offer you can't afford to refuse."

"David, she'll pay us the $350,000 right away," Jasmine said, "and we can keep whatever is left of the money she says you stole. The farm will stay with Maureen, and she won't mention that you took her retirement money. Isn't that right, Maureen?"

"Yes, I'll keep it to myself, but he has to admit what he did."

"All right." David threw his hands up in the air. "I'll accept the offer only because we need the money right now. For the record, I couldn't care less about the farm staying in the family."

"For the record, what else do you have to say?" Maureen recognized the infuriated expression flashing across David's face, one she had often seen during their marriage.

"I took the money." David's words didn't sound remorseful at all to Maureen, but he said them out loud and that was what mattered.

Jasmine shook her head, but she placed her arms around David, pulling him close.

"I'm Maureen's attorney," Jeffrey said, "so let's discuss this together and figure out what's going to happen and when."

Maureen was grateful Jeffrey was getting down to business, hoping the agreement would be finalized before Jasmine and David left that evening.

With his yellow legal pad already in front of him, Jeffrey took over. In the next several hours they had worked out the details, printed the legal documents and signed the papers, insuring everyone was satisfied with, or at least accepted, the arrangement. When Jasmine and David were gone, Maureen and Jeffrey opened one of Dill and Summer's nicer wines and celebrated the deal.

"Here's to the $350,000 you happened to have sitting around, and to the genius and generous way you used it." Jeffrey clinked his glass against Maureen's and took a drink. "You are a lady full of surprises."

"I'd spent years saving the money for retirement, but I need to think about living life now. Investing in the farm is a risk I'm willing to take." Maureen swirled the wine in her glass, studying its movement. "If David hadn't helped himself to a sizable chunk of my money, there might have been some left over to help me get the farm up and running."

"He's a real piece of work, isn't he? I cannot picture you with him at all."

"Neither can I." Maureen tapped her glass against Jeffrey's again and took a long drink.

"I'd say things turned out as good as possible, all considered," Maureen said.

CHAPTER 48

W hen Maureen heard the sound of Dill's truck pulling into the yard, she told Jeffrey she had some of her mother's things to go through, grabbed her glass and the wine bottle, and scurried upstairs. Once in the bedroom, she closed the door and clicked the lock.

The box filled with her mother's things remained on the bed, its flaps folded open, inviting her inside. Pulling out the banded envelopes, Maureen found the two she hadn't yet opened. In one of them was her mother's Last Will & Testament, dated a week prior to Peggy's death. She had named one primary beneficiary, Maureen Henderson (formerly named Darla Jean Whitcomb). In case Maureen was deceased, Jasmine was named as the contingent beneficiary.

"Thank you, Momma. It only cost me more than $350,000 to claim my inheritance." Maureen couldn't help but laugh at the irony of the entire situation. "However, I am enjoying this box full of your treasures, and it didn't cost me a dime."

The fifth envelope was not sealed. She pulled out the papers and unfolded them, pressing them flat against the bed. It was another Last Will and Testament and began "I, Stanley R. Nowak." It sickened Maureen to be in the presence of something with Stanley's signature on it, something he had touched. She started to fold the sheets and put them away, but her curiosity got the better of her.

She skimmed through the bequest from beginning to end, and then read it out loud, word for word, to be certain she had not misread it. In Article II, Money and Personal Property, Maureen read:

I give all my land and property, including residences and buildings located on said property, subject to any mortgages thereon, and all policies and proceeds of insurance covering such property, to my life partner, Peggy L. Whitcomb.

If this was a legitimate will, Crooked Creek Farm, the place Dill claimed he inherited from his grandparents, didn't belong to Dillon after all. This could mean that ever since Stanley died more than twenty-three years ago, Maureen's mother was the owner, and now, after her death, the farm had been bequeathed by her mother to Maureen.

Maureen stared at the will in disbelief. If it was legal, it was odd Dill didn't know anything about it, or maybe he was pretending it didn't exist. How was he able to live for over twenty years on a farm that wasn't his? He even sold pieces of land from the farm to Sandover and offered to sell them the entire property after Summer died. Her mother must have known.

Maureen folded the papers and placed them into their envelope. Never could she allow Stanley, even as he rotted in death, the satisfaction of somehow making up for his actions with this gift. Picturing her mother's face that last day, Maureen suspected it gave Peggy a sense of justice to leave the farm to Nathaniel's daughter and Stanley's victim.

Downstairs, Jeffrey was seated at the island, working on his laptop. Maureen placed a stool next to him and sat.

"I found this in the box of my mother's things." Maureen handed Jeffrey the copy of her mother's will.

"She left everything to you," Jeffrey said as he read the will.

"Yes, everything, which amounted to the box I brought home from the prison."

"I'm surprised your mother bothered with a will, since there wasn't anything of any consequence to leave you."

"I also found this." Maureen handed him the other documents. "I think it's the reason for Momma's will."

Jeffrey skimmed through the legal pages once and started over, taking his time to read them with more care. A loud whistle sounded from his lips.

"Do you think this is for real?" Maureen was doubtful.

"The will appears to be valid. It has Stanley's dated signature, and there are two witness signatures, plus the inclusion of a notarized self-proving affidavit. The will was handled by one of the attorney's offices nearby, so I can check with them about when the will was presented to your mother."

"What do you think I should do?"

"Do about what?" Dill, smelling like a tavern, appeared at the kitchen door, listing a bit to the right, his eyes red-rimmed and his face ruddy. "If you're asking should you leave, I vote yes."

"I vote you should tell Dill what you found." Jeffrey gave Maureen the look and head nod that said, "Go on now, you can do it."

"Dillon, I came across something in my mother's things. It's her will dated the week before she died."

Maureen tried to give the paper to him, but he shoved her hand away.

"That doesn't have anything to do with me."

"It names me as the primary beneficiary of everything my mother owned."

"I'm happy for you. Except for the Whitcomb farm, which she gave to your sister, your mother had nothing, and that's what you got."

"Read this." Jeffrey took the document from Maureen and handed it to Dill, who accepted it with reluctance. When he finished reading, he said nothing.

"You already knew about Stanley's will, didn't you?" Jeffrey took the papers back as he confronted his good friend.

"Where'd you say you got that?" Dillon's voice was flat and void of emotion.

"I told you, in my mother's things. She left it for me. Crooked Creek Farm is my inheritance."

"It should have been mine."

"Then you did know."

"Yes, I knew. Stanley made it clear I wasn't named in my grandparents' bequest. He threatened on a regular basis to cut me out of everything he owned if I didn't do what he said. After he died, I learned he actually made good on his threat."

"What could you possibly have done to cause him to disinherit you?" Jeffrey wondered.

"Doesn't matter. He hated me, because I knew his secrets. I hated him for the same reason."

Jeffrey made coffee and poured each of them a cup. Maureen wasn't sure what to do. They were sitting in silence, drinking their coffee when Dillon started talking as though he were in the room alone, reliving his own nightmare.

"The date is seared into my brain. It was September 12, 1993, and I had turned twelve the previous spring. When Stanley brought Darla over after school, he made me follow them to the attic. After the three of us were inside the room, Stanley said he wanted to 'see how much I'd learned' as he put it, and I realized what he had planned for you and me. Somehow I got away and ran. For three days I didn't go home. When I did return, we argued, and Stanley started beating me. This time I fought back and held my own for awhile, but in the end, he nearly killed me. It was worth it, because he never beat me again, and I think it was the last time Darla was brought to the house. I'm guessing this was when dear old dad cut me out of the will."

"No wonder it didn't bother you when Stanley was killed," Jeffrey said.

"He got what he deserved."

"That same September, I would have been thirteen. It's when he stopped hurting me, and it was all because of you, Dill." Maureen was stunned by this realization. "How will I ever repay you?"

"There's nothing to repay."

"You've lost the two things you loved most in the world. I can't bring Summer back, but I can return what should be yours. I owe you that much."

"You don't. In fact, I'm indebted to you, or rather, to your mother."

"What do you mean?" Maureen said.

"After Stanley died, I had no one. Your mother let me stay at the farm with Loriano and Silvia, who became my guardians. The three of us kept things going as best we could. I stayed in contact with your mother, so she would know what was going on, even though I don't think she wanted anything to do with the place. When I was sixteen, she hired me to legally take it over."

"So Momma knew you were selling Crooked Creek, piece by piece, just like she knew Toni was . . ." Maureen stopped, her eyes fixed on Dill's face. "Wait. You had to know all along about Toni."

"Toni liked to pretend she owned the property and could do whatever she wanted. I pretended to believe her. That way, I kept an eye on her for your mother."

"Later on, did Momma approve of your plan to sell all of Crooked Creek Farm?"

"Yes. I couldn't believe she was willing to let it go. She understood how devastating cancer can be." Dill paused. "I don't know if I would have gone through with the sale, because the place didn't belong to me, and this land is Summer's final resting place. As things turned out, I didn't have to make that decision. It all belongs to you, fair and square."

"There's nothing fair about any of this, and, even if it was, I could never accept something from Stanley."

"You're like your mother in that way," Dill said.

"Promise me one thing, though. If I give the farm back to you, you won't let Sandover or another sand mining company have any of it."

"That's something I can't promise. The debts piled up from Summer's illness would close the business in no time. They'd take everything, and then neither of us would have Crooked Creek Farm."

The three sat for awhile in silence. Maureen watched Jeffrey, deep in thought.

"I have an idea of how to solve the problem." Jeffrey's voice was calm, but Maureen could tell he was excited by the gleam in his eyes.

"Maureen will retain ownership of Crooked Creek Farm and will hire Dill as farm manager. He'll run the business like he did for your mother."

"What about if my creditors come after the farm? You can't imagine how much money we owe."

"They could try, but you don't own the farm, never owned it. We have the will to prove that. A lien has to be attached to 'your property' in order to make a claim against you."

"What happens to Dill and Summer's debts?" Maureen was trying to grasp how Jeffrey's plan might work. "They won't simply disappear."

"I hate to do it, but I guess I could declare personal bankruptcy." Dill was shaking his head. "It's just something my grandparents would never have done."

"There's no shame in it. You have the right to declare bankruptcy." Jeffrey placed his hand on Dill's shoulder. "You should be able to file Chapter 7 bankruptcy since your income is so low. Without any burden of debt, you can start over."

"I guess there's no other way out of this mess. Personally, I have nothing to lose, because Summer and I put every spare penny back into the business."

"Dill, I want you to remain in the farmhouse. It's your home." Maureen was sincere about her offer.

"Are you serious? You don't know how much that means to me."

"Okay, so Dill will live in the house and run the farm. Both of you will need some working capital to get started again. I suggest you sell off some of the equipment you've been working on. Keep only what is absolutely necessary." Jeffrey was jotting notes onto a legal tablet. "I do have some money I've been saving until I found something I wanted as an investment. I think I've found it."

"That's amazing! Are you sure?" Maureen said.

"We'll work out some sort of plan for sharing the profits from the farm, if there ever are any profits." Jeffrey laughed.

"No, I don't want a nickel from anything connected with Stanley." Maureen was adamant. "With the exception of Jeffrey's investment, Crooked Creek belongs to Dill, in every way except on paper. You have my word."

"I don't know what to say, Maureen." Dillon's voice was quiet.

"Say you want to be my farm manager. Say you will make the farm a success and make Summer and my Momma proud."

Maureen watched Dill's somber face break into a smile.

"All right, it's a deal." He reached out and the two shook hands. "I accept your offer."

It was late when they finished roughing out a draft of their business arrangement, establishing Dill as Maureen's employee, working in the capacity of her farm manager, with Jeffrey as a contributing partner. After Dill retired to bed, Maureen and Jeffrey took Samuel and Road Dog outside, where the cool night was already filled with the smell of fall fires. Jeffrey piled logs into the fire pit, and soon it was snapping and sending red orange flames into the evening sky. Pulling the adirondack chairs close to the pit, Maureen opened a beer for each of them and handed one to Jeffrey. They sipped their beer and stared into the fire.

"If you decide to stick around," Maureen said, "I know a farm or two where you could find a job."

"I might take you up on that. Sometimes, I do miss practicing the law, though."

"Maybe you could do both," Maureen said.

"Interesting idea. I'll have to think about it."

"It could mean a whole new life for you."

"Speaking of a new life, here's to your new life, Maureen and to the life you gave to Dillon." Jeffrey tapped his brown bottle against Maureen's. "You are an amazing and generous human being."

Maureen caressed Road Dog's wonky ears, the dog's wide muzzle resting on her lap. "Guess I've come a long way from the woman in free-fall who picked up a hitchhiker one stormy night."

"I wasn't hitchhiking. I was walking, remember?"

"No, I'm pretty sure you held out your thumb, hitchhiker style."

"I was waving you to go past me. There was no thumb involved."

"Agree to disagree." Maureen tapped her bottle to Jeffrey's again.

"Thumb or no thumb, I'm glad you stopped." He gave Maureen a thumb's up sign.

"Me, too."

THANK YOU

I'd like to express my gratitude to my editor, **Barbara Lobermeier**, for her constructive, knowledgeable input. Her help and insight were invaluable during the writing of this novel.

Many thanks to my friend, **Jan Hughes**, who helped with the legal aspects of my story.

Thank you to my friend, **Lois Preusser Krawczyk**, for reading the novel and giving me her thorough and honest analysis.

ABOUT THE AUTHOR

Judith lives in Wisconsin with her husband, Greg, and their three rescue dogs.

Check out Judith's website at: http://jstaponkus.com

Other books by the author: Long Time Coming, May, 2019